"You seem to have a problem with control, Morgan."

He shook his head. "I always maintain absolute control."

Misty quirked a brow and stared at his fly.

Morgan grinned. "That's an aberration, an involuntary reaction I have around you."

"Well, whatever it is," she replied, "you don't hesitate to shock me all the time, embarrass me."

He slid his hand over her bottom and lifted her so she fit against him. His voice went husky and deep. "I just want you to know how much I want you."

She knew it was dangerous to make herself vulnerable to him, but at the moment she didn't care. "Thank you."

Morgan's fingers caressed and excited. "You want to know how you can thank me?"

Just then a tentative knock sounded on the door. Misty jumped and shoved him away. "Good grief, my first time in your office and look what happens."

With a wry smile, Morgan turned and headed for the door. "Unfortunately, not a thing."

D0465247

Dear Reader,

I hope you enjoyed the first book, *Sawyer*, in my Buckhorn Brothers miniseries. It was out last month, and the next two brothers—*Gabe* (Temptation #794) and *Jordan* (Temptation #798) will follow in August and September. But this month is Morgan's month—and what a guy he is!

I just love it when a woman can confuse a man a little, turn him on a lot, and in the process steal his heart. From the moment poor Morgan—who's strong as an ox and doubly determined—meets Misty Malone, he's fighting a losing battle. Add the heckling of his brothers and a mischievous nephew, hunks all, and you get lots of fun.

Morgan's is also one of the sexiest stories I've ever written. But the credit for that goes all to the man himself. He made it impossible to tone things down.

I hope you like Morgan, and I hope the glimpses of Jordan and Gabe tantalize you just a bit.

Happy reading!

Lori Foster

P.S. You can write to me at P.O. Box 854, Ross, Ohio, 45061

Lori Foster
MORGAN

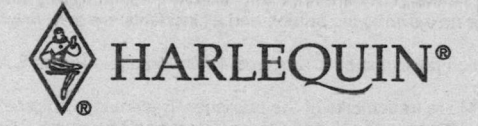

HARLEQUIN®

TORONTO • NEW YORK • LONDON
AMSTERDAM • PARIS • SYDNEY • HAMBURG
STOCKHOLM • ATHENS • TOKYO • MILAN • MADRID
PRAGUE • WARSAW • BUDAPEST • AUCKLAND

To my son, Jake.

If a strong will can make the world right, there's no doubt
you'll have it fixed in no time. I don't know anyone who
possesses more sheer determination or a keener mind.
What's so fun is the incredible sense of humor wrapped
around it all! You make me laugh so much with that quick,
dry wit, and you awe me with your unshakable logic.
I love you, Jake, very, very much.

ISBN 0-373-25890-9

MORGAN

Copyright © 2000 by Lori Foster.

Prologue

IT WAS one of those sweltering hot weekend mornings when a man had nothing better to do than sit outside in his jeans, feel himself sweat and wait for a breeze that wouldn't come. The sky was the prettiest blue he'd ever seen, not a single cloud in sight. He loved days like this, and looked forward to viewing them from his own house once he finished it. If all went well, it would be ready for him to move in by the end of summer.

Morgan Hudson tilted his chair back and closed his eyes. Everyone was gone for the day, and the house seemed strangely quiet, not peaceful so much as empty. He hoped he didn't feel that way when he got moved in. Living with three brothers and a teenage nephew got a man used to chaos, especially with *his* brothers.

Sawyer, the oldest, was the only doctor for miles around, and he had patients coming and going through the back office attached to the house all day long—sometimes even through the night. It was one reason the brothers had all hung around together for so long. Sawyer was an excellent father, but when Casey was little, they'd all pitched in to cover dad duty so the rigors of med school, and later being the town doc, didn't overwhelm him. It had been a pleasure.

Jordan, his younger brother, was a vet, and that meant the house and yard were always filled with stray animals. Morgan didn't mind. More often than not he got attached to the odd assortment of mangy, abandoned or just plain homely critters. 'Course, he didn't tell Jordan that.

Gabe, the youngest brother, was a rascal, with no intention of settling down anytime soon. And why should he when half the female populace of Buckhorn County, Kentucky would be bereft if he ever did? The women had spoiled Gabe something awful, and he indulged them all. Gabe just plain loved women, young and old, sweet or sassy. And they loved him back.

Casey, Sawyer's son, was constant chatter. He was at that awkward age of sixteen, half man, half kid, when females fascinated him, but then, so did driving and stretching his independence. Casey, as well as the brothers, was thrilled when Sawyer decided to marry again, adding a female into the masculine mix. The adjustment to Honey Malone had gone surprisingly smooth.

Morgan smiled. Damn, but he liked Honey. Mostly because the woman had snared his brother with a single look. Sawyer had fought it, Morgan'd give him that, but it hadn't done him a damn bit of good. He'd gone head over arse in love with Honey almost from the first day. And once Casey had decided he loved her, well, that had put a bow on the package. Sawyer would do anything for that boy, so it was a good thing Casey had taken to Honey the way he had.

Morgan wanted to have a son just like Casey some day—if he ever found a woman he wanted to marry. At thirty-four, he figured he'd waited plenty long enough. He almost had the house done, and he sure as hell was settled enough now, despite what his brothers thought. He had a respectable job and plenty of money put away. It was time for him to get on with his life, his hell-raising days long over.

A bird landed on the porch, right next to where Morgan's bare foot was braced on the railing. He cocked an eye open, whistled softly to the bird, then watched it take flight again. Obviously the bird hadn't known he was human—or else it'd thought he was dead. With a grin, Morgan closed his eyes again. He was like that, so still sometimes it set people on edge. To Morgan, it was all about control, taking charge of his life and seeing that things fell into place. He had the future mapped out, and he had not a single doubt that things would be just as he wanted them. He controlled himself, he controlled his future.

Whenever possible, he controlled those around him.

THE MAN was sound asleep when Misty pulled up in front of the huge, impressive log house. It seemed to go on and on forever, sprawling over incredibly beautiful land. On the way in she'd seen a lake surrounded by colorful wildflowers, an enormous barn and several smaller outbuildings. In the distance, sitting atop a slight rise, was another house, but apart from that, the home was isolated.

Honey had told her a little about the property, but mostly she'd talked of her marriage. Sawyer, her husband-to-be, had rushed things through, and Honey was putting a wedding together in just under three weeks. It had taken Misty a few days to gather her things and join her sister so she could offer some last-minute help. The timing couldn't have been better, and Misty had given a silent prayer of gratitude that she actually had a place to stay for a short time. Otherwise, she'd have been homeless.

Honey had warned her that the testosterone level would be enough to strangle a frail woman, but still, Misty hadn't been prepared for the sight of the hard, dark man sitting on the porch. He wore tight faded jeans, the waistband undone—and nothing else. She gulped, seeing a flat, six-pack, slightly hairy abdomen.

Besides being massively built and layered in solid muscle, he was breathtakingly gorgeous. Not that it mattered to Misty, who was twice burned. She'd written men off, and they'd stay written off. But that didn't mean she couldn't look. And appreciate what she saw.

She inched closer, wondering exactly how to wake him or even if she should. She'd arrived a day early, so Honey might not be expecting her. But surely there was someone else in the house, and maybe if she knocked quietly...

She was right beside him, practically tiptoeing in her sandals, trying to decide what to do, when suddenly he opened his eyes.

Oh, Lord.

She felt snared, like a helpless doe in the headlights of a semi. She stared, swallowed and stared some more. The man seemed as surprised as she was, and then he suddenly moved, jerking upright. He lost his balance, and his chair went crashing backward with jarring impact.

The string of curses that emerged should have singed her ears, but instead it amused her. She smiled widely and leaned down to where he lay sprawled on the polished boards of the porch. "You all right?"

Still flat on his back, he ran one hand through his dark, wavy hair, eyes closed, and Misty had the distinct feeling he was counting to ten. When he turned his head to face her, she prepared herself for the impact of his gaze again.

It didn't help. The man had the most sinfully beautiful blue eyes she'd ever seen.

"Is there some reason why you're sneaking up on my porch?"

The chuckle came without warning. She was nervous, damn it, and she couldn't be. She didn't want Honey to know of her troubles, not when Honey had just found so much well-deserved happiness. Misty had already decided to act as if nothing had happened, to resolve her difficulties—*what an understatement*—on her own. Having the invitation to stay with Honey for a little while was a reprieve from heaven, and hopefully would give her a chance to get her bearings and make some very necessary plans.

"Now, I didn't sneak," she lied easily. "You were just snoring so loud you didn't hear me."

His blue gaze darkened to purest midnight. "I don't snore."

"No?"

"Any number of women can tell you so."

Uh-oh. She was on dangerous ground. This obviously

wasn't the kind of man you could easily flirt with. He took things too seriously. And she sensed he wasn't exactly going to behave like a gentleman. Misty brushed her bangs out of her eyes and gave him a cocky grin. "I'll take your word for it. Must have been distant thunder I heard." She looked pointedly at the clear blue sky, and he scowled, quickly prompting her to add, "Did you break anything?"

Without her mind's permission, her gaze drifted over his big, hard, mostly bare body, and her pulse accelerated.

The man pushed himself into a sitting position off to the side of the chair. He let his arms dangle over his bent knees and narrowed his eyes in what she took to be a challenge. A very small, very sensual smile tilted his mouth. "You want to check me over to see?"

The idea of her hands coming into contact with all that exposed male skin made her fingertips itch. Distance became a priority, especially with the husky way he'd asked it. Misty came swiftly to her feet, but that just redirected his gaze to her legs, so close he could kiss her knee by merely leaning forward.

He looked as if he were considering it.

She quickly stepped back. Perspiration dampened her skin and caused her T-shirt to stick to her breasts. It had to be over ninety degrees, and the humidity was so thick you could choke on a deep breath.

Trying to lighten the suddenly charged mood, she asked, "How in the world can you sleep in this heat?"

He pushed himself to his feet and righted the chair. He was a good head taller than her, with sleek, tanned shoulders twice as wide as hers. She felt equal parts fascination and intimidation. She didn't like it. She would never let another man affect her in either way. When he looked down at her, his expression somewhat brooding, she gave her patented careless grin and winked. "Out all night carousing and now you're too exhausted to stay awake?"

He stepped forward, and she quickly stepped back—then

had to keep stepping back until her body came into contact with the wood railing. He towered over her, not smiling, taking her in from head to toe. If Misty hadn't known for a fact that she had the right house, and if Honey hadn't assured her that all the men were beyond honorable, she'd have been just a tad more worried than she was. "Uh, is anyone else here?"

"No."

"No?" *Now* she was getting worried. "What about your brothers? And wasn't your mother supposed to be visiting, too?"

He frowned, but didn't back up a single pace. He was so close she could smell the spicy scent of his heated skin.

She held her breath.

"My mother had a slight emergency and she won't be able to make it after all. My brothers and my nephew are all in town together, enjoying a Saturday off."

They were alone! She could barely form a coherent sentence with him deliberately crowding her so. She had a suspicion that was why he did it. She swallowed and asked, "What about Honey?"

His gaze sharpened and his dark brows pulled down in a ferocious frown. "She's with them." He looked her over again, very slowly this time. To her, it seemed as if he was savoring the experience. Then he asked, "Just who the hell are you, lady?"

His expression was bland, but there was something in his tone, a mixture of heat and expectation. Misty bit her lip, then stuck out her hand, warding him off and offering a belated introduction. "Misty Malone." Her voice broke, and she had to clear her throat. "I'm Honey's sister."

His expression froze, then abruptly hardened as he stepped away without taking her hand. "Ah, hell." He glared an accusation, then added, "That wasn't at all what I wanted to hear."

JUST LOOKING AT HER MADE HIM SWEAT.

And in the damned tux for his brother's reception, sweating was more than a little uncomfortable. Even the air-conditioning didn't help. He should look away, but he couldn't seem to drag his gaze from her. The sensuous way she moved, her deep black hair swaying to the music, looking almost liquid it was so silky, her husky laugh, all worked to make him crazy and put a stranglehold on his attention. Morgan loosened the tie around his throat and undid the top two buttons of his white shirt. But that didn't help the restriction of his pants, and he just knew if he started loosening them up, his new sister-in-law would have a fit. And he'd sooner kick his own ass than upset Honey.

"If you stare any harder, you're liable to set her on fire."

Morgan jerked, then turned to glare at Sawyer. "Aren't you supposed to be with your bride?"

"Jordan's dancing with her."

Great. Just great. After meeting Misty that first day on the front porch, Morgan had done his best to avoid her. Hell, he'd almost seduced his new sister-in-law's sister. And worse, she'd egged him on. What kind of woman did a thing like that?

He felt infuriated every time he thought about it. All his lauded control seemed to be paper-thin these days, especially with the way Jordan and Gabe adored the woman. They doted on Misty, every bit as fascinated as Morgan had been by her sensual looks and careless smile, only they seemed genuinely interested in her, and that really put a crimp in his mood.

Morgan didn't particularly like her. She was so brazen, so sassy and unrestrained, it was almost impossible not to be drawn to her on a sexual level. But where her sister was discreet and gentle, Misty was bold and outgoing. It was no wonder he hadn't figured out who she was on the spot; he'd expected the sister to be more like Honey, not the exact opposite.

With her come-on lines and lack of inhibitions, Misty could put any male on edge, and that wasn't at all the type of woman he was determined to be interested in these days. No, he wanted a woman like Honey, one he could settle down with, one that was as interested in becoming domestic as he was. Not that he wouldn't indulge in a little dalliance here and there before he found the wife, just not with Honey's sister. No way. That would be crossing the familial line.

Trying to sound disinterested rather than disgruntled, Morgan said, "I'm surprised Jordan could pull himself away from Misty. He and Gabe have been crowding her all night." Then he shook his head. "Hell, they've both been dogging her heels like lovesick puppies all week."

"And that bothers you, does it?"

Morgan snorted. "Hell, no. Except that she's a far cry from Honey and I don't want to see them get stuck in an awkward situation."

That made Sawyer laugh out loud. "Jordan and Gabe? I hate to break it to you, Morgan, but they're grown men and they've been handling their fair share of female companionship for some time now. Hell, Gabe started earlier than you did."

"He lied."

Sawyer laughed again. "Nope, I caught him at it, out in the barn that first time, so I know exactly how old he was."

Diverted for the moment, Morgan turned to Sawyer with a grin. "You're kidding?"

"Don't I wish. I think that's what started him on the path of debauchery."

Morgan chuckled at that. The youngest brother was a regular Lothario, to the delight of the female population of Buckhorn. "Details?"

Shrugging, Sawyer said, "The girl was four years older than him, and since then, it's like he's irresistible to women."

"Honey resisted him."

Sawyer's grin was very smug. "Yeah. I was glad to see it. Good for his ego."

"'Course, he wasn't really giving it his all, seeing as you'd already staked a claim." Before Sawyer could object to that, Morgan turned to Misty. "Does it amaze you how two sisters can be so damned different? I mean, Honey is just so kind-hearted and innocent."

Sawyer had just taken a sip of his champagne, and he choked, but when Morgan gave him a suspicious look, he just raised his brows, as if encouraging Morgan to continue.

"Misty is..."

"What?" Sawyer seemed intent on digging in. "Sexy?"

"Hell, yeah, she's sexy. But then so is Honey."

Sawyer blinked at that, then frowned ferociously. "I'm not at all sure I like—"

"Oh, give it a rest, Sawyer. I'm not blind. And I just appreciate the fact she's so sexy—for you."

After downing the rest of his champagne in one gulp, Sawyer demanded, "Your point?"

Sawyer was being damn entertaining again, but Morgan couldn't take advantage of it because he couldn't pull his gaze away from Misty. Gabe had just swept her up into a new dance. She complained for just a moment about her feet, and Gabe, the rascal, merely went down on one knee and pulled her shoes off, tossing them aside. Misty seemed charmed, and they began a rather heated, intimate dance.

The floor cleared to give them room, and Misty behaved totally uninhibited. Gabe was no better, showing off, making the women cheer, but that was his damned brother and he wasn't interested in looking at Gabe.

Misty was something altogether different.

Morgan had to grind his teeth together. "Will you just look at her?"

"I'd rather look at you looking at her. More amusing that way."

"It's like, Honey is so sweet and gentle, and Misty's all spice and fire. What is it with her, anyway? Does she think she has to seduce every guy around her?"

"She's not seducing, she's dancing."

Morgan snorted. "The way she dances, it's the same damn thing."

Sawyer snickered. "For you, at least."

Just then, Jordan interrupted Gabe and stole Misty away. She laughed, as willing to partner him as Gabe, and Morgan nearly ground his teeth into powder. "It's not right, I'm telling you. She's playing with them both."

Deliberately adding oil to the fire, Sawyer said, "It seems to be a game they're enjoying." Then he clapped Morgan on the shoulder. "Relax, will you? She's just dancing, nothing more. Oops. Here comes Honey, so I better get this out quick. She's concerned because you're avoiding Misty. I was supposed to tell you to go dance with her."

"*Ha.*" Morgan was positively appalled by that idea, but not for the reasons his brother would likely assume. "I'm not getting near her." He was afraid if he did, he'd explode. He couldn't recall ever wanting a woman quite the way he wanted this one.

She was staying with them at the house, so he saw her at breakfast, looking all sleepy but still full of smiles for his brothers. He saw her at bedtime, wishing everyone—but him—a good night's sleep. He even saw her in the afternoon, though he did his best to avoid it. She would be painting her toenails right out on the back patio, or puttering around the kitchen, giving the illusion of being domestic when he'd be willing to bet she didn't have a domestic bone in her entire lush little body.

It didn't matter what she did, he liked it—a little too much. And she knew it, which was why she avoided him as much as he did her. They were far too sexually aware of each other for comfort.

But it was all physical, and a fast, easy, physical relationship with his sister-in-law's sister would never do. Sawyer, damn him, had made the woman a relative with his marriage, and that put her off-limits for every single thing Morgan would like to do with her. And the things he'd like to do...

He almost groaned out loud. The vivid images of him and Misty together, naked, overheated, carnal, would amuse his brothers and shock the hell out of Honey. She was overprotective of Misty—why, he couldn't fathom. He had a feeling his sexual thoughts wouldn't shock Misty at all. He had the taunting suspicion she'd be with him every step of the way.

"Damn." Morgan felt the start of an erection and had to fight to control himself. Not easy to do when Misty was laughing and looking flushed from all that dancing. Jordan whirled her in a wide circle, and Morgan wanted to flatten him.

"Damn is right. You're in for it now."

Morgan turned to see what Sawyer was blathering on about and was met with Honey instead. She looked incredibly beautiful in her white wedding gown, her long blond hair loose and her face glowing. Morgan smiled at her. "Have I kissed the bride yet?"

"About a dozen times, I think." She grinned at him, and twin dimples decorated her cheeks.

"*Morgan...*" Sawyer's beleaguered tone didn't bother Morgan one whit. Annoying each other was the brothers' favorite pastime. And Sawyer, love-struck from day one though he fought it pretty damn hard, had made himself a prime target.

Honey laughed and patted her husband's chest. "Oh, Sawyer, relax. Your brother is just a big pushover."

Sawyer choked again.

Morgan, amused by her insistent misconceptions of him, grinned. Not another soul in Buckhorn, male or female, thought of him as a pushover—pretty much the opposite, in fact.

His grin fell flat with her next words.

"I want you to dance with Misty."

"Ah..."

"Morgan, it almost seems like you've been avoiding her. She told me just this morning at breakfast that you didn't like her."

They'd talked about him? Morgan wanted to ask exactly what had been said, but he didn't want to look too interested. "I don't dislike her."

"Of course you don't! But she thinks you do because you've spent so much time at work since she's been here, and you've barely said two words to her."

Morgan tugged on his ear, beginning to feel uncomfortable. He wanted to sock Sawyer, who stood behind his bride, smirking. "It's been really busy this week and being that I'm sheriff I can't just..."

"But you're not busy now. And look, she just finished a dance. It's the perfect time for the two of you to talk some more and get better acquainted."

Sawyer, ready to get back a little of his own, said, "Yeah, the timing is *perfect*. And with your, er, charm, you should be able to put her right at ease." Then he grinned, glancing at his wife. "You'd do that for Honey, wouldn't you, Morgan?"

Honey, playing along, gave him her most endearing smile.

He tried, but not a single rebuttal came to mind. "Well, hell." Morgan stomped away, resigned to his fate and unfortunately, in some ways, pleased to be forced into it. He saw

Misty look up from across the room, as if she'd somehow sensed his approach. She did that a lot, seeming to know the second he entered a room. And then she'd get quiet and withdrawn—but only with him.

Her dark blue eyes, so bright and clear they still had the effect of making his heart skip a beat, widened. He saw her soft lips part, saw her cheeks darken with color. She turned, looking, he knew, for an avenue of escape. But she'd already been surrounded by every eligible bachelor in Buckhorn, and they were in no hurry to let her leave.

Morgan stopped right behind her. She didn't turn to face him, but she knew he was there; her shoulders stiffened the tiniest bit and her normally husky voice became a little bit shrill as she asked the men who would dance with her next.

Morgan looked at every man there, and he fashioned a grin. A very hard, unmistakable expression. Several of the men, eyeing him closely, began to back up, quickly making their excuses.

Morgan took advantage of their retreat. "I believe that'd be me, Malone."

She hated it when he called her by her last name. He'd found that out the first day they met. He'd been calling her by Malone ever since, because it helped to maintain the small distance necessary for his sanity.

"I don't think so, *Hudson*." She reached for Gabe's hand. He was one of the few men who wasn't intimidated by Morgan's darkest stare. In fact, Gabe looked highly entertained. He was a gentleman and would have assisted her, if Morgan hadn't beat him to it, reaching around her and snatching her slim fingers in his own before she could get a solid hold on Gabe. The reach brought his chest up flush against her slender back. He could smell her, warm woman and sweet sexiness. Her scent was like an irresistible tonic to him, and like any basic male animal, he reacted strongly to it. Her hair, so silky and luxurious, brushed his chin, and it was like having fire lick down his spine. He caught his breath.

They both froze.

Gabe chuckled. "You two going to stand there doing the statue imitation all night, or do you intend to dance? I have to tell you, Honey is frowning something fierce over the show you're giving the guests, and I think she's about to start this way."

Morgan drew in a deep breath, searching for control. "Get lost, Gabe."

"No way. I don't get to see you this rattled too often."

"I'm not rattled." He stepped back a safe distance but retained his hold on Misty. Trying to sound reasonable, rather than rattled, he said, "Your sister wants us to dance."

Misty's pink tongue darted out to lick nervously at her lips, and Morgan wanted to groan. He glanced at Gabe and saw that his brother was every bit as alert and fascinated as he was. *Damn.* He started backing out to the middle of the dance floor, tugging Misty along with him. Everyone could see she was a reluctant participant, and after the way she'd accepted every other partner, Morgan was peeved. "Come on, Malone. I won't bite you."

"Can I have that in writing?" Gently, she tried to disengage her hand. Morgan stared at her, refusing to let go and refusing to respond to her sarcasm.

She sighed. "Look, Morgan, this isn't a good idea."

Perversely, he asked, "Why not?"

"You don't like me! That was easy enough to figure out from the moment we met."

She was so...lovely, he couldn't help but study her face, the narrow nose, the high cheekbones, her small rounded chin. If he looked any lower, he'd never survive the dance, so he brought his gaze to hers. "I liked you well enough...at first."

"All right. Then from the moment I introduced myself. I have no idea what you've got against me, and to tell you the truth, I really don't care."

"You don't, huh?" It was amazing how she went straight

to the heart of the matter. Most women wouldn't have been so bold.

He wondered if she'd be that bold in bed.

"No, I don't," she said. "Truth is, I'm not at all crazy about you, either."

The grin took him by surprise. Strangely, Morgan realized he was enjoying himself. Beyond being turned on, he felt challenged, and that didn't often happen with women anymore. "Why not?"

Before she could reply, the music changed, turned sultry. Misty gave such a heartfelt groan of despair, he chuckled. "Oh, no. I'm outta here." Again she tried to pull loose, but Morgan swept her closer and wrapped one arm around her waist.

Near her ear, he whispered, "Quit fighting me, Malone. It's only one dance." One dance that felt closer to foreplay. Just holding her was making him nuts, and this close, he could see a few damp, glossy black curls clinging to her forehead and temple. Her upper chest, visible over the scooped neckline of her maid-of-honor gown, was dewy with perspiration. She was warmed up and flushed all over. The vigorous dancing, he thought, leaning subtly forward to breathe in her heated scent. The thought of any other man in the room, especially his damn younger brothers, being this close to her, being affected the same way, made him want to growl.

Misty frowned at him. "What's the matter with you, anyway? You look like a thundercloud."

She pulled back, putting a few more inches between their bodies, but Morgan could see the added color in her cheeks and knew she was feeling the effects of the closeness, same as he was.

When he didn't answer, just continued to stare at her, she sighed. "Don't pretend my honesty bothered you, Morgan. I won't believe it."

Going for the direct attack, he surmised, and smiled. "You

haven't offended me.'' Then he made his own direct attack. "You wanna know what I don't like about you, Malone?"

"*No*."

Her naturally husky voice dropped another octave in her irritation. Where his hand rested on her back, he could feel the satin of the dress, warmed by her body, and the supple movement of her muscles. She was slim, but still stacked like a Barbie doll, with lush breasts and a narrow waist. Her legs seemed to go on forever, long and sleek and sexy. Her bottom, though small, was perfectly rounded and just bouncy enough to make him catch his breath whenever she walked away. He'd spent far too many hours obsessing over her bottom.

And those breasts. He could spend at least an hour enjoying her just from the waist up. Unable to stop himself, Morgan looked down at the pale, firm flesh and imagined the formal dress around her waist, her breasts naked for him to see, to touch and taste, to enjoy. He groaned. It was almost too easy to imagine his mouth on her, considering how much cleavage was showing, more so than any of the other women in the wedding party, though they were all wearing similar gowns in different colors. With the shape of the neckline there was no way she could be wearing a bra, or at least, not much of one.

Almost burning up, he growled, "You're Honey's sister."

She blinked, wary surprise evident in her expression. "So?"

"That puts you off-limits. And I don't like it."

Her eyes widened. "Good grief! You make it sound like if you decided to...to—"

"Yeah, all that you're imagining and more."

Her breath caught, and she choked on her anger. "Like I'd be agreeable! Well, let me put your mind at ease here, Morgan. The answer would be no!"

Annoyed all over again, he said, "I'm not buying it, Malone. You flirt all the damn time. Not just when you talk, but when you move, when you eat." He looked at her breasts again, which were trembling with her ire. "Hell, even when you breathe."

His words made her sputter before she managed to spit out, "That's absurd!"

"Do you realize every guy here has been ogling your breasts?"

Her mouth dropped open, then abruptly snapped closed. "You're disgusting."

"I'm not the one showing so much skin."

Through her teeth, she ground out, "Every woman in the bridal party is showing the same amount of skin, you idiot. Why don't you go lecture one of them?"

Easily, knowing it was true, he said, "None of them looks like you." Then he pulled her closer despite her slight resistance. "And I don't want any of them."

She looked flabbergasted. "Why, you...you arrogant bas—"

"Shh. Keep your voice down. I don't want your sister's reception ruined by a scene." She glared at him and her eyes looked hot enough to roast him, her cheeks rosy with color. He wanted to kiss her, but had at least enough sense to hold back from that.

Actually, Morgan wouldn't have been at all surprised if she'd socked him one, right there in the middle of the hall. And he was honest enough to admit he'd deserve it. He wasn't sure why he goaded her, but he couldn't seem to stop himself.

She huffed, then jerked against his arms. Very low, with clear warning, she said, "If you don't want me to cause a scene, then kindly get your paws off me and leave me alone."

With relish, he said, "Can't. Honey is determined to see us get acquainted."

She rolled her eyes. "Oh, for heaven's sake... I'll talk to her."

"Why bother?" He stared into her incredible eyes and felt a twisting in his guts as he muttered, "You won't be here much longer, and then it won't matter."

She quickly looked down and bit her lip.

Above the lust, suspicion blossomed. Morgan whispered, "Misty?"

Her gaze jerked to his face, and he realized he'd called her by her first name. Misty suited her, all dark and mysterious, except for those direct, intense blue eyes. "You *are* leaving soon, right?"

She swallowed, looking away once again. "I hadn't really thought about it."

Frowning, Morgan half danced, half steered them toward the patio doors. Misty didn't seem to realize his intent, she merely clutched at him to keep from losing her footing as he danced her first one way, then another, moving easily around the other couples.

When he opened the patio door and stepped outside, Misty started to hold back. Then he saw her square her shoulders and follow him. Evidently she'd decided they needed a showdown.

He thought she was exactly right.

He closed the door behind her, then said, "Come on."

The night was warm, heavy with humidity. Moonlight fell over her like a pale blush and formed a halo around her midnight hair. She tilted her head, ignoring his outstretched hand. "Where are we going?"

"Someplace more private. I know my brothers, and one or all of them will be out here in under two minutes to see what I'm doing."

"You won't be *doing* anything," she said.

He answered her with a shrug, then merely waited.

After a long moment, she sniffed, but took his hand and stepped cautiously forward. He realized then she was still barefoot. Irritation filled her tone when she said, "Obviously your brothers don't trust you any more than I do."

Morgan smiled in the darkness and stepped off the patio to head toward one of the gazebos decorating the back lawn of the town hall. "Oh, they trust me, all right. They're just nosy as hell and can't ever pass up an opportunity to needle me."

Misty paused outside the ornate gazebo, staring at it and breathing deeply of the scent of flowers, planted in profusion around the white wood and trellis structure. The entire county of Buckhorn was big on flowers. "I love gazebos. I think they're so quaint."

Morgan opened the door and cautiously entered the dim interior. "Yeah, I guess Gabe feels the same because he built one—bigger and sturdier than this—down by the lake at home."

"I saw it. Gabe really built that?"

"Yeah. He's a handyman of sorts, among other things." The door banged shut behind them, sealing them inside where the air suddenly crackled with awareness. Morgan refused to believe he was the only one who felt it.

Just enough moonlight filtered in to show the way to the white bench seats lining the inside. He stared hard, seeing the dull glimmer of Misty's eyes, the sheen of her white teeth. "Would you like to sit down?"

"What I'd like is to find out what you want so I can get back to my sister's celebration."

What he wanted? Now that was a loaded question. From the second she'd taken his hand, he'd had a throbbing erection. Morgan seated himself, stretching out his long legs on either side of her, caging her in. His eyes quickly adjusted to the darkness, and her pale skin and the light color of her dress made her visible. She didn't so much as move a muscle. He crossed his arms and considered her. "You're different from Honey."

"Night and day," she admitted without hesitation, then explained, "we're also very close. So what's your point?"

"I wouldn't want to see her hurt."

Misty stiffened again, but the rigid posture just caused her breasts to be more noticeable. "Anyone who hurt her would have to answer to me."

"Yet you think nothing of coming in here and flirting with my brothers, coming on to them—"

She suddenly inclined closer, and her voice was a near hiss. "I haven't *come on* to anyone! I danced, but then so did everyone else at the reception. It's what's expected at a—"

Morgan leaned forward and caught her shoulders in his hands, keeping her bent close. Her skin was silky and warm, and he flexed his fingers almost involuntarily. "You also parade around the house all day without a bra, and barefoot."

Her eyes narrowed, and he could feel her tremble. "It's ninety degrees outside, Morgan! Most every woman I've seen since I arrived has been wearing a sundress or tank top without a bra." She poked him in the chest, hard. "Maybe *you* should try wearing one to see how horribly uncomfortable they can be in this weather before you start judging me."

Morgan thought that was the most ludicrous thing he'd ever heard. He opened his mouth, but she quickly cut him off.

"And as for my bare feet, what of it? Don't tell me you have a foot fetish?"

He hadn't, not until he'd met her. He'd never even noticed a woman's feet before. But Misty had small, narrow feet, and she painted her toenails a bright cherry red. They looked sexy as hell, and every time he saw her pretty little feet, he imagined them digging into the small of his back while he rode her hard, making her scream with intense pleasure.

He also knew in his gut he wasn't the only male noticing. "You're entirely too comfortable around my brothers."

"Ha! I don't think it's your brothers you're worried about at all."

Because that was so close to the truth, even if he didn't want to admit it, Morgan slowly stood. Misty tried to back up, but he had hold of her shoulders and she didn't get far away from him. "You don't think so?"

She hesitated, going cautious on him now that he was so close and towering over her. But then she lifted her chin with her usual bravado. "No. I think it's...you."

He nodded, and his pulse thrummed in his veins. "You're right. It is me. But it's also you."

"No, I—"

He stepped so close her back came up against the smooth painted wall.

All the anger, all the frustration, abruptly shifted to pure sexual tension. Morgan couldn't resist one second longer. With his fingertips, he touched her cheek, then her lips, gently, barely brushing, savoring her softness and the way she trembled in response. Touching her felt so right and made him feel downright explosive. She went utterly still, not moving, not even breathing.

In a raw whisper, he said, "There is absolutely—" he leaned closer "—no possible way—" her eyes drifted shut and she panted for breath "—I'm feeling all this on my own."

"*This?*" The word was a mere whisper, sighed against his mouth.

"Lord, you make me hard, Misty." And then he kissed her.

She held herself stiff for all of about two seconds before her mouth opened and her hands fisted on the lapels of his formal jacket. She moaned, a low, hungry, needy sound.

Morgan, who'd been successfully avoiding her for an entire week, was a goner.

2

INSANITY, Misty thought, feeling the hot delicious stroke of Morgan's tongue, the slide of his large rough hands down her spine. He had her pulled so close, their bodies were practically fused together. She hadn't expected this, hadn't known *this* even existed. Lord, the man knew how to kiss, knew how to move his hands and his legs and his...hips. Everything he did, every place he touched her, made her too hot, too hungry. Made her want more. And so far he hadn't even let his hands wander that far.

But no sooner did that thought filter into her fogged brain than one of those large hands came up over her rib cage to close on her breast.

Her nipples immediately drew tight, and she pulled her mouth away to gasp at the incredible sensations his touch caused.

He groaned harshly, and a rough tremble traveled through his big body.

Stunned, somewhat disoriented by the unbelievable intensity, Misty whispered, "No..."

At that single word, not even said with much conviction, he froze. His hand opened slowly, as if it took great effort to get his fingers to obey. With his face pressed to the place where her shoulder and neck met, he struggled for air, and every muscle—pressed so closely to her—stiffened.

Then he stepped away.

The air positively throbbed between them, but still, he'd stopped the second she'd asked him to. The significance of that didn't escape her; he was a remarkable man, very much in control of himself. Misty did her best to catch her breath, to stop staring at him in the darkness. She should leave, right now, but she couldn't seem to get her feet to move. Every nerve ending in her body was still alive in a way she hadn't known was possible.

"I won't apologize."

He sounded breathless, frustrated, on the verge of anger, and she swallowed hard, trying to calm her galloping heart. "I...I didn't ask you to."

Still without moving, he added, "This is going to be a problem."

Again, she asked, "This?"

Several beats of silence passed, then suddenly he moved away from her and he actually laughed. "Come off it, Malone. You felt it as much as I did." He turned back, looking for verification.

It she assumed was the incredible sexual pull. "If you mean..."

Through his teeth, he said, "I mean I touched you and you got so hot I feel singed. I kissed you and you sucked on my tongue and rubbed up against me and it was like throwing a match on gasoline. There's enough goddamned heat in this room to start a bonfire."

Misty sucked in her breath, shocked at the words, at the harsh vehemence of his tone, but unable to deny them. Part of her new determination in dealing with men was to be brutally honest—with herself and them. Sugarcoating things, *faking* things, had caused at least half of her present problems. Being too timid, too naive, had caused the other half. In order to get on with her life, she had to start facing things head-on.

A rough warning growl rumbled from deep in his throat. "Malone—"

"You're right," she hurried to assure him, unwilling to let him shock her with more of his brutal honesty. "And I'm sorry. You took me by surprise."

"Bull." He propped his hands on his hips and glared at her. "I've known from the day I met you how it'd be. Why the hell do you think I avoid you?"

Oh. That certainly explained a few things, she supposed. "I see. Well, I must not be as clever as you, because I thought you were a totally obnoxious, thoroughly unlikable jerk and I was thankful that you ignored me. I had no idea this—" she waved a hand, trying to come up with a word suitable to the loss of control and depth of sensation he'd sparked "—*chemistry* was between us. I wasn't even aware something like *this* existed."

He cursed again, but she didn't let him interrupt her. "Now that I do know, trust me, I won't let it happen ever again."

Morgan seemed to measure her words. And then she saw his eyes narrow, his expression darken. He looked at her breasts, and she knew her nipples were still painfully hard. Without a word, he reached out a hand and gently brushed the backs of his knuckles across one sensitive tip, gliding easily over the satiny material of the dress. Misty drew in a sharp breath and felt a small explosion of erotic stimulation throughout her body.

Morgan whispered, "Oh, it'll happen again, sweetheart, if you hang around. That's why you need to finish your little visit and hightail it out of town just as fast as you possibly can. My control only goes so far, and it seems you have no control at all."

The words were like a cold slap, reminding her of all her troubles, of how gullible she'd been, how utterly stupid.

She jerked away and bit her lip hard to keep herself from tearing up. No way would she let the big jerk see her cry. Much as she had hoped to regroup in Buckhorn, she could see that was now impossible. What she would do, she hadn't a clue. But he was right, leaving was imperative. She had absolutely no desire to get involved with a man again, for any reason. Especially not a domineering, bullheaded behemoth like Morgan Hudson, a man who didn't even like her, and in fact, seemed to disdain her.

Keeping her back to him, she drew a long, steadying breath. Then she reached for the door. "I'll leave first thing tomorrow morning." Despite her resolve, her voice quavered tenuously.

There was a slight pause. "Misty..."

He sounded uncertain, but she had no intention of discussing things with him. There was no one she could trust except Honey, and she wouldn't ruin her sister's current happiness for anything. After she got her life straightened out and made some plans that would hopefully carry her through the coming months, she could begin making confessions to her sibling.

The open door offered no relief from the heat; there wasn't a single breeze stirring. Misty stepped onto the dew-wet grass, then felt Morgan's hand settle on her shoulder. "Wait a minute."

She flinched at his tone but didn't bother trying to move away from him. Just that simple touch, his hand on her shoulder, made her acutely aware of him as a man. She almost hated herself. "What now?"

She turned to face him, trying to look irritated when she was actually breathless. The moonlight was brighter. She could see his every feature—the strong, lean jawline, the harshly cut cheekbones. He was by far the most impressive male she'd ever seen, but then, his brothers were nothing to sneeze at. There must have been a mighty impressive gene pool somewhere to create all that masculine perfection.

He stared at her, not answering at first. He shook his head, distracted, and just when he started to speak, another voice intruded.

"There you are."

Morgan looked up. "Casey. What in hell are you doing out here?"

Misty turned to see Sawyer's son. At sixteen, Casey already showed signs of his own masculine superiority. He was tall, nearly six feet, and had the bone structure that promised wide shoulders and long, strong limbs.

"Dad wanted someone to find you and haul you back inside."

Morgan shook his head. "And of course, you just naturally volunteered for the job."

Casey chuckled. "Actually, Uncle Jordan and Uncle Gabe beat me to it, and they did seem pretty anxious to come out here and fetch you in, but Dad told me to go instead, on account of he said you wouldn't slug me."

Morgan threw an arm around his nephew, held him in a brief headlock and then started them all toward the door. "Don't be too sure of that, boy. My affection for you is kinda thin at the moment."

With a laugh, Casey said, "I'm not worried. I can still outrun you."

"You think so, do you?"

"Yeah, 'cause I'm fast—and you're getting old." Casey ducked quickly under Morgan's arm and came to Misty's side. Walking backward, his grin wide, he said, "Dad also told me if you didn't want Honey to get after you, I should walk Misty in and you should come in after."

"He said all that, did he?"

"He said you wouldn't want to shatter Honey's skewed illusions, being as she doesn't know the real you, yet."

Casey was having a fine time of it, pestering his uncle. Misty smiled to herself, amused at their close camaraderie and a little wistful. Her own family consisted of Honey and her father, since her mother died when they were young. Her father had been overbearing and overcontrolling, cold, without the foundation of love that would have made those personality traits more bearable. If it hadn't been for Honey, she didn't think her childhood would have been at all tolerable.

Casey seemed to have a fantastic family foundation. It was

easy to see why Honey had fallen in love with the whole clan.

Morgan stopped just out of reach of the patio, still in the shadows where the lights didn't reach. "You go on in, Casey, and tell your dad I expect him to control his wife. We'll be there in just a moment."

"Dad said you'd say that, and then I was supposed to tell you he's sending Uncle Gabe and Uncle Jordan out in two minutes."

Morgan made a playful grab for Casey, but he jumped back, laughing. Holding up his hands, he said, "Hey, it was Dad, not me!"

Morgan reached for him again and Casey hurried to the door. After he opened it, he yelled back, "Two minutes, Uncle Morgan!"

"Damn scamp."

Misty was still smiling, though she felt great sadness inside. "You're all very close."

"We helped to raise him. Sawyer got full custody when Casey was just a little pup, and between raising him and finishing med school, he would have been frazzled for sure if we hadn't all pitched in. Not that it was a chore. Hell, Casey's always been a great kid, even if his sense of humor is sometimes warped."

Misty stared at him, dumbfounded. "*You* helped raise him?"

"Yeah, sure. Along with my mother and the others. What'd you think, that I was too reprehensible to be around a youngster?"

Actually that was exactly what she thought, but she kept the words to herself. "I was just...surprised. The idea of four men raising a baby..."

"Yeah, well, like I said, my mother taught us what we needed to know. But she felt real strong about Sawyer being involved as the dad, and that meant the rest of us just kinda chipped in. I was...let's see. Nineteen at the time. I'll admit, the diaper thing threw me for a while there, and having formula spit up on me wasn't exactly a treat." Then he grinned. "But the whole uncle bit really turned the girls on. Hell, every time I took Casey into town with me, they'd come on like a mob."

Misty rolled her eyes. "What a lovely image."

Morgan laughed, but then his laughter died. "Look, about what happened..."

"You already made yourself pretty clear, Morgan. I don't think we need to beat it into the ground. I said I'd leave in the morning, and I will."

He ignored that and sighed. "Malone, I care a lot about your sister. I wouldn't want her upset."

She could only stare at him. "You're worried I'll say something to Honey? What? Am I supposed to go tattle on you, is that it?"

Even in the dim light she could see the way he locked his jaw. "She wanted us to be friends."

"Good God!" she exclaimed, and when he frowned she added, "All right, forget the disbelief. For your information, I happen to love my sister."

"Glad to hear it."

"I wouldn't do *anything* to hurt her, and that includes disillusioning her about her new family." She poked him in the chest, her frustration level going right out the window. Her entire life was presently in the toilet, and Morgan Hudson was worried about her discretion? Ha!

"As far as I'm concerned, Honey can think we got along like best pals. But until I can get out of here tomorrow morning, stay the hell away from me."

She turned and stalked in, but at the door, she couldn't resist looking back one last time at Morgan.

He stood there in the moonlight, head tilted toward the dark sky, eyes closed, jaw clenched. His big hands were knotted into fists on his hips. Misty felt herself shiver, even though the evening was oppressively hot.

She knew then that he was right. Tomorrow morning she would leave Buckhorn behind. Hopefully, she'd think of somewhere to stay in the meantime.

She'd spent all her savings fighting the criminal conviction, and lost. She was homeless, out of a job and with no prospects.

And that was the least of her problems.

IF MORGAN HADN'T been lying there awake, his body frustrated, his mind disturbed by sensual images, he might not have heard it. But he hadn't slept a wink all night, too busy remembering the sweet taste of Misty, the way she'd felt pressed against him. Perfect. Willing. *Hot.* Though his head told him things had ended when they should, his imagination had insisted on conjuring up a different ending to the tale, and he'd been rock hard and hurting for more hours now than he cared to admit. It was like suffering the curse of wretched puberty all over again, and he had Misty Malone to thank for it.

The squeak came again, and Morgan recognized the sound as the porch swing that hung in the huge oak at the back of the house. Throwing off the sheet that covered him, he stalked naked to the open window and listened. His room was at one end of the house, opposite to Sawyer and Casey's, with the entire living quarters in between so they all had privacy.

Morgan's bedroom faced the lake, as did Sawyer's. As did the porch swing.

Someone was out there and his gut instinct told him it was Misty. He felt it in his bones, by the way his heart beat faster, by the way his stomach knotted. Only Misty had ever had that intense effect on him, and he figured it was mostly because he had to deny himself. If she wasn't related by marriage, if he could have spent a long, hot weekend with her, indulging all his cravings, he'd be able to get her out of his system.

But he couldn't, and that was the only reason for his obsession. He was sure of it.

Morgan saw that the moon hadn't completely set, even while dawn was struggling to break. He glanced at the clock, surprised to see it was barely five-thirty. What was she doing up so early, hanging around outside? Looking for more ways to torment him?

It took him a mere two seconds to decide to go see her. He knew all the reasons he shouldn't, but something overrode them all, some basic need to spar with her one more time before the rest of the family would be there to pull him back.

He was still buttoning his favorite pair of worn, comfortable jeans, and wearing nothing else, when he stepped out of his room. At the last minute, he stopped, went back into his bedroom and then into his bathroom. He brushed his teeth, giving a disgusted glance at his morning beard and disheveled hair, then decided to hell with it and headed out. But when he passed the kitchen, he halted again and concluded a cup of coffee was definitely in order, if for no other reason than to help him get his bearings before facing her again. She threw him off balance with just a glance, and set his teeth on edge with blinding lust.

As he hurriedly measured the coffee, being careful to be quiet so he wouldn't wake anyone else, he thought about Misty and how she would look so early in the day, her dark hair still tousled, her eyes soft and warm. He imagined her still in her nightgown, something thin and slinky, and he almost dropped the carafe of water. The anticipation he felt was ridiculous, but real.

For at least a few hours this morning, he'd have her all to himself.

Jordan had an apartment above the garage and would be oblivious to anything and everything until at least ten o'clock. He liked to sleep late on the weekends, his only chance to catch up from his busy week.

Gabe might not even be back yet. He'd been surrounded

by the single women of Buckhorn when last Morgan had seen him. But if he was home, his rooms in the basement would insulate him from the normal busy-house noises.

As for Sawyer, he was no doubt occupied with his bride. Morgan wouldn't be at all surprised if he didn't leave the bedroom all day. He grinned at that thought, remembering how Casey had told his father to feel free to linger, that he'd take care of all the chores for him.

Morgan was still grinning and feeling a little too anxious when he silently stepped outside with two steaming mugs of coffee. His bare feet didn't make a sound on the wet morning grass as he walked to the swing. It was a bit chilly, a heavy fog hanging over everything, which turned his first sight of Misty, her back to him, curled up on the swing, into a whimsical, almost ethereal picture. He was only two steps away from her when he heard her give a delicate sniff.

Everything masculine in him froze, and he experienced that incomparable dread men suffered when women turned to tears. He didn't know what to do. He strained to hear, hoping he'd misunderstood the sound, hoping she had a cold.

She sniffed again, then dabbed at her eyes with a wadded tissue. *Oh, hell*. Morgan felt a hard, curling ache around his heart and closed his eyes for a moment. The fact that her tears bothered him so much was a sure sign that things were out of control. Just physical attraction, he insisted to himself, despite his burgeoning sympathy and concern. Shoring up his nerve, he announced himself by clearing his throat.

Turning around so quickly she nearly upset the swing, Misty stared at him. She had glasses on, which he'd never seen before, and her hair was tied back with a plain elastic rubber band, long tendrils carelessly escaping. Even in the gray predawn light, he could see that she blushed.

Truth was, she looked like hell, and he hadn't thought such a thing was possible. Her nose was red and her eyes were hidden behind the reflection of the glasses. His simmering lust died a rapid death, not because of how she looked, but because he knew she was upset, and he was horribly afraid that *he* was the reason.

Not knowing what else to do, he held out one cup of coffee, for the moment ignoring her distress. "I heard the swing and figured you could use this."

She glanced at the cup as if it might hold arsenic. Morgan sighed. "It's coffee. Lots of sugar and cream. I figured since Honey drank hers that way, you likely did, too."

She took the cup, sipped, then quietly thanked him. Without another word, she turned her head to stare toward the lake, which could barely be seen through the fog. She had simply and plainly dismissed him. Her wishes couldn't have been any more clear than if she'd come right out and said, *Go away*.

Nettled, Morgan pretended not to notice.

He moved to sit beside her, never mind that there wasn't really enough room. She quickly scrambled to get her legs out of the way, and it was then he noticed she was wearing a soft old cotton housecoat. No belt, just fat buttons all the way down the front. It looked loose and comfortable, like something that his sixty-year-old mother would wear when she wasn't feeling well. All the buttons were done up except the top one, and Misty clutched that small span of material together with a fist.

Morgan pushed a bare foot against the ground, making the swing sway gently, mindful of the coffee they each held. He kept his gaze on her profile. "You wear glasses."

She didn't answer him.

"I guess that answers the mystery of your big blue eyes, doesn't it? I always figured the color was a little too clear, a little too good to be real. Colored contacts?"

Her shoulders stiffened and she turned to him. Over the rim of the glasses, she glared and gave him a view of those perfect, clear, startling blue eyes, unadorned.

Morgan stared into her eyes, then whispered, "I guess I was wrong."

She turned away again, but muttered, "It's not the first time."

Ignoring that, he touched the rubber band sloppily knotted in her hair. "Rough night?"

One hand clutched the coffee mug, the other a damp tissue and the top of her housecoat. She hesitated, then slanted him another look over her wire-framed glasses. "If that's what you want to think, why not? I mean, you left before me, so it's entirely possible that once you were gone, I staged an orgy in that nice little gazebo you showed me."

Morgan sipped his coffee while keeping his gaze on her. His free arm rested over the back of the swing, his fingers almost touching her. *Almost.* "I somehow doubt your sister would have tolerated that."

She started to jerk to her feet, but Morgan caught her elbow. "No, don't let me run you off. I didn't come out here to harass you."

"No, you came to see if I was ready to leave. Well, don't worry. As soon as it's light, I'll get dressed and go. I packed last night so I could get an early start. I just wanted to watch the sunrise first."

Her words made him feel almost as bad as that time Jordan needed help treating an ornery mule and it kicked him in the gut, breaking two of his ribs. Morgan rubbed a hand over his chest, which didn't do a thing to help this particular ache, then muttered, "It's for the best and you know it."

"I'm not arguing with you, Morgan."

"Good, because I didn't come out here to argue."

"No? Then why?"

Hell, why *had* he come out? Whatever warped reasoning he'd used to justify his actions, he couldn't remember it now. Because he didn't have an answer, he tried changing the subject. "You look like you're...upset."

She shook her head in denial. "No, not at all."

But there was that tissue clutched in her hand, and her red nose and watery eyes. His conscience bothered him, and that had to be a first. In the normal course of things, he didn't bother with a guilty conscience. He was always rock certain of his decisions. "I don't have anything personally against you, Malone."

She snorted.

Morgan clenched his jaw, but he was determined to have his say. "It'll be best for all concerned if you leave soon."

She sighed, then turned to stare at him. "Yeah, well, you seem to be the only one who thinks so. Gabe spent half the night trying to talk me into hanging around, and Jordan even offered me a job."

In angry disbelief, he said, "You told them I asked you to leave?"

His anger didn't faze her. "No. But they knew I'd go sooner or later." Then she mumbled, "Though sooner seems to be on your personal agenda."

Morgan struggled to control his temper. "What did you tell Jordan?"

"That I'd think about it."

His muscles bunched in infuriated reflex. He wanted her gone. He did *not* want her hanging around his brother. "Like hell."

She shrugged nonchalantly, egging him on. She had a habit of doing that, deliberately pricking his temper—and his lust. Hell, half the time he was around her he didn't know for sure what he felt, just that he felt it too keenly and he didn't like it one damn bit.

Jealousy of his brothers was a unique thing, but he absolutely couldn't bear the thought of Misty being with one of them. Besides, he knew if she hung around, they'd eventually be involved, he had no doubt about that at all. Acting on gut instinct, he said, "Forget the job with Jordan. I'll pay you to go."

Her mouth fell open and she stared at him.

"How much do you want?" he asked, forcing the words out through his teeth.

"You're not serious."

"Why not?" He felt goaded and angry and out of control. He absolutely hated it. "You'd use Jordan, taking his infatuation with you to finagle a job. Well, why not use me instead? Hell, at least I know what I'm getting into. So name a price."

Her lips pinched shut, her eyes narrowed and an angry blush rose from her neck up. Then, as he watched, she gathered herself, and anger was replaced by deliberate belligerence. "Hmm, well now, I know what it was Jordan wanted in exchange for the job. But...exactly what would you expect in return for cash, Morgan? Or do I even need to ask?"

Her innuendo goaded his temper, but more than that, it stirred his desire for her, sending him right over the edge. He broke out in a sweat, his gut clenched, his body hardened. He reached for her, not even sure himself what he would do once he had hold of her. But she surprised him by her reaction. She leaped to her feet with a gasp. The coffee mug fell from her hand to the soft ground with a dull thud, spilling the coffee and rolling a few feet away. Misty covered her mouth with both hands. Her face was pale, and she swayed.

Morgan stood also and caught her to him, ignoring her feeble struggles. "Damn it, are you all right?" He shook her slightly, his alarm growing. "What the hell is wrong with you? Answer me, Malone."

Staring at him in horror, she opened her eyes wide and then pushed away, ran several feet to a line of bushes and dropped to her knees.

Morgan was dumbfounded. He started after her, but halted when he heard the unmistakable sound of retching. Never had he felt like such a complete and utter ass. He'd been harassing her again, when that hadn't been his intent at all. He'd argued with her after telling her he wouldn't. And she was sick. He made a false start toward her, then pulled back, as uncertain of what to do as he'd been on his very first date.

He'd hated the feeling then; at thirty-four, he hated it even more.

She probably drank too much last night, he thought, staring at her slim back as she jerked and shuddered. Some people just couldn't hold their liquor—though he didn't remember seeing her imbibe. Mostly she'd just danced and laughed and driven him crazy with an inferno of lust.

When she was done being sick, sitting there on her knees on the damp ground, her arms wrapped around her stomach, he inched closer. He felt totally out of his element, not quite sure what to say or do. But he knew he had to do something. She kept her back to him, no doubt mortified. He knew women could be unaccountably funny about such things. Finally, feeling like a fool, he knelt behind her. "You want me to go get you something to drink?"

She moaned and clutched herself a little tighter. "Just...go...away."

Morgan hesitated, then lifted one hand to her shoulder, gently rubbing. Touching her made *him* feel immeasurably better, whether it did anything for her or not. "I bet Sawyer has something he could give you for the hangover."

She laughed, a raw, broken sound that was close to a moan. "A hangover, Morgan? When I didn't drink a single drop?"

Way off base with that one, obviously. He nodded. "Okay, not a hangover."

She shook her head, and more silky strands of midnight hair escaped her rubber band to curl around her cheeks. A few tangled in the armature of her glasses, and he gently pulled them away.

Without looking at him, she said, "You always think the worst of me, don't you?"

He didn't know what to say to that.

"I should be used to it. God knows, men always... Oh, just

go away." Her voice was thin, washed out; she sounded too tired to argue.

He couldn't stop his deep frown or his concern. "If you're sick, then—"

Her hands fisted on her thighs in a sudden startling display of frustration. Still without looking at him, she hissed, "Damn it, why can't you just leave me alone?"

He wouldn't let her rile him again. "Look, Malone, my mother would skin my hide if I left a sick woman wallowing out in the dew, without—"

"I am not sick!"

Her stubbornness annoyed the hell out of him, even as he continued to gently stroke her back. "Oh, then I'm hallucinating? That wasn't you just puking your guts up in my bushes? Because I have to tell you, Malone, if you're hoping to be a martyr to get my sympathy, it's not at all necessary. Hell, I already—"

She turned to him with a feral growl, momentarily startling him, then practically shouted, "I am not sick, you idiot! *I'm pregnant.*"

3

OH, GOD. Misty stared at Morgan, horrified by her statement, and ready to be sick all over again. She slapped a hand over her mouth and gulped air through her nose, determined to hold it back. She'd thought the fresh air would help, and it really had, but then Morgan had joined her....

She frowned, her queasy stomach almost forgotten. It was all his fault, and she said, without the demonic tone this time, "I don't suppose you'll just forget I said that?"

Dumbly, he shook his head, his eyes still wide, his jaw still slack. For once he wasn't scowling. He looked too stunned to scowl. "Uh, no. Not likely."

Her temper snapped. "Oh, of course not. That would be too easy, wouldn't it?" She frowned ferociously, wishing she could hit him over his hard head. "Well, it's none of your business, anyway. And if you tell my sister, I swear I'll make you regret it."

Morgan's expression hadn't changed. It was a comical mix of surprise, chagrin and helplessness. Something else, too, something bordering on anger, but she couldn't be sure. He blinked, but didn't say a word. With a sound of disgust, Misty rolled her eyes and started to get to her feet. "Look, I'm sorry about your bushes. Really. Do you think anyone will notice?" Before he could answer, she added, "But in a way, you're the one to blame. If you hadn't kept prodding me... But that doesn't matter now. I'm feeling much better, fine, in fact, so I'll just go get dressed and get on my way. Please thank your brothers for me. And tell Honey I'll be in touch."

She was rattled, which accounted for the way she was blathering on and on. She wanted to bite her tongue off. She wanted more coffee.

She wanted away from Morgan Hudson.

He'd slowly stood when she had, and now he stepped in front of her, blocking her attempt at a strategic retreat. "I don't think so, Malone. You're not going to make a confession like that and then just creep off."

She was too tired, too mind weary to deal with him now. As if speaking to an idiot, she said, "I didn't exactly have creeping in mind. I thought I'd dress, pick up my bags, walk out the front door and drive away. There's a big difference."

"You were crying. Your eyes are all puffy."

He said it like a heinous accusation. She waved a negligent hand, not about to explain herself to *him*. "Don't be silly. I always look like hell in the morning. Lucky for you, you won't have to get used to it."

She started around him again, and this time he picked her up. She would have screamed her head off, she was so exasperated, except she sure as certain didn't want the other brothers witnessing her this way.

Gabe was such a comedian, he'd probably start joking about the whole thing. And Jordan, with that mesmerizing voice Honey claimed could put a cow to sleep, would do his best to comfort her, which would make her cry again.

And Sawyer—she had no idea how he'd react to his new wife's sister showing up pregnant.

So instead of screaming, she held herself stiff and tried to ignore how easily Morgan carried her, his incredible strength, the delicious way he smelled this morning and her twinge of ridiculous regret when he sat her on the swing.

It had been so long since she'd been held, so long since she'd felt anything like caring or concern or gentleness, she was almost starving for it. Even Morgan's aggressive, demanding concern felt like a balm.

But she was also more savvy now, and she knew beyond a

shadow of a doubt that Morgan Hudson was not a man to take comfort from.

"Uh, Morgan..."

Hands on his thighs, he leaned down in front of her until their noses nearly touched. "I'm going to go get you some juice. If you move so much as your baby toe before I get back, you won't be happy with my reaction. I mean it, Malone."

He looked more serious than she'd ever seen him. Not that she was afraid of him and his threats, but again, a ruckus might wake everyone else.

She turned her head away. "Bully."

"Damn right."

He sauntered off, but as if he hadn't trusted her to stay put, he was back in less than a minute. Misty hadn't moved, only because she was so tired. For weeks now she'd been trying to come up with a solution, but the problems just kept adding up, and she hadn't a clue what to do. Finding a job was obviously top of the list. Then she could sell her car to make the first month of rent once she found a place she could afford.

Borrowing money from her father was out of the question. She wouldn't ask him for a nickel. They had never been close and she knew without approaching him what his reaction to her most recent problems would be. Probably even worse than his reaction to her pregnancy, which predictably had been disappointment. He'd give her money, but that's all he'd ever give, never understanding or emotional support. She had enough to deal with without his overwhelming condemnation on her shoulders.

No, she'd rather go it alone than go to her father.

She was still frowning, deep in thought, when Morgan handed her a tall, cold glass of orange juice. The juice looked wonderful, and she accepted it gladly. Sipping, she said, "I thank you—at least for the drink."

Morgan seated himself beside her and crossed his long arms over his massive chest. With his dark frown and set jaw, he looked belligerent and antagonistic. She didn't like his attitude at all.

She liked him even less.

Knowing he hated it when she acted brazen, and hoping he'd go away and leave her alone with her misery, she said, "You know, you really should show a little more decorum. Running around half naked is almost barbaric. Especially for a man built like you."

He blinked in surprise, and his brows smoothed out. "A man built like me?"

"Yeah, you know." She glanced at his hard, hair-covered chest, felt a shot of heat straight through the pit of her stomach and raised her brows. "All muscle-bound. You do that to attract the women? Because while I appreciate the sight of your sexy body, I'm not at all attracted."

He narrowed his eyes. "Are you trying to distract me, Malone?"

She sighed. "No, I'm being honest. You're an incredibly good-looking man, Morgan. And evidently a pushy one, too. But I'm not interested in any man, for any reason. I'm through with the lot of you—for good. Besides, I'm leaving today, and with any luck, you'll be long married with kids of your own and moved away before I ever visit again." She nodded at his chest once more. "You're wasting the excellent display on the likes of me."

"Oh, I don't know about that, considering most of what you just said was bunk. You are interested—at least in me." His voice dropped, and he looked her over slowly. She felt the touch of his gaze like a stroke of heat, from the top of her thighs to the base of her throat. "Last night proved that."

Misty swallowed hard, feeling a new sensation in her belly that wasn't at all unpleasant. "Last night was an aberration. I've had a lot on mind and you took me by surprise."

He let that slide without comment. "The part about me moving out is true enough, though. But I won't be far. The house on the hill? That's mine. It'll be ready to move into soon."

She couldn't see the house from here, but she remembered admiring it when she first arrived. It wasn't quite as large as this one, but it was still impressive. She wondered if he already had the wife picked out, too, but didn't ask. "Good for you."

Tilting his head, his look still far too provocative, Morgan said, "I'm curious about this professed disinterest of yours, especially considering your condition."

"My *condition?*" She hated how he said that—just as her father had, just as her fiancé had—with something of a sneer. She wanted the baby and she wouldn't apologize for having it, not to anyone, and certainly not to him. "It's not a disease, you know."

His gaze hardened. "When're you getting married, Malone?"

The words were casual, almost softly spoken, but they sounded lethal. And his stare was so intent, so burning, she looked at his chest instead of meeting his eyes. "None of your business."

"I'm making it my business."

The juice did wonders for settling her nausea and she finally felt more herself. Morning sickness was the pits, and she hoped she got past that stage soon, though now that the worst had happened and she'd been sick in front of Morgan, anything else had to be an improvement. "You do that a lot, do you? Butt in where you've got no business being? I bet that's why you took the position of sheriff. It gives you a legal right to nose around into other people's affairs."

He looked off to the distance, and Misty, following his gaze, saw that the sun was beginning its slow climb into the sky. It was a beautiful sight, sending a crimson glow across the placid surface of the lake, bringing a visual warmth that had her feeling better already. She sighed, knowing she'd never forget this place and how incredibly perfect it seemed.

Then Morgan spoke again, reminding her of a major flaw to the peaceful setting. Him.

"We can sit here until everyone else joins us if you want, but I got the impression you're keeping your departure a secret."

She sighed again, actually more of a huff. "You've got no right to badger me about something that is none of your damn business, Morgan."

"You're family now," he explained with a straight face. "That gives me all the rights I need."

Something that ludicrous deserved her undivided attention. She stared at him, almost speechless, but not quite. "*Family?* Get real."

He looked her over slowly, and she knew, even before he told her, that he was making a point. "Oh, you're family, all right, because if you weren't, we'd never have left that damn gazebo, that is, not until things ended in a way that we'd both have enjoyed. A lot."

The tone of his voice, both aggressive and persuasive, sank into her bones. Her stomach flip-flopped and her toes curled. Damn him, how could he do this to her now, when she'd just been sick, when she didn't like him, when he didn't much care for her? It wasn't fair that of all the men in all the world, Morgan Hudson had this singular effect on her.

But then, little in her life had been fair lately.

She shook her head, denying both him and herself. "You're twisting things around—"

"I'm stating a fact."

"The fact is that you want me as far from your family as you can manage!"

His shrug was negligent, but his gaze was hard. "As you pointed out, everyone else feels differently. Jordan even offered you a job."

"Which I refused."

His brows shot up. "You did?"

He sounded surprised, but then, she had been purposely

harassing him by letting him think otherwise. That had been childish, and not at all smart. She sighed. "Of course I did."

"Why?"

Exasperated by his suspicious tone, she explained, "This'll be a shock, I'm sure, but I'm not the party girl you seem to think I am, Morgan. I realize both your brothers were likely just fooling around, but I don't intend to take any chances. I'm not interested in fun and games, and as I already told you, I'm even less interested in being serious with someone. I didn't want to accidentally encourage either of them, so I thanked Jordan for the offer, but declined, and I told Gabe I had other responsibilities and couldn't hang around any longer. So you can relax your vigil. Both your brothers are safe from my evil clutches."

He didn't react to her provocation this time, choosing instead to hark back to his earlier question. "When are you getting married?"

He wouldn't give up, she could tell. He looked settled in and disgruntled and determined. She was so tired of fighting men, her ex-fiancé, her ex-boss, even the damn lawyers and the judge. Maybe once she told Morgan everything, he'd be glad to be rid of her. She slumped into her seat, all fight gone. "I give up. You win."

He didn't gloat, and he didn't sound exactly pleased with himself. He was simply matter-of-fact in his reply. "I always do." Then more quietly, "When are you getting married?"

"I'm not." She felt him studying her and she twisted to face him so she could glare right back. "I'm not getting married, okay? There's no groom, no wedding, no happily ever after. Satisfied now?"

There was a sudden stillness, then Morgan relaxed, all the tension ebbing out of him, his breathing easier, his expression less stern. She hadn't even realized he was holding himself so stiffly until he returned to his usual cocky self. He uncrossed his arms to spread one over the back of the swing, nearly touching her shoulder, and he shifted, all his big muscles sort of loosening and settling in.

In a tone meant to clarify, he asked, "You're *not* getting married?"

"What, do you want it written in blood? I'm not getting married. The very idea is repugnant. I have absolutely no interest in marriage."

"I see." The aggression was gone, replaced by something near to sympathy, and to Misty, that was even worse. "What happened to the father of the baby?"

Why not, she thought, fed up with fending him off. "He found out he was going to be a father and offered me money for an abortion." She wouldn't look at him. The humiliation and pain she'd felt that day was still with her. It had been the worst betrayal ever—or so she'd thought, until she'd lost her job. "I refused, he got angry, and we came to an agreement."

"What agreement?"

"I wouldn't bother him with the baby, and he wouldn't bother with me."

The swing kept moving, gently, lulling her, and though Morgan was silent, it didn't feel like a condemning silence as much as a contemplative one. Finally he asked, "How long have you been sick in the mornings?"

"Only for a few weeks. And before you ask, yes, I'll tell Honey. But not now. She has a tendency to worry about me, to play the role of big sister even though I'm only a year younger than her. She's so happy with Sawyer now, she doesn't need to hear about my problems just yet."

His fingers gently touched her hair, smoothing it. It was clearly a negligent touch, as if he did it without thought. When she glanced at him, she saw he was watching her closely.

"Will the baby be a problem?"

"No! I want the baby."

His gaze softened. "That's not what I mean."

Lifting her chin, she said, "If you're asking me if I'll be a good mother, I hope so. I don't have much experience, but I intend to do my absolute best."

"No, I wasn't accusing you of anything or questioning your maternal instincts." He smiled slightly. "I just wonder if you know what you're getting into. Babies are a full-time job. How do you intend to work and care for it, too, without any help?"

She shook her head. Since she didn't even have a job at present, she didn't have an answer for him.

"Will you be able to get a leave of absence?"

The irony of that question hit her and she all but laughed. Instead, she turned her face away so he couldn't see how lost she felt.

Morgan touched her cheek. "Malone?"

"Isn't this interrogation about over?"

"I don't think so. So why don't you make it easy on yourself and just answer my questions?"

"Somehow I don't think this conversation is going to be easy on me no matter what I do."

He got quiet over that. "I don't mean to make things difficult for you."

"Don't you?"

"I didn't create this situation, Malone, and the attraction isn't one-sided. Will you at least admit that much?"

She didn't want to, but saw no point in denying it. "Yeah, so? I think the fact I'm pregnant and without a groom shows my judgment to be a bit flawed, so don't let it go to your head."

His large hand cupped the back of her skull, his fingers gently kneading. The tenderness, after his previous attitude, was startling. "Everyone makes a mistake now and then. You're not the first."

"Which mistake are we referring to? Me being pregnant, or my response to you?"

Again, he was quiet.

She decided to make a clean break, to finish her confessions and get away before she became morose again. She slapped her palms on her thighs, turned to him with a take-charge air and said, "Okay. You've worn me down. Besides, the sun is almost completely up. Everyone will be waking soon, and I hope to get out of here before that. I'd just as soon avoid the lengthy goodbyes if I can. So tell me, Sheriff, what other intrusive questions do you have for me before I'm formally dismissed?"

Again, he easily ignored her sarcasm. "How far along are you? You sure as certain don't look pregnant."

She laughed shortly. "Yeah, just think, if I did look pregnant we probably wouldn't be having this conversation right now!"

"Malone?"

"Three months." She gave him a crooked grin. "From what I understand, I may not start to show until my fifth, maybe even my sixth month. By then, I'll be a distant memory for you, Morgan."

"But you're sure you are—"

"Had the test, so yes, I'm sure. Besides, I feel the pregnancy in other ways."

His gaze went unerringly to her breasts, now thoroughly hidden beneath her sexless robe. Still, she practically squirmed with the need to shield herself with her hands. She resisted the telltale reaction. "Yep, I'm bigger now," she said, doing her best to sound flippant, unaffected. Trying not to blush. Her glasses slipped a bit, and she pushed them back up.

"What about your job?"

Hedging, she asked, "What about it?"

"It occurs to me that I don't know all that much about you."

Her eyes widened and she laughed. "Now there's a revelation for you. Of course, anytime you don't know something, you just fill it in with fiction."

He touched her cheek with the back of one finger and his

expression was regretful. "I admit to making some pretty hasty assumptions. But you haven't helped, Misty, coming on the way you did."

"I didn't—"

"Yeah, you did." He smiled just a little, making her heart twist. "You flirt with everyone."

She sighed. "True enough. I was trying to act cheerful and worry-free so Honey wouldn't suspect anything. Maybe I overdid it just a bit."

"And maybe I want you bad enough that all you have to do is breathe and it seems like a seduction. At least to me."

Her gaze shot to his face; she was speechless.

"It's true, you know. I don't think I've ever wanted a woman the way I do you." His hand opened and his palm cupped her cheek. "Even now, with you looking like a maiden aunt and after you tossed your cookies in the bushes. Even knowing you're pregnant with another man's baby, I still want you."

She shook her head, words beyond her.

"I know. It's a damnable situation, isn't it?"

"No, it's not." She was resolute, driven by her emotional fear. "I'm leaving, this morning, right now if you'll just stop questioning me and let me leave without a fuss."

"It's not that easy, Malone, now that I know you're in trouble."

"Such an old-fashioned sentiment! Unmarried pregnant women are no longer in *trouble.* They're just...pregnant." She gave a negligent shrug.

"All right, if you say so." He looked far from convinced. "So quit hedging and reassure me. Where do you work?"

Knowing that, as sheriff, it would be easy enough for him to check, and not doubting for a moment that he probably would, she sniffed and said, "I only recently left Vision Videos."

"Vision Videos?"

"A small, privately owned video store. It's located in the

town I...used to live in." She sincerely hoped he missed her small hesitation. The idea of being homeless was still pretty new to her. "It's very small scale, only three employees besides the owner, but the store did incredible business. He'd planned to open another location by the end of the summer and I was going to run it for him."

"But you're not now?"

"Now, I'm in the process of reevaluating my options."

He stared, and his softly stroking fingers went still. With disbelief ringing from every word, he said, "You're unemployed?"

"Momentarily, yes."

His eyes narrowed. "By choice? Because I'll tell you, if your boss fired you for being pregnant, that's against the law...."

"No, he didn't fire me for that."

Morgan's back stiffened, and his scowl grew darker. "But he did fire you?"

"Actually...yes."

"Why?"

"He...well, he accused me of doing something I didn't do."

"Damn it, Malone," he suddenly burst out, his irritation evident, his patience at an end. "It's like pulling snake teeth to get you to tell the whole—"

"All right!" She shot to her feet, every bit as annoyed as he was. Hands on her hips, she faced him. "All right, damn it. I was convicted of stealing from him. Three hundred dollars. But I didn't do it, only they believed that I did!"

Morgan stood, too, and now he looked livid. "They?"

She waved a hand. "The owner, the lawyer I had to hire, the despicable judge. Everyone."

Very slowly, Morgan reached out and took hold of her shoulders. "Tell me what happened."

Misty had no idea if he was angry with her or the situation. She tried to shrug his hands away, but he held on. Her temper was still simmering, though, and she was in no mood for his attitude, so she jerked away and then sat on the swing, giving a hard kick to make it move. Morgan grabbed the swing to stop it and sat beside her. "I'm waiting."

She crossed her arms over her breasts. He made her feel vulnerable and defensive when she had no reason to feel either one. "Not long after I found out I was pregnant and Kent, my ex, bailed out, I was at work and the cash came up short. The woman who'd worked before me had signed out and made her deposit, so the money had to have been taken during my shift. Only I didn't take it and I don't know where it went. I was in the bathroom—" She glanced at him. "Pregnant women spend a lot of time in the bathroom."

He made a face. "Go on."

"Anyway, there was no one in the store, so I made a quick run to the bathroom, and when I came back out, my boss and his girlfriend were just coming in. He was royally ticked that I'd left the counter, even after I explained that the store was empty and that I'd hurried. We argued, because he said I'd missed too much work lately, as well. See, I'd come in late twice, because of the morning sickness. Anyway, he was in a foul mood and being unreasonable, to my mind. I'd never been late or missed work before. Not ever. That's why he was going to make me a manager of the new store, because I was a good worker and dependable and all that."

"Get to the point, Malone."

She wanted to smack him. Instead, she said, "He checked the drawer and found out the money was missing. I still can't believe he accused me of stealing it. I'd been working for him for two years. I did everything, from inventory to decorations to promotion to sales to orders. I'm the one that helped that business do so well! I thought he trusted me."

"He called the cops?"

"Yes." The police had arrived, and she now knew firsthand the procedure used for thiefs. She shuddered with the memory, which wasn't one she intended to share with Morgan. "To make a long story short, the lawyer I hired said they had a good case against me. I was the only one in the store at the time the money was taken, and they found out I was pregnant, that the father of the baby had taken off. They painted me a desperate woman, with plenty of motive to take the money. He suggested I plead guilty to save myself a bundle in lawyer fees and court costs. I...I refused. So my lawyer suggested that I go with a trial to the bench, since that would get it over with quickly."

"I gather that wasn't the best decision possible?"

She shook her head. "A jury might not have been so autocratic or sexist."

"*Sexist?*"

"Yes. The judge was a stern-faced old relic who saw me as a femme fatale just because I'm young and I don't exactly look like a college professor."

One brow shot up, and his mouth quirked. "You mean because you're sexy as hell and he noticed?"

"That's not funny, Morgan."

"No, it's not. Sorry."

He still looked amused, though, which annoyed her no end. The judge's reaction to her had been salt in the wound. She could still remember how exposed she'd felt, standing before him.

She looked away and said quietly, "He gave me six months probation, made me pay back the three hundred dollars I hadn't even taken, as well as court costs and legal fees, then finished up with a scathing lecture about my responsibilities and morals and hoping I'd learned my lesson." She snorted. "The lesson I learned was that men see things one way, which is seldom the right or honorable way, and they sure as hell can't be trusted."

"Misty..."

"Don't use that tone on me, Morgan Hudson. You got what you wanted, all the nitty-gritty details. Well, now I'm done. I want to get out of here. I need to go find a job, and I'm

just plain not up to fighting with you anymore, so if you'll
excuse me—"

"No."

"*No?*" Incredulous, she turned to face him. "What do you
mean, no?"

He stood, then caught her arm and pulled her to her feet.
Still holding her, his gaze intent on her face, he said softly, "I
mean you're not going anywhere, Malone. You're going to
stay right here."

4

MORGAN STARED at Misty, knowing that despite her outraged frown, there was no way he could let her go, not now. Her shoulders felt narrow and frail beneath his big hands, and he wished like hell she looked pregnant, so she'd be easier to resist. But she didn't. She looked soft and sexy, even with a red nose and those hideous glasses. He wanted her more than ever, but that was beside the point.

At least she wasn't planning on getting married. Though it wasn't any of his damn business, the very idea had set his teeth on edge. She could certainly do better than settling for some clown who didn't want his own child. He swore to himself that was the only reason it bothered him. Then he called himself a fool.

"You can't be off on your own right now. You said it yourself, you don't have a job, and you're sick."

She gave him a blank stare, as if he was a stranger.

"Damn it, Misty, you know I'm right!"

"I know you're nuts, that's what I know." He made a grumbling sound, and she said in exasperation, "It's morning sickness, Morgan, that's all. I'm fine the rest of the time. I'm perfectly capable of finding and working a job. Pregnant woman do it all the time, you know."

Actually, his mind was buzzing with possibilities. If she stayed—and she would because he didn't intend to give her a choice—he could give her a job. He'd long since figured they needed someone to answer the phones at the office, but more often than not folks just called him directly. It was a small county, and the crime level was amazingly low, so he'd been in no rush to hire a new deputy. But a secretary of sorts, someone to keep track of his schedule and forward calls and take notes, that'd be a blessing.

He'd put off the hiring for some time now. He hadn't really wanted anyone else mucking around his offices. But now…

He eyed her belligerent expression and winced. Better to tell her about the job later, when she wasn't so annoyed with him. He gave her a slight shake. "So what do you intend to do?"

"I intend to punch you in the nose if you don't stop manhandling me!"

His fingers flexed on her shoulders, very gently, and he saw her eyes darken. He hadn't hurt her, would never deliberately hurt her. No, her complaint was for an entirely different reason. "Manhandling, huh?" he asked softly. "And here I thought I was being all that was considerate and caring."

She bit her lip in indecision, then resolutely shook her head. "Not likely, Morgan. You're up to something, I just haven't figured out what yet."

Her opinion of him was far from flattering, with good reason, he supposed. He dropped his hands and turned to think, only to hear her stomping away. He caught the back of her robe and drew her up short. "Whoa. Now where are you off to? We have to finish discussing this."

Through gritted teeth, she said, "There's no *we* to it, and there's nothing to discuss." She swatted his hands away and jutted her chin toward him. "I'm going in to shower and dress, and then I'm leaving. You won't have to worry about me at all, and your precious brothers will be safe from my lascivious tendencies."

Damn it, she was trying to make him feel guilty—and succeeding. "You let me think the worst about that, Malone. Admit it."

"You always assume the worst," she argued. "I'm not responsible for the way your mind works."

"No, you're not. But in a way, it is your fault." She looked ready to erupt, so he added, "I get around you, Malone, and I can barely think at all, much less with any logic. In case you haven't noticed, I've got the hots for you in a really bad way."

Her face went blank for a split second, and he braced himself for an attack. Then suddenly her mouth twitched, and she burst out laughing. "Is that your way of saying you're sorry?"

Hearing her laugh was nice, even if she was laughing at him. "I suppose you think I owe you that much?"

"Nope." Her glasses slid down her nose and more hair escaped the rubber band. She looked disheveled and vulnerable and so damn female he felt rigid from his neck all the way down to his toes. "I don't think you owe me a darn thing, Morgan, except to butt out of my business."

Shrugging in apology, he whispered, "I can't do that."

"You," she said with emphasis, "have no choice in the matter."

"I can help you, Malone."

"You want to help?" She turned away from him, then said over her shoulder, "Leave me be."

Why, Morgan wondered as she stalked away, would she steal money from an employer, but not take money from him when it was freely offered? Especially considering the situation she was in. And not only had she refused the money, she'd been downright livid over the idea. Somehow it didn't fit, and he damn well intended to find out what was going on.

Later. Right now he was busy plotting. She had turned down the money, but maybe she'd accept his help in other ways once he talked her into staying. He wasn't raised to turn his back on a woman in her predicament, especially considering that she *was* part of the family. Whether she liked it or not, that excuse was good enough for him.

He picked up the coffee mugs and her empty juice glass,

then headed into the kitchen. He had a few things to take care of before she finished showering, so he might as well get to them. First was that ragtag little car of hers. Removing a few spark plugs ought to do the trick. Getting his brothers out of bed would be a little harder, considering the night they'd all had, but they would rally together for a good cause, and he definitely considered Misty Malone a good cause. Given how all his brothers had doted on her the past couple of weeks, he had no doubt they'd feel the same.

Twenty minutes later, Morgan was sitting at the kitchen table with a bleary-eyed Casey when Misty walked in. The others hadn't quite made it that far yet, but Morgan knew they'd present themselves shortly.

Casey, with his head propped in his hand, glanced at her and yawned. "Morning, Misty. What're you doing up so early?"

Misty stopped dead in her tracks. Her hair was freshly brushed and twisted into a tidy knot on the top of her head that Morgan thought made her look romantic and amazingly innocent. Her glasses were gone—thank God—and she no longer had a red nose. She wore a yellow cotton camisole with cutoff shorts and strappy little sandals and she looked good enough to eat.

Morgan drew in a shuddering breath with that image and steered his wayward thoughts off the erotic and onto the essential.

Rather than answer Casey, her accusing gaze swung toward Morgan and there was murder in her eyes. He grinned. He'd rather have her fighting mad than looking morose any day. Leaning against the counter with his arms crossed over his chest, Morgan said, "What's with the suitcase, Malone?"

Casey, who hadn't noticed the luggage yet, sat up straight. His gaze bounced back and forth several times between the suitcase and Misty's face, and he looked more alert than he had only five seconds ago. "You're not leaving, are you?"

Misty ground her teeth, then whipped around to face Casey with a falsely bright smile plastered in place. "'Fraid so, kiddo. I have things to do. But I did enjoy my visit. Tell your dad thanks for me, okay?"

She started to move, but Casey jumped up, looking panicked, and all but blocked her way. "But Dad'll kill me if you leave without saying goodbye! I mean, Honey will be upset and that'll upset Dad. Just hang around for breakfast, okay?" He glanced at Morgan for backup. "Tell her, Uncle Morgan. Shouldn't she stay and have breakfast?"

Morgan nodded slowly. "I do believe you're right, Casey."

"Ah, no... It's better if I—"

The kitchen door swung open and Jordan dragged himself in. He was wearing a pair of unsnapped jeans and scratching his belly while yawning hugely. His hair was still mussed and he looked like he could have used another six hours of sleep, at least. The last Morgan had seen him last night, three of the local women were trying to talk him into taking each of them home. It was a hell of a predicament for his most reserved brother.

Morgan had not one whit of sympathy for him.

Because Jordan had taken the path from the garage—where he kept his apartment—to the kitchen, the bottoms of his feet were wet. When he saw Misty packed up and ready to go, he nearly slipped on the linoleum floor in his surprise.

Morgan caught him, then pushed him upright. If Jordan knocked himself out, he'd be no help at all.

In his usual mellow tones, Jordan asked, "What's going on here?" He dried his feet on a throw rug while quietly studying everyone in turn.

Morgan feigned a casual shrug. "Misty says she's leaving."

Casey crossed his arms, ready to add his two cents' worth. "She's not even going to tell anyone goodbye."

Looking from Casey's disapproving face to Misty's red cheeks before finally meeting Morgan's gaze, Jordan frowned. Not a threatening frown, as Morgan favored, but rather a contemplative one. Jordan was no dummy and caught on quickly that this was the reason he'd been summoned from his bed. He fastened his jeans now that he knew there was a lady present, then took several cautious steps forward, making certain not to slip again. Holding Misty's shoulders, he asked softly, "What's wrong, sweetheart? Why are you sneaking off like this?"

Morgan didn't like his brother's intimate tone at all. And he sure as hell didn't like Jordan touching her. He glowered at Misty as he said, "I don't think she wanted anyone to know she was going."

Jordan glanced at Morgan, then crossed his arms over his chest and regarded Misty with quiet speculation. "Is that true?"

After a long, drawn out sigh, Misty dropped her heavy bag and propped her hands on her hips. "I'm not sneaking, exactly. You all knew I was going to be leaving today."

Gabe spoke from the doorway where he'd negligently propped himself, unnoticed. "Not true." He gave Morgan a look, then came into the kitchen and dropped into a chair with a theatrical yawn. He, too, was bare-chested, but he wore loose cotton pull-on pants. "You said you couldn't stay, Misty, but you didn't say a damn thing about taking off today at six-thirty in the morning. Hell, the birds aren't even awake yet, so I'd definitely call that sneaking. What's up, sweetheart?"

Misty looked ready to expire. Morgan took pity on her and pulled out a chair. "Why don't you at least sit down, Malone, while you do your explaining?" He reached for her arm, but she sidestepped him. Breathing hard, she glared at them all, then said, "I'm leaving, that's all there is to it. I'm already packed and I want to get an early start. I'm not good at long goodbyes, so...if you'll excuse me?"

She picked up her bag and headed for the door. Her car was parked at the side of the house, close to the back door. There was a flurry of arguments from Casey, Jordan and

Gabe, but Morgan had expected no less of them. It was why he'd so rudely dragged them out of their warm, comfortable beds. Unfortunately, Misty wasn't going to be swayed by them.

She stormed out of the house in righteous fury, and they all trailed behind, talking at once. Morgan listened to their arguments for why she should stay and even commended his brothers for making some good points.

Misty did an admirable job of ignoring them.

When Jordan realized how serious she was, he took the suitcase from her hand while stabbing Morgan with curious looks, as if waiting for *him* to stop her somehow.

Morgan almost laughed. He'd known there was no way he'd be able to bring her around. If he wasn't missing his guess, he was the biggest reason she was so set on going. That was why he'd pulled the spark plugs, as insurance until he got her over her pique and could make her see reason.

After Jordan stowed her suitcase in the back seat, he reached for Misty and pulled her into a fierce hug. To Morgan, seething at the sight of Misty snuggled up against Jordan's bare chest, the embrace didn't look at all familial. He was just about to tear them apart when Jordan leaned back the tiniest bit to look at her.

"Where will you be staying?" Jordan asked. "Is there a number where we can call you?"

Misty appeared stumped for just a moment, which made Morgan very suspicious, then she brightened. "I'm sort of moving around at the moment. But I'll let you know when I get settled, okay?"

Morgan continued to study her. It was amazing, even to him, but he could read her like a book, and he knew without a doubt she didn't have any place to stay. He wanted to throttle her, and he wanted to hold her tight.

Gabe stepped up next for his own hug, and he even dared to kiss her on the cheek, lingering for what Morgan considered an inappropriate amount of time. Morgan gave serious thought to throwing Gabe back into the basement. "If you change your mind," Gabe said, "promise you'll come back."

"I promise. And thank you."

Casey shook his head. "My death will be on your hands, because Dad is still going to kill me."

Morgan silently applauded Casey's forlorn expression, but Misty didn't buy it. She actually grinned. "Your father wouldn't hurt a hair on your head, and you know it! Now give me a hug." With a crooked smile, Casey obeyed.

And even that made Morgan grind his teeth. Casey was a good head taller than Misty with shoulders much wider. Morgan didn't like it at all. Hell, so far they'd all touched her more than he had!

Misty didn't even bother looking at Morgan. He crossed his arms and waited until she'd gotten behind the wheel and pulled her door shut, then he leaned back against a tall oak tree. He considered himself patience personified.

Jordan stepped up to him with an intent frown. It was unlike Jordan to be so disgruntled, and Morgan raised a taunting brow. "Sorry to see her go?"

Jordan didn't rile easily. "You got me out of bed just to tell her goodbye? I figured you'd stop her somehow. Honey's going to be damn upset when she finds out we let her leave."

Morgan eyed his brother a moment longer, decided he didn't see any signs of lovesickness, and turned to stare at Misty. "She's not going anywhere."

Misty gave one final cheery wave to them all and turned the key. The engine ground roughly, whined, but didn't quite turn over. Frowning, she tried again. The car still wouldn't start.

Satisfied, Morgan watched Gabe saunter over to him, Casey at his side. "You tinkered with her car?" He sounded faintly approving. Gabe was the mechanic and handyman in the family. If he'd thought of it or had had time, he likely would have done the same.

Morgan gave him a wounded look. "Now, would I do a

thing like that? I'm the law around here, Gabe, you know that. Tampering with a car is illegal." He looked at Misty with a smile. "I'm sure of it."

Grinning, Gabe went to the driver's window and tapped on it. When Misty rolled down her window, he said, "Doesn't sound like she's going to start, hon."

Misty dropped her head onto the steering wheel and ignored Gabe, ruthlessly twisting the key once again. She looked so forlorn that Morgan almost couldn't stand it. He wanted to lift her out of the car, hold her, tell her everything would be okay. He wanted, damn it, to take care of her. To protect her.

Because she was family.

Because she was a woman in need.

Because it was the right thing to do.

Not because he cared for her personally. Wanting a woman and caring for her were two different things, and he was never one to confuse the issues. Yes, he wanted her, more so now than ever, which seemed odd in the extreme. But he could deal with that. What he couldn't deal with was the idea of her running off with no place to go, and the fact that she'd be alone at a time when she needed family most.

So maybe she'd gotten into some trouble? He wasn't completely convinced yet. But even if it was true, everyone made mistakes, and being a pregnant, unmarried woman was as good a reason for theft as any he'd ever heard. He didn't approve, but he did understand. She was still young, only twenty-four, and she'd found herself in a hell of a predicament.

From the sound of it, she'd more than paid for the crime, not only financially, but emotionally, as well. He didn't blame her for not wanting to own up to it if she was guilty. Few people tended to brag about their bad judgment.

Convinced that he was still in control of things, including his own tumultuous emotions, Morgan walked over to the car and opened the back door. He lifted out her bag then nudged Gabe aside. He pulled her door open and cupped his free hand around her upper arm. Gabe stood there grinning at him, while Jordan and Casey watched with satisfaction.

"C'mon, Malone," Morgan said. "Sitting out here moping isn't going to solve anything."

She smacked her head onto the steering wheel again. "I can't be this unlucky."

Morgan hesitated, but he knew damn good and well he'd done the right thing. He'd needed to buy some time to undo the damage he'd inflicted with his insistence that she should leave. Later, she'd thank him. "Rattling your brains won't help. Come inside and we'll figure something out."

She leaned back in the seat and stared at him. "I hope you're happy now."

His smile was only fleeting before he wiped it away. "I'm getting there." He urged her out of the car and kept hold of her arm even as they walked back in. He was pleased that she didn't pull away from him. That surely showed some small measure of trust, didn't it?

Unfortunately, something he *hadn't* figured on happened: they found Sawyer and Honey smooching in the kitchen, wrapped up together in no more than a sheet.

Morgan halted abruptly when he saw them, which caused Misty to stumble into his side and Jordan to bump into his back. Like dominoes toppling one another, they all ended up crammed into the tiny doorway, gawking.

Misty groaned at the sight of her sister, then turned her face into Morgan's side. "I'm cursed."

At her softly spoken words, Honey jerked away from her husband, looked up, then blushed furiously. "Oh, Lord." She clutched at the sheet, pulling it up to her throat and all but leaving Sawyer buck naked. "It's barely six-thirty! We thought everyone was still in bed!"

Sawyer grabbed for an edge of the sheet to retain his modesty in front of Misty, then turned to frown at his brothers. "What the hell is going on?" He noticed the suitcase Morgan held, and his expression altered. "You going somewhere, Morgan?"

Standing on tiptoe, Casey attempted to see over Morgan's shoulder, then stated, "Misty was going to leave, but Morgan stopped her."

Sawyer glanced at his wife, then blinked at his son. His confusion was amusing, if unfortunate. "Leave where?"

"I don't know." Casey gave an elaborate shrug. "Home, I guess, though she said she's in the middle of moving somewhere and she'd have to tell us where exactly after she got settled. I tried to stop her, Dad, honest, but she was determined—"

Morgan felt Misty tremble and said, "That's enough, Case." Then to Sawyer: "Just a misunderstanding. What are you two doing out here? We thought you'd...sleep in...till at least noon."

Grinning like a rogue, Sawyer announced, "We needed nourishment."

Honey turned bright pink and elbowed her husband, who grabbed her and kissed her hard on the mouth. Morgan couldn't help but smile at them. Though Sawyer had fought it hard, he was so crazy in love with Honey, it was fun to watch them.

Morgan wanted a relationship like that. Then he thought of Misty beside him, the exact opposite of her sister, and he scowled.

Jordan shoved his way past the others. "If you two newlyweds want to go back to bed, I'll bring you a tray in just a few minutes. Coffee and bagels?"

"Perfect." Sawyer tried to turn Honey around, but she wasn't budging.

"Misty?" Honey looked oblivious to Sawyer's efforts. "You were going to leave without telling me?"

There was no mistaking her hurt, and although Morgan wouldn't have put Misty through such an ordeal, he decided it was probably best to get it all out in the open at once. The sooner Misty got through it, the sooner she could understand that she didn't need to leave.

He was surprised and pleased when he felt Misty's hand slip into his, and he squeezed her fingers tight, then answered for her. "Well, she's not going anywhere right now because her car won't start. You don't have to worry."

Honey's brows shot up. "Her car won't start?" She sent a suspicious look at Gabe. "Did you tamper with her car like you did mine?"

Gabe straightened from his sleepy, slouched position and crossed his heart with dramatic flair. "Never touched it. Hell, I just got up. I'm not awake enough to be playing with engines."

Jordan spoke before Honey could turn her cannons on him. "Same here. I didn't even know she was planning to leave until I saw her with her suitcase."

Misty stared at her sister, and Morgan could feel her tensing. "They tampered with your car?"

Honey shrugged. "I wanted to leave, because I thought I was intruding and putting them all in danger. But they weren't worried, and they thought it'd be better if I stayed here with them. They knew I couldn't very well leave without transportation, so they kept my car disabled. I thought Gabe was fixing it for me, but instead he was making sure it wouldn't run if I tried to sneak off." Honey smiled at her husband, then added, "Their intentions were good, so I forgave them."

Misty pulled her hand away and slowly turned to glare at Morgan. Her eyes were dark with accusation and anger. "Did you ..?"

Shrugging, he said, "You didn't exactly leave me a lot of choice."

Her gasp was so loud she sounded as if someone had pinched her. She drew back her arm and slugged him in the stomach, gasped again, then shook her hand and glared at him. "How dare you!"

He tried to rub the sting out of her hand, but she held it protectively away from him. Morgan frowned at that. "You wouldn't listen," he said by way of explanation. He was more than a little aware of their rapt audience, but saw no way around it. Damn it, she was Honey's sister, and she'd been preparing to slip off without a job, without money....

He'd never heard a woman growl so ferociously before. Everyone was frozen, silent. Misty looked as if she might hit him again, then thought better of it. Her expression was angry but resolute. "Fine. I'm calling a cab. He can take me to the bus station."

Morgan glared at her. "Don't push me, Malone."

"You've done all the pushing, you—you...!"

"Bastard?" he supplied helpfully.

She growled again. "Fix my car!"

"No." He crossed his arms over his chest.

Sawyer, ever the diplomat, cleared his throat. "Uh, Morgan..."

Still matching Misty glare for glare, Morgan shook his head. "She can't leave, Sawyer, all right?"

"Why?"

Gabe spoke. "If she's that set on going—"

"I'd prefer she stay, too," Jordan added, "but—"

Morgan closed his eyes, trying to think of some way around the problems. Nothing too promising presented itself. When he met Misty's gaze this time, he knew she could read his purpose.

"Don't you do it, Morgan," she warned.

He touched her cheek and gave her a small, regretful smile. "I'm sorry, sweetheart." Then he turned to everyone else and announced, "I don't want her to go, because she's pregnant."

The reaction wasn't quite what he'd expected. Honey's mouth fell open, Gabe and Jordan both became mute, Casey's neck turned red, and Sawyer leaned on the counter with a sigh, holding tight to his share of the sheet.

Misty went ahead and hit him again. He took hold of her hands before she hurt herself. This time she didn't pull away, but chose instead to stare at him with evil intent. He supposed she'd rather look at him than face everyone else. If he could have thought of a way to spare her, he would have.

Then Morgan realized no one was looking at Misty. They were all staring at him—with accusation. It was almost too funny for words.

"*I'm* not the father," he said dryly. "Hell, I've only known her a couple of weeks, if you'll recall."

Sawyer coughed. "That's actually quite long enough."

"In this case, it wasn't!"

Everyone relaxed visibly. Honey said to Morgan, "Well, of course she can't leave, you're right about that. Hang on to her until I get back, okay?" Then she took off like a shot, dragging Sawyer along with her, given that they shared the sheet and he didn't want to be left bare-assed.

Gabe sat down at the table and relaxed, at his leisure. "All this excitement has made me hungry. Jordan, if you're fixing breakfast, make some for me, too."

Jordan nodded and began pulling out pans. "Might as well skip the bagels and go for pancakes. Casey, Misty? Either of you hungry?"

Casey glanced at Misty, then pulled out his chair. "I'm always hungry. You know that."

Misty's eyes were wide, as if she'd been prepared for an entirely different response to his statement, maybe something more dramatic than an offer of breakfast. Did she think he and his brothers were ogres? Morgan almost smiled at her. Had she expected to be stoned? To receive a good dose of condemnation? He chucked her chin, then said gently, "Didn't I tell you it'd be all right?"

Misty didn't bother answering. She looked like she'd turned to stone. Morgan held her gaze, trying to think of some way to smooth things over with her. "I don't suppose you'll believe me when I tell you that wasn't intentional?"

Her eyes darkened to navy and her lips firmed.

"Okay, the car part was," he admitted, just to rile her. He couldn't bear seeing her look so lost. "And I admit I got Jordan and Gabe and Casey out of bed."

She mumbled under her breath, no doubt something insulting, but he just pretended he hadn't heard her. "I swear, I had no idea our newlyweds would be up. And I didn't plan to let the cat out of the bag about your pregnancy, either."

Her expression remained murderous.

Leaning close, crowding her against the cabinets so his brothers couldn't see her or hear him, Morgan whispered, "I have no intention of sharing your other secrets, so you can rest easy on that score, okay?" They were so close, her scent filled him with every breath he took. He braced his hands beside her hips on the counter; she braced her hands on his chest. She didn't quite push him away, and he saw her lips part. It amazed him the effect they had on each other. Even when she was likely thinking of ways to bring him low, she still responded to him. When they did finally come together—and he was certain it would happen sooner or later—he could only imagine how explosive it would be.

His heart thundered. "Misty?" She slowly looked up and met his gaze. "There's no reason for anyone to know about the rest unless you want to tell them, okay?"

Misty shivered, but before she could answer Honey came whipping into the room in her robe and skidded to a halt when she saw Morgan's nose practically in Misty's ear. "Hey, now, none of that. Get away from her, Morgan. I want to talk to my sister without you trying to intimidate either of us."

Morgan slowly straightened, wondering what Misty was thinking, if she'd believed him. "I've never intimidated you, Honey."

"Not for lack of trying." She caught Misty's arm and pulled her aside.

Morgan lifted the suitcase. "I'll just take this back to her room."

Misty shook her head to refuse him, while Honey gave him her sweetest smile. "Thank you, Morgan. Misty and I will be in the family room, talking."

"I'll call you when breakfast is ready," Jordan said, and Misty seemed unaware of the concern in his tone.

After the sisters left, Morgan felt both his brothers watching him. He turned to glare at them. "What?"

"Not a thing."

"Didn't say a word."

Casey made a show of studying a bird outside the kitchen window.

"Damn irritants," Morgan muttered. He lifted the suitcase and carried it out of the room. He knew his brothers each had at least a dozen questions, wondering what he was doing mixed up in the middle of Misty Malone's affairs, and why he was the only one privy to her startling news. But he wasn't about to betray her trust any more than he already had. They could just go on wondering.

When Morgan got to the room Misty had been using, he found the bed neatly made and everything very tidy. He pictured her sleeping in that bed last night, or rather, not sleeping. Just worrying. He'd told her she should leave, and this morning she'd been crying.

His stomach cramped and he idly rubbed his hand over it, but the ache continued. He could easily imagine what she'd been thinking, how she'd felt—how he'd made her feel—and he hated it. She probably hadn't slept at all last night, worrying about what she'd do, worrying about finding a job and about the baby.

A baby, a little person that would look like Misty, with dark hair and big blue eyes... He smiled at the thought, then caught himself and scowled.

What kind of job could a woman with a record get? He didn't know the terms of her probation—he'd have to ask her about that—but he knew it wouldn't sit well with an employer, especially not when she'd supposedly stolen from the last guy who'd hired her. Would she be able to earn enough to take care of herself and a baby?

She was certainly stubborn enough to make it work somehow, but she had a hard road ahead of her. And that route wasn't even necessary.

Morgan considered things for a moment, then came to some decisions. He opened her suitcase, emptied it on the bed, took the case to his room and shoved it under his bed. If she wanted to try sneaking out again, he wouldn't make it easy for her. At least until he knew she had a decent plan. Then, he told himself, he'd let her go.

He also intended to do a little investigating. Getting the details of the theft wouldn't be hard, and then he'd make his own conclusions.

He felt like a warlord, holding her against her will, but damn it, it was only stubborn pride that had her wanting to leave in the first place. That and his big mouth. He had the feeling if he hadn't asked her about leaving, if he hadn't pushed her, she'd have stayed on for a while, using the time to make new plans. She had a lot to deal with, and until he'd started harassing her, she'd probably seen this as an ideal situation, a place to regroup and be with her sister without anyone knowing what had happened.

Except that she'd told him everything. He took immense satisfaction in that small success, discarding the fact that he'd bullied the information out of her. Misty wouldn't have told him if she hadn't trusted him at least a little.

He remembered stories of her father that Honey had shared. That man wasn't one to coddle or offer comfort, so Morgan had no doubt she hadn't even tried going to him for help. According to Honey, neither of them was overly close to the man, and with good reason.

Everything would work out, he was certain of it.

On his way to the kitchen Morgan passed the family room and was brought up short by a disgruntled, *"He hates me."*

Morgan stalled, his heart jumping, his muscles pulled tight. He waited, eavesdropping like a maiden aunt to hear what Honey would say in reply.

Her soft voice was soothing, just as Morgan had known it would be. "Morgan doesn't hate you, Misty. He kept you here because that's just how they all are. They're a little on the gallant side, and Morgan wants to protect you."

There was a rough, disbelieving laugh. "Right. If you say so."

Morgan could tell she didn't believe her sister and he pulled his hands into fists. Even his toes cramped. Hate her? Hell, no. What he felt was as far from hatred as it could get, and a whole lot steamier than that cold emotion. He wanted to devour her, to make love to her for a week so he could get her out of his system.

He hated the effect she had on him, but he didn't hate *her*.

"I do say so," Honey insisted. "I know them all better than you do."

"It doesn't matter what Morgan thinks or how he feels about me, Honey. The point is, I didn't mean to intrude on you. The last thing you need right now is to start worrying about me."

"There, you see? I won't worry as long as you're around so I can see you're doing okay. Morgan probably knew that, too."

Morgan lifted his brows. Sounded good enough to him, though thoughts of Honey hadn't much entered into his mind while he was trying to think of ways to keep Misty around.

"But..." Misty floundered, then insisted, "I need to get back to work. I can't just stay here indefinitely."

Morgan hustled through the doorway before Misty could convince Honey that she should leave. He surveyed both women cozied up on the couch, and Misty's eyes widened in alarm.

There was no way for him to reassure her right now, so he didn't bother trying. He'd already given her his word that he wouldn't tell about her stint with the law. It wouldn't hurt her to trust him just a bit.

He got right to the point. "I heard you mention your job."

"Morgan." Her tone said she'd kill him if he said one more word.

The threat didn't worry him. After all, the woman had hurt her hand just smacking him in the stomach. And she had shared her secrets with him, which he chose to see as a sign of trust whether she realized it or not. "I have a solution."

Misty moaned again. He noticed she'd been doing a lot of that lately.

Undaunted, he held up his hands and pronounced, "You're going to come to work for me."

MISTY STARED at Morgan, wondering what he was up to now. Somehow, in the short time it had taken her to shower, he'd done something to her car so it wouldn't start, shaved so that he looked refreshed and ready to take on the day instead of looking like a dark savage, and he'd pulled on more clothes.

She was eternally grateful for the clothes part.

Even when he made her so mad she wanted to club him on top of his handsome head, she couldn't seem to ignore him. The man filled up the space around her with his size, his scent, his pushy presence. When he was there, he was really there, and she doubted any sane woman would be oblivious to him, especially not when he was flaunting his bare, muscled chest.

Morgan had the type of body that had always secretly appealed to her. He was tall and powerful and immeasurably strong—but he could be so gentle.

She shook her head. Just because he distracted her didn't

mean she'd let him off the hook. What she'd most wanted *not* to happen he'd made sure *had* happened. Never mind that she was now in the situation she'd originally wanted, with a safe place to stay, close to her sister.

How the circumstance had come about was totally unfair—and all Morgan's fault. Honey deserved some carefree time, but now she'd worry endlessly. Honey had a horrible tendency to mother her, a habit she'd gotten into because their mother had died long ago and their father was so cold and undemonstrative. Though Honey was only slightly older, she'd taken the big-sister role to heart.

She'd have told Honey the whole story eventually, of course, because they didn't keep secrets from each other. But not now, not when Honey had just gotten married and found so much happiness. It wasn't fair to drop such a burden in her lap.

She should have choked Morgan instead of punching him in his rock-hard middle, she thought, surveying his dark frown. But judging by his thick neck, that wouldn't have done him much damage, either. The man was built like a pile of bricks and was just as immovable.

And now he'd offered her a job. Or more precisely, he'd demanded she take a job. *With him*.

He hadn't precisely told Honey that Misty didn't have a job anymore. No, he'd made it sound as if he was only offering her an alternative so she could stick around. Did that mean he'd been sincere when he'd promised not to tell anyone about the rest of her troubles? God, she hoped so. It was all too humiliating, and though she knew Honey would believe her innocent, she had no idea how the others would feel.

Being pregnant was one thing; she wanted the baby and couldn't really regret its existence. And the brothers had been very accepting about the whole thing—almost cavalier, in fact. But surely they wouldn't want a jailbird in their home. She felt sick at the idea of them finding out.

"I already have a job," she stated forcefully, when Honey gave her a nudge for sitting there and staring.

Morgan lifted one brow and proceeded to settle himself into the stuffed chair adjacent to the couch. Contrary to how Misty felt, he looked at his ease and without a care in the world. His dark blue eyes were direct, unflinching.

"Now Malone," he said easily, "you were just telling me that you hate that job, that you planned to look for something else. Why not look here, so you can be close to your...family?"

"I never—" Misty bit her lip, stopping her automatic protest in mid-sentence. How could she dispute his enormous lie without telling the actual truth? He'd cornered her, and he knew it.

After clearing her throat, she smiled sweetly. It always worked for Honey. "I never meant to imply *you* should give me a job."

Morgan waved his hand in dismissal. Apparently the big ape was immune to her smile. "Of course you didn't. I know that. You'd never hint around that way. You're much too...up-front and honest for that." His eyes glittered at her and he added, "But I want you to take the job."

She glanced at Honey, saw no help there and resolutely shook her head. "No."

"How can you refuse when you don't even know what the job is yet?"

Through set teeth, she growled, "What is the job?"

Morgan actually smiled, which put her even more on edge. "I need an assistant. Someone to act as sort of a secretary and a dispatcher, when necessary. No, don't look like that. You won't need special training. Buckhorn is a small county and we do things just a bit differently. You'd need to take calls, keep track of where I am and forward on the important ones, but make notes for the ones that can wait. Mostly just for mornings and afternoons. Your evenings will be free, and just think, you can spend more time with Honey."

Honey leaned forward in her seat, already excited by the prospect. "Morgan, that's a great idea!" To Misty, she said, "It only makes sense, Misty, for you to be with family now. This is no time to let your pride get in the way."

"Of course it isn't," Morgan agreed.

Honey sighed. "Didn't I tell you he was wonderful?"

Misty almost choked, especially when she glanced at Morgan and saw his amusement. She thought she might throw up again. She drew a deep breath and tried to sound reasonable. "I don't know anything about working for a sheriff..."

"I'll tell you everything you need to know, sweetheart."

There was only so much she could take and remain composed. "I am not," she said in lethal tones, "your sweetheart."

Honey patted her hand. "They all use endearments, so you might as well get used to it. I swear, at first I thought they knew my name before I'd even given it to them. Then I realized everything female is a sweetheart or a honey to these guys, even the hodgepodge of animals Jordan keeps around." Honey gave Morgan a fond smile. "They're very old-fashioned in a lot of ways."

Under her breath, Misty muttered, "You mean they're overbearing, macho, autocratic—"

"What's that, Malone? I couldn't quite hear you." Morgan looked ready to laugh.

"Not a thing." She stood, and both Honey and Morgan came to their feet, too, as if they thought she might topple over at any moment. Good grief, she wasn't even showing yet. "I'll think about the job, Morgan."

He gave her a slow nod, looking at her from his superior height in a way that made her feel downright tiny. "That's fine. But make it quick, okay? I need you to start tomorrow."

Her eyes widened. She didn't want to start tomorrow! She didn't want to start at all. If anything, she hoped to make some solid plans tomorrow that would appease everyone so she could be on her way. "But..."

"Will you, Misty? Please?" Honey hugged her close, and Misty had no choice but to return the embrace. Since meeting Sawyer, her sister was deliriously happy and she wanted everyone else to feel the same. Over Honey's shoulder, Misty glared at Morgan. He winked at her, the obnoxious brute.

Misty pushed her sister away slightly and drummed up a reassuring smile. "Why don't you go have breakfast with that new husband of yours? I want to discuss this...job, with Morgan."

"But you haven't even told me about the baby yet, or how far along you are, or anything!"

Misty thought about moaning again, but with Morgan watching her so closely, she held it in. To her surprise, he took Honey's arm and said, "One thing at a time, hon, okay? If she takes the job and sticks around, you'll have all the time in the world to chat."

It was obvious Honey didn't want to, but she finally agreed to leave. She gave Morgan a warning look on her way out that had Morgan chuckling in a deep rumble.

Misty saw nothing funny in the situation, but he didn't give her a chance to light into him. No sooner was Honey gone from the room than he walked to her and said, "I told you I won't say a word about the job or the conviction. You have my word on that."

It was as if he'd deliberately taken away her steam. But Misty had more than one grievance and she was nowhere near ready to give up her anger. "Why should I believe you?"

His hesitation was plain before he lifted a hand and smoothed her cheek. He was so gentle, so warm, she couldn't get her feet to step out of his reach. "I didn't want to hurt you, Malone. You must know that."

She managed a rude laugh. "You couldn't hurt me."

Her disdainful tone never fazed him. His mouth tilted in a

wry, regretful smile. "I think you're wrong about that. I think you've been through a hell of a lot and you're vulnerable right now."

Because he was right, she felt twice as determined to deny it. "Don't get all mushy on me, Morgan. My stomach can't take it."

He lifted his other hand so that he framed her face. "You're so tough, aren't you, Malone? Ready to take on the world all alone. I admire that kind of courage, you know."

"So my insults aren't having the desired effect, huh? You must have a thicker skull than I figured."

Morgan whistled. "You really are ticked, aren't you?"

"Ticked? I'm a whole lot more than *ticked*. What you did was reprehensible."

"What I did," he said, his thumbs gently smoothing her cheeks, "was try to keep you here since I was the one who had run you off."

Misty blinked at him. He felt guilty? Is that what this was all about? Caught between disbelief and annoyance, she struggled with her fading anger. She really hadn't wanted to go, but neither had she wanted her personal business sallied about for the entire family to hear. Facing them again was going to be incredibly tough. She already knew there'd be dozens of questions, most importantly about the absent father.

As if he'd read her mind, Morgan made a tsking sound. "Come on, Malone, stop beating yourself up. There's no reason to be embarrassed, you know. My brothers won't judge you. If anything, they'll rightfully blame the guy who got you pregnant and then walked away. Like Honey said, we're old-fashioned about things like that. A guy should take responsibility for his actions."

She appreciated the sentiment, if not the interference. "Yeah, well, this guy didn't. And believe me, things are better with him out of the picture."

Morgan laughed. "I'm not disputing that. If he was around, I'd be tempted to beat him into the ground."

"Really?" That wasn't an altogether unpleasant thought. She'd felt the same many times after the way Kent had reacted to her news.

Morgan nodded, then said gruffly, "He hurt you. The least he deserves is a good beating."

Misty was speechless. Morgan had sounded almost like he cared, like he didn't despise her, after all. She said facetiously, "How...sweet of you."

Morgan's look was stern. "Look, Malone. The last thing you'd want is to be married to a loser."

"The last thing I want is to be married, period." Misty stared at his chest and muttered, "I've had my fill of dealing with men, thank you very much."

"I think you've just been dealing with the wrong men."

"Such an obvious truth." She looked at him pointedly.

He let her implication pass without comment, then leaned down until his forehead touched hers. She could feel his warm breath on her lips, his body heat seeping into her, his gentleness flowing over her. She sighed.

"It's also obvious," he said very softly, "that Honey loves you to death. Nothing will change that."

Oh, how could he make her feel like this when she was rightfully angry? "I know my sister loves me, Morgan. But telling her wasn't your decision to make."

"Maybe, but it was the right decision. You were just being stubborn, admit it."

"No, never."

He laughed. "At least this way you're with family, and I'm talking about all of us. We are family now, Malone, whether you like it or not. You don't have a job, you don't even have a place to stay."

Alarmed, she finally managed to dodge his soothing hands and move out of reach. She tried for a credible laugh, but it sounded more like a weak snicker. "Don't be ridiculous."

His eyes narrowed. "It's no good, Malone. I know you too well."

"You hardly know me at all!"

"But we're getting there." Then in a softer tone, "Just where the hell did you think you were going to go?"

The best she could come up with was a shrug.

"That's what I figured. So why not stay here?"

Misty felt like screaming in frustration. "For crying out loud, Morgan, you *told* me to leave!"

He shook his head. "Damn it, that was before."

"Oh, I see. A pregnant woman isn't so risky. You're no longer worried that I'll seduce your brothers? After all, I thought that was your overriding concern."

Morgan leaned against the wall by the fireplace and crossed his arms over his chest. Misty recognized that stance and the accompanying expression all too well.

"No, my overriding concern was the chemistry between us. And your pregnancy doesn't change that much. You're still too damn sexy, and only a dead man wouldn't be tempted."

She wished she hadn't brought it up. "That's ridiculous."

He very slowly shook his head. "It's true. You have to know how gorgeous you are, how you make a man feel. But I have an idea on how to handle that."

The words, along with the way he'd looked at her as he spoke, made her skin flush and her belly tingle.

She didn't want to be attracted to him! He was arrogant and stubborn, but he was also very dedicated to his family, protective and so incredibly good-looking she imagined women had been chasing him for most of his life.

She mustered up a bored look to hide her reaction to him and asked, "So what's it going to be? Bundle me up in burlap? Paint a big red A on my forehead to ward off the innocent? What?"

"Nothing so drastic as that." He paused for a long moment, as if measuring his words, then he met her gaze and his eyes were hard...determined. "I'll just tell everyone that we're involved, so you're off-limits."

"What?"

He smiled at her reaction. "Believe me, Malone, that'll be enough to keep all other men away, which is what you wanted, right?"

Ruthless...

5

MORGAN WAITED until Misty looked at him, then snagged her gaze and refused to let her look away. There was a soft blush to her cheeks that about drove him crazy. He had a gut feeling that blush was a combination of anger, embarrassment and excitement.

He understood the anger and wished for some way to spare her the embarrassment. The excitement he relished.

"It's a good plan, Malone."

"For me to pretend to...to be your..." Her stammering ceased, and she stared at him blankly.

"My woman. Yeah, that's the plan." He wanted to walk closer to her, to touch her again, but he didn't dare. She looked skittish enough to jump out of her skin if he even breathed deeply. "Here's how I see it," he said, trying to sound reasonable. "You do need a job, but it won't be easy to find one without employers knowing you were convicted of stealing from the last place you worked. And once they know that, they'll be reluctant to hire you, right?"

"Maybe."

"And you're still on probation?"

She nodded hesitantly. "For a few more months."

"That's what I figured."

She gulped, and her hands fisted. In shame? In regret? He just didn't know, but he hated to see her feel either emotion. He intended to do what he could about her conviction as soon as possible. But for now, he had other things to contend with. "The job I'm offering gives county wages, which aren't great but neither are they piddling. And the fact you worked for a sheriff's office will have to look good on your résumé, and to your probation officer."

She didn't appear quite convinced. She stared at her feet in deep concentration.

A niggling sense of panic seeped in. Misty had been very clear about her feelings on involvement of any kind. The only way Morgan could see around that was to wrangle his way into her life. Keeping her here, hiring her on, showing her she could trust him and rely on him was part of a great plan. He'd just have to make damn sure it worked. "As I said, it's not a hard job—"

Her head shot up and she glared at him. "I'm not afraid of hard work."

"I didn't mean that." Sometimes Morgan wished he was as good at soothing frazzled nerves as his brother Jordan. Jordan could talk the orneriness out of a mule, whisper a baby bird to sleep. He was one hell of a vet, but his talents carried over to people, as well. Morgan, on the other hand, usually relied on rigid control to get his way. He managed things, taking on other people's problems and resolving them so they didn't have to worry. Most people appreciated that.

Only it didn't work with Misty. She bucked him at every turn, refusing to accept what he was best at offering.

"All I meant," he continued, "is that you could easily do the job. You don't need any special training or skills. And by accepting it, you can stay here indefinitely, which rids you of the cost of room and board."

She was already shaking her head before he'd finished. "I can't just stay here free, Morgan."

He straightened. "Why the hell not? You hadn't been in a hurry to leave until I prodded you along."

"That's not entirely true." She looked flabbergasted by his persistence, but he'd be damned if he'd back off. "Sure, I had hoped to hang out for a week or two more while I figured out

what to do next, but then I'd have left. I never intended to
stay here any longer than that."

He scowled at her. Everything had changed the moment
she'd dropped to her knees in front of those bushes. She
should stay, which meant he no longer had to fight himself
for wanting her to stick around.

She'd said she wasn't as outgoing as she'd pretended. He
wasn't buying that for a single second. She might not be such
a real flirt, only using that as a way to cover her worries. But
she was brazen and outrageous and beautiful. She was also
strong and proud, qualities he'd always admired in men and
women alike. But for right now, he wished she wasn't quite
so proud.

"Honey wants you to stay." That was the only argument
he could think of that might convince her. Telling her *he*
wanted her to stay didn't seem to be such a great idea. She'd
ask him why, and beyond telling her he wanted to ravish her
senseless, he'd have no excuse. Even knowing she was pregnant by another man, now that she'd admitted she wouldn't
be marrying that man, hadn't dampened his lust. In fact, he
admired her courage, which seemed to add a keen edge to
his feelings.

In a mumble totally unlike her usual decisive tone, Misty
said, "My sister is new here. This is Sawyer's house and—"

"Honey is new, but permanent. She can invite anyone here
that she wants." Misty had a lot to learn about them, first and
foremost what *family* meant. When Honey became Sawyer's
wife, she became an equal member of that family.

Actually, Morgan thought, smiling a little inside, she'd
been an accepted member of their family as soon as they'd all
realized Sawyer loved her.

"But Sawyer might not care for—"

"Sawyer will love having you here. But truth is, the house
belongs to all of us. My father built it back when he and my
mother were married. When she and Gabe's father retired,
they decided to move to Florida, and we took over the up-

keep of the house. Since grown men need some privacy, Gabe converted the basement into an apartment, and Jordan did the same with the rooms over the garage."

She looked him over as if trying to figure him out. "But you still live in the house."

"Yeah." He could see the questions in her eyes and grinned. "I don't, however, bring women here for overnight, if that's what you're asking. Casey is almost sixteen now, and *he* thinks he's all grown up, but I still wouldn't flaunt lovers in front of him. I remember being sixteen. Guys that age don't need any help in the raging hormone department."

She looked startled for a moment, then frowned. "Being raised in a house full of males must be ideal for a boy his age."

Morgan shrugged. "We've done the best we could. But I know Casey loves the idea of having Honey around. Just as he'll love the idea of you sticking close, too."

"I don't know, Morgan. I mean, the others..."

"It won't be a problem. The only problem would be if I let you get away."

She still didn't look convinced, then she harked back to what he'd said earlier. "Gabe is your half brother?"

Morgan grinned, suddenly knowing how he'd reassure her. "Come here, Malone. I have a nice long tale to tell you."

She snorted at that, but she did go ahead and seat herself—in a chair so he couldn't sit beside her. He chose the couch, and realized they'd switched positions from earlier. He couldn't remember ever grinning so much, but damn, she amused him with her constant advance and retreat. She was a mix of bravado and prudence, and he realized it was a potent combination, guaranteed to drive any man crazy.

"My father died when I was just a baby." Her eyes widened and he laughed. "I know. Tough to imagine me as a squalling infant, huh?"

"The squalling part I can believe, but the idea of you ever being little boggles the mind. You're just so—" her gaze skimmed his chest, his shoulders, then down to his thighs "—massive now."

Because he had her attention, Morgan settled back and stretched out his long legs, then laced his fingers together on his stomach. Misty swallowed and slowly closed her eyes, so she didn't see his grin. "I was still little when my mom remarried and had Jordan. But things didn't work out and she divorced him."

Her eyes snapped open. Looking more fascinated by the moment, Misty said, "After she had Gabe, you mean?"

"Nope." He laughed outright at her confusion. "My father died in the war. He was my mother's first real love, and she had a hard time getting over him. Then she met Jordan's father. She was lonely and she had two sons to raise. She thought she loved him and married again. But not long after that he lost his job and started to drink. Things went from bad to worse. It wasn't easy for her to work a job, care for three kids and put up with the small-town stigma of being a divorced widow with three sons."

"I don't imagine it would be." Misty picked at a thread on her shorts, then admitted, "Even in this day and age, being a single mother has its problems. Not to mention being a mother of three. She must have a lot of courage."

He said softly, "You have your own share of courage, sweetheart. Deciding to have the baby shows a lot of guts and determination."

She changed the subject, or rather got it back on track. "Do you remember much of Jordan's father?"

"Not really. I was only two when she married him, and I've never heard my mother complain much about those times. All she says is that he gave her Jordan, so she doesn't regret a moment of it. But I've lived here my whole life and lots of people talk, mostly about how strong she was and how she'd gone off men completely after losing one and divorcing another." He watched her closely. "I guess sort of like you claiming you don't want anything to do with men now. A woman gets hurt like that, and it's hard to ever trust again."

He stared at her until she slowly lifted her gaze to meet his.

"I'm not hurt, Morgan. I keep telling you that. I'm just a little wiser, is all. My priorities right now are a job and security for the baby. I don't need a man for that."

But he wasn't just any man, and he damn well wanted her to realize it. He went on with his story as if he hadn't been sidetracked. "You know what I do remember? Sitting with her in the evening and reading books, coloring pictures or sometimes making cookies. She worked damn hard, but she was never too tired to talk with us or to give us hell if she caught us fighting."

Misty gave him a pointed look. "Us, meaning *you* most likely. Somehow I don't see the others getting into as much mischief as you likely did."

Morgan shrugged. "True. I've always been a bit of a hell-raiser—something Mom claims I inherited from my father's side of the family, though I've seen her riled a few times so I'm not buying it. As to the others, Sawyer's always been serious and a bona fide overachiever. There aren't too many men I know who could have cared for a baby and finished up med school without missing a beat. Even with our help, he had his hands full, but he never complained."

Misty sighed. "Sawyer is the exception. Most men would run from that kind of responsibility."

For some reason that observation irritated Morgan beyond all reason. "You haven't known enough good men to make that judgment."

Her laugh was a little sad. "That's true enough, I suppose." Then she smiled at him, a real smile that affected him like a stroke in just the right place. "I think it's wonderful that you're all so close. My father isn't that way at all. If it wasn't for Honey..."

"I know. She's told me a lot about him, and about how

close you both are because of it." Morgan wished she'd open up a little with him, but her smile was gone and she now had that closed look on her face that he recognized all too well. He said carefully, "Being that you are so close, aren't you just a bit pleased by the idea of having her nearby?"

She ignored his question to ask one of her own. "So what about Gabe? I gather he wasn't found under a rock?"

"Sometimes I wonder. But my mother is still married to Brett Kasper, and he's Gabe's father."

She studied him closely. "You all look different, but I never realized.... I mean, well, you and Sawyer do have similar looks, except that you're an imposing hulk and he's not."

"Gee thanks."

She waved that away. "You have the same dark hair, and there's something about the shape of your jaws. Stubborn, you know?"

"I've heard that, yes."

"But now Gabe, with that blond hair and those incredible electric blue eyes—"

"Malone," he said in warning.

"And Jordan has brown hair and green eyes and his voice is so—" she shivered "—seductive."

"You're pushing me again, Malone."

Misty started laughing, and Morgan realized she'd been deliberately baiting him. He smiled with her. "Do I need to start worrying about my brothers' virtue again?"

"Ha! None of you have any virtue left, and you know it."

"Not true. Virtue and chastity are not the same thing at all."

She chuckled again, shaking her head in feigned disbelief. Whether she realized it yet or not, she liked him, and she'd like being with him. Morgan spoke his thoughts aloud without even thinking about it. "Hearing you laugh is much nicer than hearing you cry."

Just like that, she stiffened up on him. Color darkened her cheeks, and her eyes narrowed. "If you hadn't been sneaking around this morning, you wouldn't have been subjected to hearing me cry."

Embarrassing her hadn't been his intent. He lowered his voice to a soothing growl. "I wasn't complaining, Malone, except that I don't like seeing you unhappy."

She sat forward, her brows lifted in mock surprise. "Oh, I see. That's why you announced to everyone that I'm pregnant, because you thought it would somehow make me happy?"

"No. But I knew going off on your own wouldn't make you happy, either. If anything, it would've made you more miserable."

"I am *not* miserable."

He raised his hands in surrender. "I stand corrected. And before you run away in a huff, do you want me to tell you the happy ending to my mother's story?"

"With your idea of *happy*, I'm not at all sure."

In a persuasive tone, he suggested, "Try trusting me just a little, Malone."

"No, never."

She was determined not to give an inch, and it frustrated him beyond measure. "You're awfully fond of that particular saying."

"Only when I'm around you."

He gave a drawn-out sigh at her stubbornness, then went on. "It took a long time, and Brett Kasper had to work real hard to get around my mother's resolve after losing one man and divorcing another, but he finally won her over. You never saw a more dedicated man than Brett. When my mom gave him the cold shoulder, he cozied up to us boys instead. Mom didn't stand a chance."

"You mean he manipulated events like you're trying to do with me?"

"Whatever works, Malone." When she growled, he gave her a small smile. His mother had supposedly been as against involvement as Misty, but she'd gotten turned around by the right man. He liked to think the same could be true of Misty. "I'll have you know, they've been married for some time now. You'd have met them at the wedding except Brett had a few health problems and couldn't travel, and my mom wouldn't leave him. He's okay now, nothing serious, but the doc still wants him to rest and Sawyer seconded that, so they missed the wedding. As soon as they can, though, they'll come for a visit."

"She sounds…incredible."

"She's as stubborn as a pit bull when you get her nettled, which luckily doesn't happen often. But for the most part, she's a woman who likes to laugh and isn't afraid to show how much she cares. She's going to love Honey. She's been waiting for one of us to give her a daughter by marriage. I think she's hoping for lots of granddaughters, too." He grinned. "She says I was such a trial, she's ready for something easier—like girls."

"I can believe that!"

Morgan leaned forward and caught her hand. "Do you see the point, Malone? You aren't the first person to make a mistake, but in time, you'll forget your reservations about men."

She started to speak, but he cut her off, already knowing what she would say. Her insistence that she wanted nothing to do with men was almost more than he could take. "So what do you say we join the others?"

She closed her eyes and groaned. "I don't know. The thought of facing your brothers again is enough to make my stomach jumpy."

Morgan considered that, then shrugged. "So don't face them. At least, not for long, and not today. Tell me you'll take the job, then we can go into town and get things set up for you. It's a good excuse and you can have a few hours to get used to the idea before sitting down with them all at dinner tonight. I can show you around town, and all in all, we can waste most of the day."

She bit her lip while scrutinizing him. "You don't have anything else you need to do?"

"Nope. Sunday is my day off. If anything comes up, someone will call, otherwise I'm free."

She still hesitated. "I don't know. It seems pretty fishy to me that this job just suddenly came available."

He still held her hand, and now he smoothed her knuckles with his thumb, marveling at how such a stubborn and defensive woman could feel so soft and delicate. He could just imagine those small hands on his body, and it made him crazy. He cleared his throat. "The job was always there, only I didn't want to hire anyone for it."

"Why?"

"Too many women were applying just to get close to me." She laughed hilariously and he waited, pretending to be affronted. When she finally quieted, he cocked a brow. "It's true. I'm considered something of a catch, only I'd rather do the catching for myself."

"That's right. You said you're looking for a wife."

Her bald statement gave him pause. She didn't seem particularly bothered by the idea. "Not actively," he muttered, "just giving it some thought." The idea of a wife wasn't something he wanted to discuss with Misty, especially since he'd all but forgotten that plan since meeting her. She kept him far too preoccupied for rational contemplation of the future. "And the last thing I need while I'm trying to work is a woman who's set on seducing me."

"I suppose if she breathes, you'd consider it a come-on?"

"Ah, you have no faith in me, Malone. I told you, the effect you have is totally unique. Contrary to your dirty little mind, I don't run around jumping every woman in the area. Hell, I have to live here, and I'm the sheriff—a respected position, you know. I have to set an example." He squeezed her hand. "Unfortunately I can't seem to remember that around you."

His honesty had her pink-cheeked again. He loved how she blushed, how her eyes turned bluer and her lips pressed together in a prim line. She was bold, and she gave as good as she got, but any talk of intimacy flustered her.

Damn, but he wanted to kiss her silly.

"If all that's true, Morgan," she fairly sputtered, "if I really affect you like that, why in the world would you want me around the office?"

"Because it solves a dilemma for both of us." He used his in-command tone, the one that made people sit up and take notice of his official position as sheriff. "You need a job, and I need a worker who won't be jumping my bones, interfering with my schedule and causing a scandal. You've made it pretty clear you plan to resist my bones, so..." He didn't admit his hope that her resistance wouldn't last long. "It's an ideal trade-off."

She considered that for a long moment, then finally nodded. "Okay. I can try the job, I suppose. On one condition."

The restriction in his chest immediately lightened, though he hadn't even noticed how tight it felt until she said she'd stay. "Let's hear it."

"I want you to fix my car. I will not be left here without transportation."

She stared at him defiantly until he nodded. "I can do that, but I have a condition of my own."

"Why am I not surprised?"

He tugged her slightly closer, holding her gaze. "I want your promise that if you decide to leave, you'll tell me."

Her eyes narrowed. "You can't keep me here against my will, Morgan."

"I'm all too aware of that unfortunate fact. And I won't even try. But if you decide to leave I want to know it."

"I wasn't really sneaking this time—"

"Malone."

"Oh, all right. I promise. But fix my car today."

He nodded. "And my other suggestion?"

"What other suggestion?"

He looked at her mouth, so sweetly lush and very kissable,

then at her full breasts pressing against the pale yellow camisole—just as kissable. He saw how she tucked her long slender legs beneath her, how smooth her thighs were, lightly tanned. Even her shoulders were sexy, making his tongue nearly stick to the roof of his mouth. "I'll stake a claim for all to see, and that'll keep interested males at bay."

Dark lashes swept down over her eyes to avoid his gaze. She subtly tugged her hand away from his and stood. "I don't know, Morgan."

He got up and stood very close behind her. "We will be involved, Malone, in an arrangement." She stiffened and he caught her shoulders before she could move away. "The type of arrangement is nobody's business but our own. I'm not coercing you into bed."

"As if you could."

"Is that a challenge?"

"No!"

He smiled at her anxious tone. "We'll be partners of a sort. You said you were through with men."

"Completely."

"Well, pretending to be mine ought to take care of other men hitting on you, and I'll have some much needed help at the office."

She shook her head while he stared at her nape, exposed by her upswept hair. He imagined kissing her there, watching her tremble. He couldn't push her now or she'd walk out the door, and she was right, there wasn't a damn thing he could do to stop her.

"That attitude is archaic, Morgan."

His newfound possessive streak was archaic, but he was dealing with it. Barely.

He rubbed her shoulders, relishing the warmth of her skin. His thumbs brushed the back of her neck to the base of her skull, lulling her, soothing her. "Look at it this way, Malone," he added in a whisper, "all your problems will be temporarily solved. And if you think this would be hard on you, just think of what it'll do to me."

"What?"

She sounded intrigued, and he hid his smile. "I want you, so you can figure it out, I'm sure. Given that you seem to take sadistic delight in making me miserable, the idea ought to appeal to you."

The torment would be worthwhile, he thought. He could spend a good deal of his time shoring up their ruse by getting closer to her. He knew, even if *she* didn't, that they'd eventually end up in bed. The chemistry between them was just too strong, no matter how hard she tried to deny it.

And he was tired of even trying.

With a wide, impish smile, she turned to face him. "Well, since you put it that way..." She patted his chest. "Making you miserable does hold a certain attraction."

He caught her hand and flattened it against his body. "So you agree?"

"You've convinced me."

Morgan stared at her, his heart thumping so heavily in his chest he thought for sure she'd felt it. He leaned toward her and saw her eyes widen. "Why don't we seal it with a kiss?"

MISTY BRACED HERSELF for a sensual assault. The memory of his last kiss in the gazebo was still fresh in her mind. But instead of being overwhelmed, she felt Morgan's mouth, warm and dry, brush very lightly over her own. She opened her eyes slowly and looked at him. His dark blue eyes were filled with heat, but also with tenderness, and she almost melted.

For a man of his size, he could sometimes be so remarkably gentle. She gave him a slight smile that he returned.

"Am I interrupting?"

They both jumped apart, she in guilty surprise, Morgan with a curse. He turned to face Jordan, leaning in the doorway with a contented smile.

Jordan tipped his head. "Breakfast is getting cold."

"Did you ever hear of knocking?"

"What fun would that be?"

Morgan turned his back on his brother and faced Misty. His wide shoulders completely blocked her from Jordan's view. Using the edge of his hand, he tipped up her chin, then asked, "What's it to be, Malone? Breakfast with the family, or do you want to go into town?"

"I'm not really hungry." She saw Morgan's understanding and quickly added, "I'm not being a coward. I really just don't have an appetite. I'll go in with you, though. No reason you should do without food, and I have to face them all sooner or later. It might as well be now."

"Get it over and out of the way, huh?"

His frown was back, but she had no idea why. "Something like that."

He glanced at Jordan over his shoulder. "We'll be right there."

Accepting the dismissal, Jordan chuckled and ambled off. The moment he was gone, Morgan framed her face and kissed her again. Before she could say much about it, if indeed she could have gathered her scattered wits to offer a protest, he took her hand and hustled her from the room.

Everyone was in the kitchen when they strolled in, still hand in hand. Like the audience at a Ping-Pong match, all eyes moved in unison to their entwined hands, to their faces, then to each other. Brows climbed high.

Morgan shook his head. "The lot of you remind me of monkeys in a zoo—not you, Honey. The masculine lot."

Honey frowned. "Is everything okay, Misty?"

"Everything is fine." She tried subtly to take her hand from Morgan, but he wasn't letting go, and shaking him off might bring on more speculation. She knew he intended to announce their involvement, but did he mean to do it right now? At this rate, no announcement would be necessary! There was no way she could continue to stand there and let everyone stare at her with concern. She had to get hold of herself and the situation. She glanced at Sawyer, then Jordan and Gabe. "Morgan insists it'll be all right if I stay here for a little while longer—"

"Absolutely."

"Of course!"

"You know you're welcome here."

Misty smiled at their combined assurance and even felt a little teary over it. "That's very generous of all of you."

Sawyer, with his arm draped over the back of Honey's chair, said, "You're family now, Misty. Family is always welcome for as long as they want to be here. Remember that, okay?"

Honey squeezed him in a tight hug. "Didn't I tell you they were all incredible?"

Gabe laughed. "Nothing incredible about welcoming beautiful women into your home." He eyed their clasped hands and added, "In fact, if you want some privacy, Misty, I have extra room in the basement." He bobbed his eyebrows at her.

Jordan looked mildly affronted. "I was going to offer to share my apartment with her. With Morgan always looming over her, it's for certain she won't get any peace and quiet around here."

Casey, looking like an imp, turned to the side to face his uncles and said, "Hey, if you guys have extra room, I'll move in with you."

Sawyer reached over and clapped his laughing son on the back. "They'll both strangle you for that, Case." Then to Morgan: "Stop letting them bait you. You look ready to do bodily harm, and then what will Misty think of you?"

"She'll think I'm possessive."

"And you have the right to be?"

"Damn right." Morgan released her hand and put his arm around her, hauling her up so close she felt her ribs protesting. "We've come to an agreement."

She gave Honey a helpless look, but Honey just rolled her eyes, as if she'd expected nothing less from Morgan.

In between bites of pancake, Gabe asked, "Is the baby's father aware of this *agreement*, or is he likely to show up here any time soon, demanding to know what's going on?"

Jordan scoffed. "If he has any sense, he'll show up. I know I would. 'Course, I wouldn't have let her get away in the first place." Then he eyed Morgan, and added, "Not that it's likely to do him any good if he does come here."

Misty had never felt so overwhelmed in her life. Not only did they seem to accept her pregnancy without hesitation or condemnation, but they also championed her and complimented her and apparently welcomed her involvement with their brother. There were no prying questions.

She was totally speechless.

Morgan was not. "He's out of the picture, and I say good riddance. But if he does ever show his face here, believe me, I'd love to have a minute or two alone with him."

"He doesn't know where I am," Misty pointed out.

Morgan gave her a level look. "Perhaps you could tell him."

"Oh, for heaven's sake." Honey shook her finger at Morgan. "You're always looking for a reason to pound on somebody."

"Sometimes you don't have to look for a reason."

Honey turned to Misty. "Don't pay any attention to his threats. It's like a dog growling, all for show. He's actually very sweet."

A round of masculine grunts disputed Honey's description. Obviously nobody else thought Morgan to be sweet.

"He is!" Honey protested. "At least, once you get to know him better—" She stopped and laughed. "But I guess you know him well enough already, huh?"

Morgan paid them no mind. "I think I do a pretty good job of not pounding on people most of the time, which is why I was elected sheriff." He grinned. "Total control of my temper."

"As I remember it," Jordan said, "it was your ability to take control of everyone else that gave the townsfolk assurance you could handle just about any situation."

"I don't seem to have control over your mouth, brother."

"No." Jordan chuckled. "But then, I've been fighting with you all of my life and lived to tell about it."

"Can we get back to the subject at hand?" Gabe asked. "What's this agreement you two have? I'm dying of curiosity."

Misty held her breath, uncertain as to what Morgan might come up with by way of explanation. None of them seemed particularly surprised that they were supposedly involved, which to her was no less than amazing. All they'd done since they first met was antagonize each other. Or at least that's all any of his family had seen. If anything, they should have believed that they despised each other. But of course, his brothers knew Morgan better than she did, and maybe grousing and growling was part of his normal temperament.

Heaven knew, he seemed to wear a perpetual frown when he wasn't laughing with her or trying to kiss her. She glanced at him and saw that indeed, his brows were pulled down and his expression was dark. It irritated her. She moved away from his side and gave him a look to let him know that if he spelled out their agreement completely, there'd be hell to pay.

To her surprise, he laughed, then kissed her loudly, right there in front of everyone. "Quit scowling, Malone. You're going to get wrinkles."

"Yeah. Or worse, you'll start looking so forbidding, we'll confuse you with Morgan." Gabe ducked when Morgan reached for him, then laughed as he resettled himself in his seat and went back to work on his pancakes.

"Misty is going to help me out around the station."

Sawyer sat back in his seat. "I thought you didn't want to hire a woman because she might get ideas."

"In this case, it's a moot point. The ideas are mutual." He looked at each brother in turn. "Any objections?"

Jordan lifted his glass of milk and said mildly, "With the two of you competing for the darkest frown, who would dare?"

Casey stood and took his empty plate and glass to the dishwasher. "I think it's great. So can I be excused? I want to go into town today."

Sawyer glanced at his son. "A date?"

"Sorta."

Morgan snagged Casey and roughed up his hair. "You're taking after your uncle, boy."

With a twinkle in his eyes, Casey asked, "Oh, yeah? Which one?"

Gabe held out his arms. "If she's gorgeous, then obviously me!"

Honey reached over and slapped Gabe's arm. "Thanks a lot!"

The moment Misty had dreaded seemed to have come and gone without much notice. She was a tad bemused at that.

"No offense, Honey," Gabe said after blowing her a kiss, "but you're married into the family now so I can't make lecherous jokes about you."

Still holding Casey in a way that made Misty wistful over the easy familiarity, Morgan said, "We can give you a ride. Misty and I are going into town ourselves."

Misty, a little surprised that he'd even suggest it, thought she'd have a slight reprieve from Morgan's isolated attentions until Casey shook his head. "Thanks, but I'd rather ride Windstorm. Jordan said she needs the exercise and I was planning on cutting across the field."

Morgan explained to Misty, "Windstorm is a new horse. Jordan brought her home not too long ago."

"I'm meeting up with friends, then we're all going to the lake for a little while."

"Anybody I know?" Morgan asked.

Casey struggled to hide his grin. "Just some girls, mostly."

Sawyer took one look at his son's innocent expression and groaned. "Lord, he is like Gabe."

At that, Casey laughed. "We're just going to swim. We won't get into any trouble."

Gabe sent mock glares around the room. "I didn't always get into trouble, you know."

"Just often enough," Jordan said with a raised brow, "to keep everyone on their toes."

Sawyer raised a hand. But before he could interject anything into the conversation, Honey stood and took Casey's arm.

"Never mind your overbearing, interfering uncles." She slanted her gaze toward Gabe. "You're *nothing* like them, except for the good looks, of course. Go and have a good time, but be careful, okay?"

Casey lifted her off her feet in a bear hug. "I'll be home by three o'clock."

"That's fine." And once he left the room, she glowered at Sawyer. "Quit comparing him to your disreputable brothers. You'll put ideas in his head."

"Would you all quit talking about me like I was the scourge of the area? Disreputable, indeed."

Honey pointed at Gabe. "And proud of it, from what I can tell."

To Misty's surprise, Sawyer didn't look at all put out by Honey's audacity toward his son. Instead, he grinned. "You're turning into a rather ferocious mother hen."

"Oh, no," Misty said, "she's always been that way. Even when she was just a little girl."

There was a round of laughing comments on that, all teasing Honey until she blushed.

Morgan pulled up a chair next to Misty and propped his

head on his fist to stare at her. "You look a little numb, sweetheart. You okay?"

She shook her head, watching Sawyer nuzzle on Honey, then Jordan and Gabe roughhousing. She didn't know what to think. "The way you all carry on, it amazes me, and now here I am right in the middle of it."

Honey's lips curled into a big smile. She said to the brothers, "It takes some getting used to, since we were from such a small family. And all our meals were very formal. No one gathered in the kitchen just to chat, and there was never this much joking around."

"I wasn't complaining," Misty said, not wanting them to misunderstand. "It's...nice."

"Of course it is." Honey cuddled against Sawyer's side, and he kissed her ear. "You know, you can't get around it, so now I just chime in, too. You'll get used to it."

Misty hadn't planned on being around long enough to get used to them. But now she was having fun. It had been a while since she'd felt the honest urge to laugh.

Morgan nudged her. "You want some pancakes or do you still want to head straight to town?"

Misty thought about it. Most of her anxiety was gone, and her stomach was starting to rumble. There was still a platter of lightly browned pancakes sitting in the middle of the table, with warmed syrup and soft butter beside it.

She grinned at Morgan, feeling more at ease than she had in ages. "Let's eat."

6

IT WAS ALMOST an hour before they finally left the house. Though she'd never have imagined it, she'd enjoyed breakfast immensely. No one said too much about her pregnancy other than to try to force an extra pancake on her along with a tall glass of milk. And no one pressured her for information on the father of the baby. They seemed to simply accept that she was there, unmarried, and that they wanted her to stay.

True to his word, Morgan played the part of an interested party, holding her arm, opening the door for her. But then she thought about how all the brothers did the same, for both her and Honey, and she realized Morgan likely wasn't playing at all. He was flat out mannerly, no way around it, and she had to admit she rather liked it.

"Are you sure I don't need to change clothes?" She wore her camisole and cut-offs, but Morgan had insisted she looked fine. The way he'd stared at her, though, giving her such a slow, thorough perusal, made her uncertain. She wore what most women wore on such hot days, but they were going to his office, and she'd likely meet a few townspeople.

"You look sexy as sin, which makes me nuts wanting to take you, but I can handle it. When you actually work tomorrow, you'll need to wear something more...conservative. Maybe jeans and a plain blouse or something. And definitely a bra. I won't get any work done if I know you're not wearing a bra."

Morgan took three more steps before he finally realized she'd stopped. He turned to face her, hands on his hips in an arrogant pose. He lifted one brow. "What's the problem now, Malone?"

As if he truly didn't know. Amazing. Even more amazing was that she felt equal parts furious and aroused. After all the condemnation she'd received from men of late, his open admiration was a balm, whether she admitted to liking it or not.

It was unnerving that of all the men she'd ever known, this particular man could make her feel such depths of excitement at such a rotten time. She didn't want to want him. She didn't want to want any man, but definitely not one who was so bold and...potent. There'd be no way to control Morgan Hudson, or to control her own erratic heartbeat in his presence.

"If this is going to work," she said, carefully enunciating each word, hoping to hide her trembling, "you have to stop being so...outspoken."

"Getting to you, is it?"

He blocked the sun with his big body, leaving long shadows to dance around her. "Annoying me, actually."

His slow smile was provoking. He strolled over to stand directly in front of her. "Is that why you're all flushed?" he asked. His gaze dropped to her chest and he groaned. Misty looked down, and she wasn't surprised to see that her nipples were pressed hard against the soft material of her camisole. She ached all over, and she couldn't stop her body from reacting.

Desperate, she turned to leave, and Morgan gently clasped her shoulders, halting her. They stood silent, motionless, for several heartbeats and then he sighed. "Give me a break here, Malone. I'm doing my best."

His best to seduce her? His best was actually pretty darn good. She turned slowly to face him and stared him in the eye, refusing to let him intimidate her.

Morgan hesitated, then ran a hand over his face in frustration. He ended with a rough laugh, taking her off guard. "You want the truth?"

"No!"

"I'm not used to women pushing me away."

"Oh, please." But she could easily believe it. Morgan had an incredible body, sensual eyes and a devastating smile that he generally hid behind a frown. She imagined any woman he looked at was more than willing to look back—and more.

"I've never known such a contrary woman," he muttered. "You want me, but you keep saying no. You make me crazy, Malone."

He looked so endearing, as if he were baring his soul, she had to fight to keep from smiling at him. She huffed instead. "You were crazy long before I stepped into the picture."

"Nope. I was in control, one hundred percent. Now I'm walking around with a semierection."

She gave a groan of frustration. "That's exactly what I'm talking about, Morgan. Your...masculine discomfort is of no concern to me."

"Well, it should be since you're the cause." She would have groaned again, but Morgan added, almost to himself, "You've shot all my well laid plans to hell."

Misty sputtered, both hurt and insulted. It was the hurt that made her sarcastic, because she knew exactly what plans he referred to. "Please, don't let me get in your way! I'll even help in the wife hunt if you want." He looked surprised, then disgruntled.

"No." He leaned over her. "I don't need your help."

"Why not? Tell me what qualities you're looking for and I'll keep my eyes open."

Morgan leaned closer, then lifted her chin with the edge of his fist. "Right now, I don't want a wife. I want you. And if you were honest, you'd admit you want me, too."

She met his gaze just as intently, determined to make him understand before she broke down and proved him right. "Sorry, Morgan, but I've sworn off men."

His hand opened, cradling her face. "That's the hell of it, Malone. You're not giving me a chance." His gaze touched on her everywhere—her eyes, her lips, her breasts. His thumb moved softly over her bottom lip. "It could be perfect, sweetheart. I'd make sure of it."

Misty wondered if she looked in the dictionary for the word *temptation* if it would feature a picture of Morgan Hudson. She could feel herself shaking inside, could feel her nerve endings all coming alive at his sensual promise—a promise she felt sure he could keep. The man was as seductive and searing as the bold stroke of a warm hand.

Wanting to give him equal honesty, she wrapped her hand around his wrist and shared a melancholy smile. "I have no doubt you...know what you're doing, Morgan. But I already feel a little used. I don't relish feeling that way again."

His fingers slid over her head to the back of her neck, cupping her warmly. "Oh, babe." His fingers caressed, kindled. His sigh was warm, his words soft. "I would never hurt you."

When she started to speak, he hushed her. "No, don't give me all your arguments. You'll make me morose."

She laughed at that. Morgan was so brutally honest, so different from the other men she knew. He didn't try to whitewash what he wanted, which was sex. He made it clear he intended to find a wife soon and that she didn't fit the role—a fact she knew only too well. He kept her aware of what he thought about things, and while she did consider him far too forward and pushy, it was nice not to have to guess about ulterior motives and hidden agendas.

Compared to Kent, a man who'd sworn undying love then dropped her the moment he found out she was pregnant, Morgan's honesty was refreshing. It was still alarming, but she'd trust it over insincere promises any day.

He released her, then rubbed the back of his neck. "You should know I'm not going to quit trying. I figure sooner or later I'll wear you down and you'll admit you want me."

"Why don't you try holding your breath?"

He wagged a finger at her. "Play nice, Malone."

"But you're the one who told me I could make you miserable, right? That's why I agreed to this farce in the first place."

She grinned at him, which made him laugh and shake his head. "Witch."

Misty wasn't offended. Somehow he'd made the name sound like an endearment.

He took her hand and started them on the way again. "Speaking of this farce...I should also point out that the job has nothing to do with your continued rejection." He glanced at her. "I'm not going to fire you if you keep saying no. I won't like it, and I'll do my damnedest to change your mind, but the job is yours as long as you're fulfilling it."

"No blackmail, huh?"

"No. I just wanted to make sure we understood each other."

For some reason, she'd never once doubted that. The way Morgan interacted with his family, treating Casey almost like a son, Honey like a sister, she knew he was too honorable to try forcing her hand. And he'd already proven that night in the gazebo that all it took was a soft, simple no to make him back off. She wasn't afraid of him. She was only afraid of herself when she was with him.

She was still pondering that when Morgan opened the garage door and she got a good look at the official car he expected her to ride in.

She backed up two steps. Granted it wasn't a typical law enforcement vehicle, but it had the lights on the roof and the word Sheriff emblazoned on the side in yellow and blue. Memories flooded back, and she winced.

To stall, she asked Morgan, "What type of sheriff are you?"

He looked up, saw her expression, then glanced at the shiny black four-wheel-drive Bronco. "Just a regular run-of-the-mill county sheriff, why? You don't like my transportation?" He wore a devilish grin.

"I've never seen anything like it." She walked around the truck, looking at it from all angles. "I thought officials drove sedans, not sport utility vehicles."

"It's for off-road driving, but there's no sport to it. There're a lot of hills in these parts. And though we don't have much in the way of big crime, just about anything that happens involves those damn hills. Last fall, a little girl got lost and we spent two days on foot looking for her. A four-wheel-drive would have made all the difference on some of the off-road searches. After that, the townsfolk got together and donated the Bronco."

Misty felt a little sick as she asked, "The child?"

"I found her curled up real tight under an outcropping of rock." His hands curled into fists and his jaw locked. "Her father had given up looking and was back at the station, drinking coffee and letting people dote on him."

He sounded thoroughly disgusted, not that Misty blamed him.

"Sawyer had rounded up about fifty people and we'd been at it all day and through the night. When I found her late the following afternoon, she was terrified, cold and crying for her daddy."

Misty put her hand on his arm, aware of the bunched muscles and his tension. Knowing Morgan as well as she did now, she could imagine how difficult that would have been for him, trying to console a child, hurting when that wasn't possible. "Her father should have been with you."

"He was a damn fool, visiting these parts and camping out when he didn't have a clue as to what he was doing. The weather was too cold for it and he didn't exactly pick the best spot to pitch his tent. The little girl wandered off because he wasn't watching her close enough."

"But she was all right?"

"Other than being a little dehydrated and scared silly, she

did great. Cutest little thing you'd ever seen. About five years old." His eyes met hers, diamond bright, and he added, "I know if it had been my kid, I wouldn't have quit looking until I found her."

"I think," Misty said, studying his intent expression, "you wouldn't have let her out of your sight in the first place."

Morgan kissed her nose. "No, I wouldn't have."

Misty wondered if he'd slept at all during those two days, and seriously doubted that he had. She gave him a tremulous smile. The man was proving to be entirely too easy to like.

Morgan stared at her mouth, groaned, then pulled the door of the Bronco open. "Let's go, Malone, before I forget my good intentions."

She clasped a hand to her heart. "You have good intentions? Toward me? I had no idea."

Suddenly his eyes narrowed. "Why are you stalling? What's up?"

"Don't be ridiculous." She eyed the truck again, then with a distinct feeling of dread, hefted herself into the seat. Morgan gave her a long look before he slammed the door.

When he climbed in on his own side, he said, "You wanna tell me about it?"

"I have no idea what you're talking about." She stared with feigned fascination at the control panel, the radio. Behind her was a sturdy wire-mesh screen separating the cargo area from the front seat—for prisoners, she knew. Unable to help herself, she shuddered.

Morgan started the engine, then reached for her hand. "When you were arrested, they cuffed you?"

"I don't want to talk about that." She tried to pull away, but he held her hand tight and rubbed his thumb over her knuckles. He did that a lot, grabbing hold of her and not letting her go. This time she appreciated the touch. She curled her fingers around his.

"I imagine you were," he said, speaking about the arrest in

a matter-of-fact way. "It's pretty much policy these days, for safety reasons."

She chewed her lip, then slowly closed her eyes, giving up. "It was the most degrading moment of my entire life. It was bad enough when Mr. Collins accused me of stealing the money, and I couldn't believe it when he actually called the cops."

"Mr. Collins?"

"My boss at Vision Videos. I kept thinking somehow things would get straightened out, that they'd realize there'd been a mistake."

"They didn't find the money on you?"

"No, because I didn't have it." She glared at him, then asked, "You think I'm guilty, don't you?"

Morgan was silent as they pulled onto the main road. He drove with one hand, still holding onto her with the other. Finally he muttered, "To be honest, I have serious doubts."

"Really?"

He glanced at her. "But if you did do it, I'd understand, okay?"

There was that damn honesty again; he wasn't convinced of her innocence, but he'd allow for the possibility. She almost laughed. For a man who wanted to get intimate with a woman, he wasn't going about it in the usual way—with lies and deceptions that would soften her up. "Even the lawyer I hired didn't believe me, not really."

"The evidence must have been pretty strong."

"Yeah, the fact that I'm a pregnant, supposedly desperate female was proof positive that I'd steal from a man I'd worked with for two years, even though I'd never been in trouble before in my life."

"Your boss knew you were pregnant?"

"Morning sickness kind of gives you away. That and the fact that I suddenly had more nights free." Misty was only vaguely aware of the beautiful scenery as they drove down the long road. The sun was bright, the day hot, but the air-conditioning in the truck had her feeling chilly.

Or maybe it was the dredging of memories that made her feel so cold inside. "I wasn't dating Kent anymore, and I knew that with the baby coming I needed to save up more money, so I'd offered to work more overtime." She slanted Morgan a look. "That made me seem guilty, too, by the way. My boss said small amounts of money had been missing several nights in a row, which was the first I'd heard of it, but he claimed that was why he'd come in unexpectedly to check on me that day, and found the money missing."

"When exactly did this all take place?"

She told him the exact day she'd been arrested.

Morgan surprised her by lifting her hand to his mouth and then turning it to gently kiss her palm. "I wasn't thinking. I didn't mean to make you uncomfortable riding with me."

Misty held her breath as his mouth moved against the sensitive skin of her palm. That, added to the gentle way he had of speaking to her sometimes, left her feeling vaguely empty and jumpy inside.

She swallowed hard. "After everything I've been through, it's silly to let a little ride get to me. But you just can't imagine what it was like. There were tons of people gathered outside the video store when I was arrested. They led me out in handcuffs and I just wanted to die. I thought I'd be glad to get in the car, where people couldn't see me, but instead, it seemed we hit every red light and folks in the other cars would stare."

Morgan slowed for a deer that ran across the road, distracting Misty for the moment. He spoke quietly, holding her hand on his thigh. "Sweetheart, people are always going to stare at you, no matter what, because you're beautiful. That's something you just ought to get used to."

Laughing helped to wash away the melancholy. "You may find this hard to believe, Morgan, but no one has ever carried

FREE GIFTS!

NO COST! NO OBLIGATION TO BUY!
NO PURCHASE NECESSARY!

PLAY THE
Lucky Key Game

Scratch gold area with a coin.
Then check below to see the gifts you get!

342 HDL C4E7
142 HDL C4EX

YES! I have scratched off the gold area. Please send me the 2 Free books and gift for which I qualify. I understand I am under no obligation to purchase any books, as explained on the back and on the opposite page.

NAME   (PLEASE PRINT CLEARLY)

ADDRESS

APT.#   CITY

STATE/PROV.   ZIP/POSTAL CODE

2 free books plus a mystery gift	1 free book
2 free books	Try Again!

Offer limited to one per household and not valid to current Harlequin Temptation® subscribers. All orders subject to approval.

(H-T-OS-07/00)

The Harlequin Reader Service® — Here's how it works:

Accepting your 2 free books and gift places you under no obligation to buy anything. You may keep the books and gift and return the shipping statement marked "cancel." If you do not cancel, about a month later we'll send you 4 additional novels and bill you just $3.34 each in the U.S., or $3.80 each in Canada, plus 25¢ delivery per book and applicable taxes if any.* That's the complete price and — compared to cover prices of $3.99 each in the U.S. and $4.50 each in Canada — it's quite a bargain! You may cancel at any time, but if you choose to continue, every month we'll send you 4 more books, which you may either purchase at the discount price or return to us and cancel your subscription.

*Terms and prices subject to change without notice. Sales tax applicable in N.Y. Canadian residents will be charged applicable provincial taxes and GST.

If offer card is missing write to: Harlequin Reader Service, 3010 Walden Ave., P.O. Box 1867, Buffalo NY 14240-1867

BUSINESS REPLY MAIL
FIRST-CLASS MAIL   PERMIT NO. 717   BUFFALO, NY

POSTAGE WILL BE PAID BY ADDRESSEE

HARLEQUIN READER SERVICE
3010 WALDEN AVE
PO BOX 1867
BUFFALO NY 14240-9952

NO POSTAGE
NECESSARY
IF MAILED
IN THE
UNITED STATES

on so much about my looks. Honey was the one the guys were always after. Men prefer blondes, you know."

"Sawyer certainly does." He turned to give her a lazy grin. "But I'm not Sawyer."

"You've got me there."

"You know what I prefer?"

She started whistling, which only made him chuckle. "I prefer dark-haired women with long sexy legs and incredible..."

"*Morgan*—" she warned.

"—smiles." He laughed at her expression. "Such a dirty mind you have, Malone. What did you think I was going to say?"

She reached over and smacked him for that, then couldn't help laughing again. "I figure I'm only slightly better than average looking—and I'm giving you the slightly better based on all this praise you've heaped on me lately."

He didn't look at her, just made a sound of disagreement. "You can ask any man and he'll tell you the same. Hell, just hearing you talk makes me hard, even when I don't like what we're talking about."

Of course she looked, then immediately jerked her gaze away. "If you don't stop being so shameless—" She sighed, unable to think of a threat that might carry any impact. It annoyed her that he'd once again gotten her to stare at him in a totally inappropriate way.

"You'll what? No, don't answer that. And for your information, I can't seem to help it."

She tugged her hand free, tucking it close so he couldn't retrieve it. "Keep your lips to yourself. That might be good for starters."

"Malone, I swear, one of these days you're going to take back those words."

She laughed again. "You're incorrigible."

"And a distraction?"

She blinked, realizing that he had, indeed, distracted her.

She nodded, giving him his due, but felt it necessary to point out the obvious. "My ride then was a little different. I was in the back, handcuffed, and the officers were in uniform—and armed."

Morgan grinned at her. "The county insists the Bronco is partly for my personal use, sort of a perk, so you're not the first woman to be seen in it."

"Did I ask for that information?"

"I just wanted you to know that if anyone stares this time, it'll be with a different kind of curiosity. And I do wear a uniform when I'm on duty, which I'm not right now. As to being armed, it's a habit." He made that statement, then shrugged.

"What do you mean?" Misty turned slightly in her seat to face him. "You carry a gun around with you?"

"All the time."

Once again she looked him over, then cocked an eyebrow. "Must be a good hiding place."

"Want to search me, Malone?"

Yes, but she wouldn't tell him that. "I'm waiting."

"You're no fun at all, but we'll work on that." He leaned down and lifted the hem of his jeans. "Ankle strap. I wear a belt holster when I'm on duty."

She'd seen him in uniform, and the sight had been impressive indeed. He looked nothing like Andy Griffith, that was for sure. When Morgan got decked out in his official clothes, he looked like a female fantasy on the loose. His shirt fit his broad shoulders to perfection, and his slacks emphasized his long, strong legs. The holster around his waist gave an added touch of danger to his dark good looks.

She imagined the females of Buckhorn County would continue to elect him sheriff just to get to see him in uniform each day.

Not that he didn't look great today in his jeans and soft T-shirt.

Misty eyed the small handgun in a leather holster. It was attached to an ankle cuff with a velcro strap. Despite herself, she was fascinated. "Do the good citizens of Buckhorn know about that gun?"

"You kidding? They insist on me holding up my image. Why, if they thought I wasn't armed, they'd be outraged. They each consider me their own personal sheriff, you know."

"Especially the women?" *Ouch.* She hadn't meant to say that.

Morgan gave her a knowing look, but thankfully didn't tease her. "Men and women alike, actually. Half my job is spent letting them bend my ear and reassuring them that the corruption of outside communities hasn't infiltrated yet."

"If corruption hasn't infiltrated, then why do they want you to carry a gun?"

He shrugged a massive shoulder. "I told you. Image." Almost as an afterthought, he added, "And I have had occasion to use it now and then."

He had her undivided attention. "You're kidding?"

"Nope. Being that we're a small town, a few of the more disreputable sorts thought it'd be the ideal hideout. To date, I've apprehended an escaped convict, caught a man wanted for robbery, and another for kidnapping."

Her eyes were wide. "Did you...shoot anyone?"

His hands tightened on the wheel. "The kidnapper, in the knee. The son of a bitch held a gun to a woman. He's lucky that's all I did to him."

Misty fell back in her seat, amazed. "I never would have imagined." Morgan seemed dangerous in many ways, and he certainly held his own when it came to taking charge of any situation. But she'd never imagined him being involved in a possibly lethal situation. He could have been killed! "This is incredible."

Again, he shrugged.

"What would the good citizens think if they knew you were consorting with a known criminal?"

"You?"

"Do you know any others?"

"Sure." He didn't allow her to question that. He gave her a speculative look, then suggested, "You could get your name cleared, you know."

"I don't see how that's possible." She bit her lip. "Once something is on your permanent record..."

"I could get it taken care of. It's a lot of legal jumble, and I can explain it later, but if you really didn't take the money..."

Misty felt her heart beating faster. "I didn't take the money." She waited for his reaction, her breath held. She wanted Morgan to believe her. It had suddenly become important to her, and not just because he wanted to help.

Seconds ticked by, and then he nodded. "I'll see what I can do."

He said nothing else, and that, she supposed, was that.

They reached the center of town, which was really no more than a narrow street full of buildings. Misty hadn't paid much attention to it when she'd been at the hall for Honey's wedding. She'd still been too nervous about Morgan and too excited for her sister. But now she had the chance to take it all in, and she wasn't going to miss a single thing.

There were two grocery stores at opposite ends of the street, a clothing store that looked as if it had been there for over a hundred years, a diner and a hairdresser, a pharmacy... She eyed the pharmacy as they drove past, wondering how awkward it might be to get her prenatal vitamin prescription filled; she'd run out of them yesterday.

One thing she didn't see was a bus station, and she wondered just where the nearest one was. After her comment earlier that she'd take a bus home, she felt rather foolish to realize there wasn't a bus around. You'd think one of the brothers could have mentioned that fact to her.

There were people sitting outside their shops, others lounging against the wall or standing close chatting. There

were even some rocking chairs sitting under canopied over-
hangs, to invite loiterers.

"This is like going back in time," she murmured as they
drove to the end of the street then turned right onto a nar-
rower side street. There were a few houses, a farm with some
cattle moving around, and a funeral parlor, which was easily
the biggest, most ornate structure she'd seen so far. Then
Morgan pulled into the circular drive of a building that
looked like an old farmhouse. It was two stories with a grand
wraparound porch, white columns in the front and black
shutters at every window.

"Why are we stopping here?"

"This is my office, darlin'." He chuckled at her as he drove
right up close to the front door and stopped. The double
doors wore a professional sign that read: Enter at Right. Evidently that didn't apply to the sheriff.

Morgan parked and turned off the engine. "The station
used to be by the county courthouse, farther into town, but it
was too small so years ago, long before I was elected, they
moved it here. Makes for a bit of whimsy doesn't it?"

Morgan climbed out, and at that moment two men came
around from the side of the house to greet him. "Hey there,
Morgan! Didn't expect to see you today. Anything wrong?"

Morgan frowned, as if surprised to see them. "Nope, no
problems. I was just showing the lady around." He opened
Misty's door and handed her out of the vehicle. Close to her
ear, he said, "Two of the biggest gossips around. They
weren't supposed to be here today, but that never stopped
them before. And since they're here, we might as well take
advantage of it."

Misty leaned away to look at him. "I don't understand."

"Anything they see makes the rounds of Buckhorn faster
than light. This'll be a good place to start letting folks know
you're off-limits."

Misty froze just as her feet touched the ground. Surely,
Morgan didn't mean to do anything in front of these nice old

men! But then she met his hot gaze and knew that was exactly what he intended.

She started to shake her head but he was already nodding. And darned if he wasn't smiling again.

7

ALL IT TOOK, Morgan thought as he watched Misty's eyes darken and her lips part, was a nice long look from him. She could deny it all she wanted, but her hunger was almost as bad as his own. When he felt it, she felt it, and right now was proof positive.

Well aware of Howard and Jesse closing in behind him, their curiosity caught, he leaned down and kissed her. It was a simple soft touch. He brushed his mouth over hers, once, twice. She drew a small shuddering breath, and her eyes slowly drifted shut, but she didn't stop him. No, she'd raise hell with him after, he had no doubt of that, but for now, she was as warm and needy as he. Her small hand fisted in his shirt, trying to drag him closer, proved it.

"Misty?" He whispered her name, watching the way her eyelashes fluttered.

"Hmm?"

His own smile took him by surprise. All his life people had teased him about his ferocious frowns, but something about Misty made him feel lighthearted, joyful deep inside. He touched the tip of her nose. "Sweetheart, we have an audience, or I'd sure do better than one measly peck, I promise."

Her eyes flew open, then widened. She peeked around his shoulder cautiously, saw the two men, and her own version of a fierce frown appeared. Her fisted hand released his shirt, and she thumped him in the chest. "Of all the—"

Morgan grabbed her hand, threw one arm around her shoulders and turned, taking her with him to face Howard and Jesse. "I thought I told you two not to work on the weekend."

"Nothing better to do today. We figured we'd get it done and out of the way."

Morgan gave Jesse a good frown to show him what he thought of that, but he knew better than to start debating with him now. "So how's the work going?"

Jesse nodded quickly, a habit he had when he was nervous, and being around women always made him nervous, especially the really pretty ones. "It's getting there. I'll have the lot of it cleared out by midweek." Though he spoke to Morgan, his eyes didn't leave Misty's face.

Howard scratched his chin, watching Misty with acute interest. "It's looking real good."

Amused by their preoccupation, Morgan nudged Misty slightly forward and said, "This is Honey's sister, Misty Malone. She's here for an extended visit and she'll be helping out around the station. Misty, this is Jesse and Howard."

Both men did a double take at that announcement, but Morgan ignored their reactions, knowing why they looked so shocked. They'd obviously jumped to the wrong conclusion. He hid his grin and decided to explain things to them later.

Jesse tipped a nonexistent hat and muttered, "Nice to meet you."

Howard stuck out his hand, realized it was covered with dirt and pulled it back before Misty could accept it. With an apologetic shrug, he explained, "I've been digging out the weeds. Messy work, that. Nice to meet you, Miss Malone."

Misty smiled. "Call me Misty, please. What exactly are you doing back there?"

It was Jesse who answered. "There's been a ton of weeds growing in the gully out back for as long as the sheriff's been stationed here. It draws mosquitoes and gnats and it's just plain ugly. Morgan wants us to clear them out and plant a line of bushes instead. We don't have the bushes in yet, but we will soon."

"I love outdoor work." Misty stepped away from Morgan and headed to the side of the house to check their progress. "I used to work with my father's gardeners when I was younger. It's hot work, especially on a day like today. But I always preferred that to being cooped up inside."

Morgan could just picture her as a little girl, hanging out with the hired help because her daddy ignored her and she had nothing better to do. It made his stomach cramp.

Howard nodded. "Know what you mean. Fresh air is good for you. I used to farm in my younger days. There's nothing like it."

She went around the corner of the house, Howard and Jesse trailing her like she was the Pied Piper. She kept chatting and they continued to hang on her every word.

Morgan was left alone with his disgruntled feelings. Odds were, he told himself, Misty had been as endearing as a wide-eyed child as she was now. The gardeners had probably loved having her underfoot. He shook his head. Gardeners, for crying out loud.

She made one simple statement about her youth and he got melancholy. It wasn't to be borne.

He heard Jesse's cackling laugh from way out back and frowned. They'd only just met her and she already had them mesmerized. He considered waiting until they came back, then changed his mind. He unlocked the front door, which only he and the deputy used, closed and locked it, then went through the converted house to the back. In what used to be the dining room, a space now housing all his file cabinets, he stared out the large picture window.

He could see Misty standing just outside the line of displaced weeds and dirt, her hands on her rounded hips as she conversed with the men. Her dark shiny hair glinted in the sunlight, and her bare shoulders and thighs appeared sleek. She looked over the still-packaged bushes while the two old codgers looked her over, eyeing the long expanse of her legs. Morgan felt like growling.

He knew he was in a hell of a predicament when two elders made him jealous. What had happened to his acclaimed control?

He went to the soda machine in the hallway outside his office and fed in quarters. Seconds later he stepped into the yard with four icy cold cans numbing his fingers. Jesse and Howard accepted theirs with relish, popping the tops and guzzling the cola. Though he'd told the old men time and again to bring a cooler with drinks, they never remembered to do it.

Misty was more restrained, using the edge of her shorts to clean the top of the can then opening it cautiously and sipping. It was so hot and humid outside that the little wisps of her hair escaping her topknot had begun to curl around her face.

She squinted against the sun, wrinkling her small nose, and smiled at him. "The bushes will look great once they're in. It'll make the yard looked bigger, too, without the tall weeds breaking up the length."

Morgan nodded, content just to look at her and drink his soda and enjoy the feel of the sunshine.

He loved the old farmhouse—and had since the moment he'd been elected and moved his things into the desk. He forced his gaze away from her and surveyed the back porch. "She's a grand old lady, isn't she?"

"She's beautiful." Misty, too, looked at the porch with the turned rails and ornate trim. "You don't see that kind of detail very often any more."

"It's solid." Morgan finished off his cola, then crushed the can in his fist. "This house is partly what inspired me to build my own home. I was forever doing improvements to the station and finally decided I needed my own place to work on. But even with my house almost complete, I still love it here."

"Somehow, I think it suits you. Especially because you're in charge."

"It does," he agreed, ignoring her teasing tone. "You want to see inside where you'll be working?"

"Sure." She turned to the men and smiled. "Howard, Jesse, it was nice meeting you."

They each nodded, ridiculous smiles on their faces. Morgan could only shake his head in wonder. Was no man immune? As they walked through the back door, he saw her smile and raised a brow in question.

"They're very sweet."

He gave her an incredulous look. "Uh-huh. You go right on wearing those rose-colored glasses, sweetheart."

She gasped at him in disapproval. "You're such a cynic. They're very nice men who are working hard for you. I'd think you'd appreciate that a little."

Morgan led her into his office, which had once been the dining room. It had a large white stone fireplace, now filled with lush ferns instead of burning logs. He'd had the arched doorway framed and fitted so he could close the door for privacy. He'd never needed or wanted that privacy more than now.

He propped his shoulders against the mantel. "Jesse was picked up for fighting two weekends ago. He broke two pool sticks and several lights after a man accused him of cheating at a game. Jesse wouldn't cheat, but he does have a terrible temper."

Misty stared at him in blank surprise.

"Now Howard, he's cooler than that. You won't catch him causing a brawl."

"You're dying to tell me, so spit it out." She mimicked his stance, leaning against the opposite wall.

Grinning, Morgan said, "He slipped into the theater without paying—five times in a row. He loves the movies, but says the prices have gotten too high. Arnold kept kicking him out and Howard kept creeping back in. No one would have known, but during the last movie, he tried stealing a bite of popcorn from the woman sitting next to him."

"And she complained over that?"

Morgan winked at her. "The woman was Marsha Werner, and he'd recently broken off a relationship with her and was, I imagine, trying to worm his way back into her good graces. She wasn't impressed, so she raised a ruckus and I finally had to arrest him. But it was Marsha who came and bailed him out, so who knows what's happening there?"

Misty tried to stifle a smile. "It's a little hard to imagine him in a relationship."

"That's only because you haven't met Marsha. Things soured between them when she wanted to get married, but they were a good couple, like the best grandma and grandpa you'd ever met." Morgan watched her smile widen and added, "Marsha's real fond of the movies, too, but as she continually explains to me in rather loud tones, she's an upstanding citizen and she pays for her entertainment."

Misty lost control of her twitching smile and laughed out loud. Morgan watched her, seeing the way the heat and humidity outside had made her shirt stick to her breasts. She'd smell all warm and womanly now if he could just get close enough to her to nuzzle her soft skin.

"So what kind of sentence did each of them get?"

He held her gaze and murmured, "Community work. That's why they're fixing the yard. I bought the bushes and they agreed to do the work. In addition, of course, Jesse had to promise to stay out of the pool hall for a month, and Howard had to pay for the movies he'd seen."

"Ah. They considered that a terrible punishment?"

"Not the yard work, but the other, yeah. With any luck, it'll make an impression this time. But I hate to see them in any real trouble. They're both pushing seventy, and even though they get around well enough to get into mischief, they don't mean any real harm. I think they're just lonely and a little bored, more than anything else."

She twisted her mouth in a near grimace, then asked, "When you arrested them..."

"No, I didn't handcuff them," he answered gently, able to read her train of thought. It hurt him to see her so hesitant, to know that her own memories ate at her. He'd fix things for her one way or another, he vowed. "I didn't stick them in back of the Bronco, either. They both rode up front with me. That way, I could give them a stern talking-to during the ride. They hate that."

Misty smiled at him for a nearly endless moment, then turned up her can of soda and finished it off. She set the can on his desk. "I'm impressed, Morgan."

"With what?"

"Your compassion. And the fact that you obviously have a soft side, which you hide pretty well, by the way."

He wasn't at all sure he wanted her noticing his soft side, not that he had one, anyway. He frowned at the mere thought.

Misty gave a loud sigh. "Now what are you scowling about? I insult you and you laugh, I compliment you and you start glowering at me."

Morgan didn't move. She had an impish look about her that intrigued him. "Come closer and I'll tell you why I'm frowning."

"Oh, no, you don't."

"Afraid of me, Malone?"

She made a rude sound, refusing to be drawn in by his obvious challenge. "Not likely. You're as big as an ox and built like a ton of bricks, but you don't beat up on women."

He made his own rude sound. "That's not what I meant, and you know it." He lowered his voice to a suggestive rumble. "You're afraid if you get too close, you won't want to move away again. But this is my office and I don't do hanky-panky here. At least, not any serious hanky-panky. So you're safe enough."

"And what constitutes the serious stuff?"

He looked at her breasts and felt his heartbeat accelerate. "Anything below the waist?"

She swallowed and he could see the thrumming pulse in her throat. "Howard and Jesse are right outside."

"Not for much longer. I only let them work for a few hours a day, mostly in the morning because the afternoon heat is too much for them."

"Then why have them doing that job at all?"

She was bound and determined to distract him, so Morgan let her. The last thing he wanted was for her to be wary of him. "Their pride is important to them, and to me. Already they've told anyone who'd listen that I've given them such a hard, impossible job, then they come here and have a great time futzing around, proving that they can do it. In fact, they complain about the short days I insist on, because Jesse used to be in construction and Howard was a farmer. They say they're used to the heat, but—" He realized he was rambling and ground to a halt.

"You're pretty wonderful sometimes, Sheriff, you know that?"

He unfolded his arms, letting them hang at his sides. In a rough whisper, he said again, "Come here."

She took one step toward him, then halted. "This is crazy."

Morgan nodded in agreement. Crazy didn't even begin to describe the way she made him feel.

She looked undecided and he held his breath, but she turned away. She pretended an interest in the office. Her voice shook when she started talking again. "This is your desk?"

She picked up a framed school picture of Casey and studied it.

"You know it is. My office is the biggest room. The cells are in the basement, though they seldom get used—and yes, I'll take you on a tour in a bit. The kitchen has been rearranged into a lobby of sorts, and there's always coffee there for anyone who wants it. The family room faces the kitchen through open doorways across the hall, and that'll be where you work. There's a lot of office equipment in there. I'll have my deputy, Nate Brewer, show you where he keeps things and how to use the file system. The upstairs has been turned into conference rooms for different community events."

He watched her inch closer to him to look at a plaque hanging on the wall. Not wanting to scare her off now that she was almost within reach, he said, "That's my mission statement."

"Mission statement?"

"My intent for holding office as sheriff. The community got to read it prior to the election." He was thankful she didn't read the whole thing. His patience was about run out and he just wanted to taste her.

"You had the plaque made?"

"Nope. The advisory board did." He saw her start to ask and said, "They're a group of citizens that bring concerns to me. Sort of a community awareness system."

She leaned closer to the plaque. "It says here that you founded the advisory board during your first term in office."

He shook his head. "I was the one who suggested a voice in the community, so they'd all feel more involved in decisions. But they're the ones who organized the board and set up the structure for it. Now they have these big elections to decide who gets to serve in the various advisory board positions."

She moved closer still, examining a trophy on the mantel beside him. Morgan tried to block it with his shoulders, but she inched around him until she could see it clearly. "What's this for?"

Feeling uncomfortable with her inquisition, Morgan cleared his throat. "That was given to me by the student council at the high school."

"It says, outstanding community leadership."

"I know what it says, Malone." He glared, but she glared right back, and he gave up with a sigh. "I started a program where the students can interact with the elders in the community, helping out with chores and such. I'd hoped to give the kids some direction and the elders some company, that's all. But now participation is recognized by the governor for qualifications to state scholarships."

She looked at him. "That's remarkable."

Morgan shifted to face her, determined to satisfy her curiosity so he could get her mind on more pleasurable topics. "Naw. The students took it a lot further than I did, making it a hell of a program. That's why I thought it deserved to be brought to the governor's notice."

She glanced at the writing on the base of the trophy. "It says here that you help supply scholarship funds, as well."

Morgan rubbed his ear and bit back a curse. "Yeah, well, that's just something I sort of thought would help...."

Misty reached up and took his hand, enfolding it in both of her own. Her blue eyes were filled with amusement and something else. He was almost afraid to figure out what. "Don't be modest, now, Sheriff."

"I'm not!"

"And don't be embarrassed, either."

He gave her his blackest scowl. "That's just plain foolish. Of course I'm not embarrassed. No reason to be. It's all just part and parcel of my job."

Misty shook her head as if scolding him, and it rankled. "I can't quite figure you out, Morgan."

Slowly, so she wouldn't bolt, he slipped his hand free and trailed his fingers up her bare arm to the back of her neck. He'd always loved the feel of women, the smoothness compared to a man's rough angles. But for whatever reason, he loved the feel of Misty more.

Just touching her arm made his heart race, his groin throb. He could only imagine how it would be once he had her naked beneath him, able to touch and taste and investigate every small part of her. He shook with the thought.

Goose bumps appeared where he'd touched her, and she

gave a small shiver. "I'm as clear as glass, sweetheart." He was aware of how husky his voice had gone, but damn, he felt like he was burning up. Gently rubbing the back of her neck, he urged her a tiny bit closer, then closer still. He stared at her thick eyelashes, resting against her cheeks, at the warm flush of her skin. "I'm just a man who wants you."

She answered in a similar husky whisper. "*That* part has been plain enough." Staring at his throat, her small hands restless, she refused to meet his gaze. "It's the rest that confounds me."

"But anything else is unimportant." And then he kissed her.

MISTY KNEW her joke about making Morgan miserable had backfired in a big way. She was the one suffering, not him. She realized she actually liked the big guy, and almost cursed. He was so cavalier about all he did, all the responsibility he accepted.

And she seemed to have no control around him at all. He was just so big and so strong and so incredibly handsome. But it was more than that.

Morgan was a nice man.

He was also an honorable man who took his job very seriously and cared about people, not just the people he called family, but all the people in his community. Like an overlord of old, he felt responsible for their safety and happiness. And that made him almost too appealing to resist.

A soft moan escaped her when Morgan touched his mouth to hers and she felt his tongue teasing her lips.

"Open up for me, Malone."

Her hand fisted in his shirt over his hard chest. She felt the trembling of his muscles, the pounding of his heartbeat—and her lips parted.

Morgan let out his own groan only seconds before his tongue was in her mouth. She'd never known kissing like this, so hot and intimate and something more than just mouth on mouth. Maybe it was because Morgan was unique, but being kissed by him seemed more exciting than anything she'd ever done.

Beneath her fingers she could feel his labored breaths, and she opened her palm, amazed by the way his hard muscles shifted and moved in response to her touch. She felt powerful—no man had ever made her feel that way before.

As if he'd known her thoughts, he caught her other hand, which had been idly clasped at his waistband, and dragged it up to his chest. "Damn, I love it when you touch me."

Misty tucked her face beneath his chin and tried to take a calming breath. Instead, she inhaled his hot male scent and renewed desire. Rather than pushing his advantage, Morgan looped both arms around her and rocked her gently.

"It's almost too much, isn't it?" he growled against her temple.

Words were too difficult, so she nodded, bumping his chin. She felt like crying and hated herself for it. She'd never been a woman who wept over every little thing, so she assumed it must be the pregnancy making her so weak.

Then again, Morgan wasn't a little thing. He was a great big hulking gorgeous thing, and how he made her feel was enough to shake the earth.

His fingertips smoothed over her cheek. "I'm trying to give you time, sweetheart. I know you've been through a lot and until this morning, I've done nothing but push you away. But it's not easy." He gave a shaky laugh and admitted, "It's damn near impossible, if you want the truth."

His words prompted a new thought, but there was no way she could look him in the eyes right now. Morgan would see everything she felt and he'd stop trying to be so considerate. If he pushed even the tiniest bit, she'd give in to him and she knew it. As much as she wanted him, she didn't know if it was the right thing to do. She needed more time.

Hiding her face close to his chest, she did her best to sound casual when she spoke. "It was a rather quick turnaround for you."

"No." He kissed her ear, then nipped her lobe, making her jump. "I wanted you something fierce the first second I saw you. I just figured it'd be too complicated if we got involved."

"Because you're looking for a wife?"

He stiffened slightly, then deliberately began rubbing her back. "Because you're Honey's sister, so you were off-limits for a fling."

It felt like her heart broke, his honest words hurt so much. Her throat was constricted, and she swallowed hard so he wouldn't know how strongly he'd affected her. "But now, since it's obvious what type of woman I am, my relationship to Honey no longer matters?"

"What the hell are you talking about?" Morgan tried to tip her back to see her face, but she held onto him like a clinging vine and he finally quit trying. His mouth pressed warmly to her temple and his arms tightened. "I don't think you're easy, Malone, if that's what you're getting at."

"No?" She forced herself to unclench his shirt. The man would wear wrinkles all day thanks to her. And his brothers would probably take one look at him and know why. "I'm pregnant, with no husband, no job. I'm a convict, for crying out loud. What's your definition of easy?"

He took her off guard, thrusting her back a good foot with his hands wrapped securely around her upper arms. His scowl was enough to scare demons back to hell. Misty held her breath, not afraid of him physically, really, but very uncertain of his mood.

He started to say something, then paused. "Damn it," he growled, "don't look at me like that. I would never hurt you."

She nodded. "I know it."

"Then why are you shaking?"

"*You're* shaking me."

He looked poleaxed by that observation, then dropped his hands to shove them onto his hips in a thoroughly arrogant stance. Misty wrapped her arms around herself and watched him cautiously.

He didn't apologize. "And you deserve it, too."

"For asking a question?" Now that he wasn't touching her, she could regain her edge.

"For suggesting something so stupid." He took a quick step toward her, leaned down in a most unnerving way and practically shouted, "I do not think you're easy!"

Misty blinked.

"Hell, woman, you're about the most difficult female I've ever run across. You fight me at every damn turn."

For some reason, Misty felt like smiling. She bit her lip, knowing Morgan wouldn't appreciate it one bit. "That's not true."

"No? I go crazy for you, and you ignore me, then flirt outrageously with every other male in the county."

That got her good and mad. "I did no such thing! And you ignored me first." She hadn't meant to bring that up; it made her sound spiteful, as if she'd ignored him to get even. She frowned at him for making her say too much.

"I tell you to leave, you argue about it. I all but beg you to stay, you argue about it."

"I did not argue about leaving."

"You got snide, I remember that well enough." He rubbed his neck and groaned. "Hell, it was all I could do to keep my hands to myself, to put up with having you in the house until Sawyer's wedding, and you just kept sniping at me, and for some fool reason that only made me want you more."

"How could I have ignored you and sniped at you at the same time? That doesn't make sense, Morgan."

His eyes narrowed. "You'd snipe with silence, by being there, making me want you, then chatting with one of my disreputable brothers as if I wasn't in the room when I knew damn good and well you were aware of me. Admit it, Malone."

This time she gave in to the grin; she couldn't help herself. "Admit I was aware of you? Sure. You're a mite hard to miss, Morgan, being so big and all."

He took another step toward her, and she backed up. In soft tones that sounded like threats rather than compliments, he said, "I admire your pride, sweetheart, I really do. But that pride is misplaced when you cut off your nose to spite your face."

"What is that supposed to mean?"

"It means you wanted to stay here, but stubbornly refused just because I'd been a pigheaded fool and asked you to go."

"I agreed to stay, Morgan," she said, feeling it necessary to point that out.

"And you refused a good job, just because you thought it was created for you."

"Uh...I took the job, too, remember?"

"I remember that I had to practically get down on my hands and knees, as well as resort to every lamebrained scheme around, to get your agreement! And you dare to say I think you're *easy?*"

"Will you stop shouting at me?"

He halted. Misty had her back to a bookcase, and Morgan was only a scant inch away. "Yeah, I'll stop shouting. As long as you promise to never again put words in my mouth."

Because he looked so sincerely put out over it, she agreed. "I'm sorry."

With his hands on the bookshelf level with her head, he caged her in. "Listen good, Malone, because I don't want to have to repeat this." His gaze dipped to her mouth, then came back to her eyes, pinning her motionless. "I do not think you're easy. I think you're a beautiful woman who got involved with the wrong guy and ended up in some trouble because of it. And no, I'm not talking about the pregnancy, because you're right, that's not real trouble. If you want the baby, then everything else will work itself out. I was talking about being blamed for the theft."

He drew a long breath, then squeezed his eyes shut. "And I'll have you know that even arguing with you makes me hot. I'm so damn hard right now I could be considered lethal."

A startled laugh burst out of her, making Morgan scowl all the more. She looked at his face, then doubled over in laughter, making an awful racket but unable to help herself.

Morgan waited patiently, crossing his arms over his chest and blocking her so she couldn't move away. His reaction made her laugh harder, and she fell against him until he was forced to prop her up.

When she finally quieted, Morgan was rubbing her back and smiling at her. "You want to tell me what brought that on?"

"You're priceless, Morgan."

"How so?"

He was such a reprobate. She smiled at him as she explained, aware of his hands drifting lower, almost to her behind. "You have absolutely no consideration for my modesty or my sensibilities. You talk about the most personal things—"

"Like what?"

"Like the fact you seem to have a problem with control."

He shook his head very slowly. "Not usually. Everyone will tell you I maintain absolute control."

She quirked a brow and stared at his fly.

With a grin, Morgan said, "That's an aberration, an involuntary reaction that can't be controlled around you."

She almost started laughing again. "Well, whatever it is, you show no hesitation in talking about it, shocking me all the time, embarrassing me."

His hands slid over her bottom completely, and he lifted her to her tiptoes so she fit against him. She caught her breath as his voice went husky and deep. "I want you to know how much I want you, sweetheart."

Contentment swelled inside her. She knew it was dangerous to make herself vulnerable to him, but at the moment, she was too touched to care. "That's just it," she said softly, "you show no hesitation about making me blush, but you're so considerate of my feelings otherwise. Thank you."

Morgan's fingers contracted on her backside, caressing and exciting. "You want to know how you can thank me?"

Misty was ready to start laughing again when a tentative knock sounded on the door. She jumped, bumped her head on the bookcase, then shoved him away. "Good grief, my first time in your office and look what happens."

With a wry look, Morgan turned and headed for the door. "Unfortunately, not a thing happened." He stepped into the hallway. Misty went to the office door to peek out and see who it was. When she saw Howard and Jesse stomping to remove the dirt from their boots, she stepped out to greet them.

"Are you all done for the day?"

Jesse shook his head. "Just taking off for lunch. Is this your first day?"

"No, Morgan was just showing me around today. I'll start tomorrow."

Jesse frowned at Morgan. "How long does she have?"

Misty didn't understand the question, and Morgan didn't help by grinning at her. "I'm not sure yet. What do you think?"

"I think it'd be nice to keep her on for good, but I don't suppose that'd be fair."

Howard agreed. "Can't imagine what she could've done—not that I'm prying, you understand. But to be here in the first place..."

Misty frowned in confusion. "I'm here because Morgan said he needed someone to answer the phone and take messages."

Jesse nodded. "That's a fact. Just about every day one woman or another comes here insisting just that. But I always wondered if it's really work they have on their minds." He gave her an exaggerated wink. "Ought to put an end to that now, what with Misty here, though."

"That," Misty said while trying to hide her annoyance at the thought, "is entirely up to Morgan."

"Yes, it is," Morgan agreed, smiling at her, "but it so happens I think Jesse is right. One female in the office is more than enough."

Misty clamped her lips together to keep from replying.

Morgan looked disappointed at her restraint. He turned his attention to the men. "You both have lunch with you?"

"Naw, we're going to the diner. Ceily promised me meat loaf today."

He glanced at his watch. "Is the diner open yet?"

"She'll slip us in through the kitchen."

Howard added, "You take it easy on the little lady, now, you hear?"

"I should explain something, here, guys—" Morgan began, and Misty knew he was going to blurt out something stupid, about how they were involved.

She rushed to his side and nudged him playfully with her shoulder, trying to act like a pal instead of an almost lover. "Morgan is a big pushover. Don't you worry, I can handle him."

Both the men stared at her in awe. Morgan rumbled, a sound between a laugh and a growl. "Malone—"

"Behave, Morgan," she snapped, giving him a telling look before forcing a smile on the men. "They're hungry. Let them go eat."

"But—"

Misty ignored him. "Run on, now. You both look famished to me. Everyone knows big healthy men need to eat a lot to keep up their strength. Especially when they're working as hard as you two are."

Jesse and Howard puffed up like proud roosters.

Misty waved them off, and after Morgan had shut the door, he said with amusement, "You certainly wrapped them around your little finger."

She didn't appreciate that comment at all, considering she'd barely managed to keep him from embarrassing her again. "They're very sweet men."

Morgan choked on a laugh. "They feel the same way about you. That's why they were trying to find out why you're here."

She didn't understand his humor at all. "Is it so uncommon for you to hire someone?"

Morgan pursed his mouth, but ended up chuckling anyway. "Actually, yeah, it is. And Malone, they don't think you were hired."

"What's that supposed to mean? Do they think I coerced the job out of you? I swear, Morgan, if people are going to talk because I'm working here..."

He leaned a shoulder against the wall, and even though his mouth wasn't smiling, she saw the unholy glint in his blue eyes. "Oh, they'll talk, all right. You see, at this moment Jesse and Howard are probably telling anyone they can find that you're serving out your time working here—same as they are."

She felt her eyes nearly cross. "That's ridiculous!"

Shrugging, he said, "That's usually why I bring someone in underfoot. Because they got into mischief and have to do community work."

"But..." She couldn't think of anything to say, then her temper flared. "You could have set them straight!"

"I believe I tried to. But you were too intent on telling them how you could handle me to let me finish."

Misty moaned and covered her face. "So now, even though no one here knows I was actually arrested, they're all going to think the same about me anyway."

Morgan pulled her hands down and kissed the end of her

nose. "Let me show you around the office, explain your duties, then we'll go to the diner and set them straight."

"We will?"

He brushed his thumb over her bottom lip. "Believe me, Malone, no one is going to have any doubts as to why I'm keeping you close, I promise. So quit your worries."

Misty followed him into the office, but his promise, and the way he'd given it, left an empty ache inside her.

Morgan was slowly getting under her skin, and that left her feeling far from reassured.

8

"Ouch." Misty bumped her head as she knelt and crawled beneath the desk. "You're sure she went under here?"

Jordan sounded slightly strangled as he said, "Yeah, she's under there."

In the farthest corner, against the back wall, Misty saw a curled calico tail. "Ah, I see her. She's a little thing."

"I found her abandoned." Anger laced Jordan's tone, and that was unusual because Misty had never heard this particular brother sound anything but pleasant. "I brought her home to heal, and your sister sort of bonded with her. Usually she's in bed with Honey, but today, well, I think she knew it was a day for shots and that's why she's running from me."

Misty bumped her head again when she tried to look at Jordan. All she could see was his feet. He'd been chasing the cat to take it to his clinic when they'd run into each other in the hallway. The cat had scurried away while Jordan kept Misty from falling on her behind.

Misty had been hoping to leave the house before Morgan. According to Honey, he'd been looking for her last night and had been disgruntled when he couldn't find her. But she wasn't yet ready to tell him where she'd been. Dodging him this morning was the only way she could think of to buy herself some time.

"So do you like your new job?" Jordan asked her as she crawled deeper beneath the desk.

"Actually, I do." She reached out her hand and the small cat, hissing at her, managed to inch a little farther away.

"That's good. I gather Morgan is behaving himself?"

"Morgan is Morgan. He never really behaves. You know that."

"Uh, yes, I see your point."

Morgan was the most forward, outspoken man she'd ever known, but he kept her smiling and sometimes even laughing. And he always made her very aware of her own femininity. The man could scorch her with a look, and in the short time she'd spent with him, she'd become addicted to the feeling.

But the entire week had been a series of near misses. Though she worked in his office, he was seldom there. She'd had no idea he kept such a horrendously busy schedule. After hours wasn't much better. When Morgan was free, she was gone. When she was free, Morgan got called away. His plan to make them look like a couple wasn't quite working out as she'd assumed. She hated to admit it, even to herself, but she'd been looking forward to his outrageous pursuit. And she missed him.

Jordan coughed suddenly, then suggested, "Uh, maybe you should just come on out of there?"

"No, I've almost got her. She's worked herself into a tiny little ball. Let me just scrunch in here a bit more."

"No, wait. I'll pull the desk out."

Misty was sure she heard repressed laugher in Jordan's voice, but the sound was muffled because most of her upper body was wedged into the seating area of the desk. "No, if you do that she'll just run off again. At least this way I have her cornered."

Jordan made a strangled sound.

"What?"

"Never mind."

Misty tried wiggling her fingers at the cat. She had hoped to be gone already, out the door before Morgan awoke. Working with him was more enjoyable than she'd thought it would be. She liked getting to know everyone in the town, and it was so obvious to her how they all adored their sheriff. He was treated with respect and reverence and a bit of awe.

"So your arrangement with Morgan is working out?"

She snorted, wondering which arrangement Jordan referred to. The work or the personal relationship. "Yes, things are fine. Although Morgan does like to complain a lot."

"Well, as to that," Jordan said cautiously, "I think he complains because things aren't going quite the way he planned."

"Things aren't going quite how I planned, either." She laughed, then added, "Morgan gripes because it's a habit, just like scowling at everyone." Misty thought of all she'd learned about Morgan in the past week, how he reacted with the various community members who liked to stop by and offer suggestions or complaints or idle chitchat. His patience was limitless, and why not? He usually controlled everything and everyone without anybody even realizing it. He was careful not to offend, strong and supportive, understanding. But the final word was his, and they all respected that about him. In fact, she often got the impression that they brought their minor gripes to him so he *would* take charge, saving them the hassle.

Overall, she admitted he made a pretty wonderful sheriff.

"You know, Jordan, Morgan would like the world to think he's a real bear, but Honey's right. Deep down he's just a big softy."

There was a choked laugh, then a loud thump. Jordan cursed under his breath.

"Now don't tease, Jordan. You know I'm right. Even though you all harass each other endlessly, you know your brother is pretty terrific."

Jordan's voice was lazy. "I think you and Honey are sharing that particular delusion. She's as misguided about him as you are." Then: "Just think. With you two singing his praises, Morgan will be known as a real pussycat in no time at all."

Laughing, Misty said, "I wouldn't go that far!"

Her laugh startled the cat, and when she tried to run, Misty reached out and scooped her up. "I've got her." She started crawling backward, inching her way out. The cat didn't fight her. Instead, it purred loudly at the attention.

Misty held the small calico close to her chest and scooted until she bumped into a pair of hard shins. Startled, she turned and looked up to see what Jordan was doing, and was met with Morgan's blackest look. He had his big feet braced, his hands on his hips and his jaw locked. He didn't move.

Jordan stood behind him, grinning.

For some fool reason, Misty felt her face heating. How long had he been there? What had she just been saying about him? She pulled her gaze away from his and frowned at Jordan. "You could have warned me."

"Warned you about what?" Jordan asked innocently.

Morgan reached down and caught Misty's elbow. "Come on, Malone, quit abusing my brother."

Judging by the way Jordan rubbed his shoulder, Misty had the suspicion Morgan had already done enough abusing, but she had no idea why. Jordan didn't seem bothered by it, though. He looked entertained. She frowned at Morgan. "What do you want?"

He didn't appear to like her question. "We need to get to work."

Misty stood, attempting to ignore Morgan's nearness and Jordan's attentive presence. "We've got a few minutes."

Crossing his arms over his chest, Morgan said, "Is that so? Then why were you trying to hightail it out of here so early?"

She couldn't very well explain with Morgan's brother standing there, so she turned to Jordan and handed him the cat. "Hang onto her this time."

"Thanks, sweetie." Jordan leaned forward and kissed her cheek, grinned at Morgan one more time, then left them.

Misty could hear his soft crooning voice as he spoke with the cat.

She had a feeling Jordan had kissed her just to provoke Morgan, and seeing the way Morgan clenched his jaw, it must have worked. They stared at each other for a long, silent moment. Finally, Morgan shook his head. "You've been avoiding me all week."

"That's not true! We've just had conflicting schedules, that's all."

"Your only schedule is working with me. Yet I haven't had one single second alone with you. That's avoidance."

She didn't want to admit that she'd missed him, too, or that she did, in fact, have another schedule. "It's not my fault that you work all the time."

"I knocked at your door at six yesterday." His gaze softened. "I expected to find you in bed still, all warm and sleepy. But you were gone already."

Misty wondered what he would have done if he'd found her in bed, and the thought wasn't at all repulsive. She cleared her throat. "Maybe it was a good thing I wasn't there."

"There you go with those lecherous thoughts again, Malone. I was just going to offer to take you to breakfast."

She winced at the very idea. "If you'll recall, Morgan, mornings are a little rough for me. I like to walk down and sit by the lake. The fresh air settles my stomach some."

He scowled over that, and his voice sounded gruff, more with concern than annoyance. "I'd forgotten. Has the morning sickness been bad?"

Oh, when Morgan was being so sweet, it was all she could do to resist him. She wasn't even sure she wanted to anymore. Thoughts of being with him had consumed her lately. When he was around, she could barely take her eyes off him, and when he wasn't, her thoughts centered on him.

Misty realized he was watching her, and she coughed. "Actually," she said, deciding to give him a small truth, "it's been better lately. Usually, as long as I don't eat, my stomach settles down fairly quick."

"So you've been skipping breakfast?"

"I was never much for big morning meals, anyway."

His frown was back, more intense than ever. "You weren't at dinner last night, either." He looked her over, then shook his head. "You know how important it is for you to eat properly right now."

"I have enough mothering from Honey. You don't need to start, too." And before he could protest that, she added, "Besides, I'm not starving myself. I ate in town last night."

He went still, then he flushed and growled, "With who?"

This was exactly the subject Misty had hoped to avoid, but now it looked as if she had no choice but to tell him. Exasperated, she pushed past him and headed down the hall. Morgan followed. "If you must know," she said over her shoulder, "I was working."

"You got off work at three o'clock, Malone. I watched you leave."

Yes, he had. She shivered just remembering. Morgan had been watching her with a brooding frown as she'd gathered her things. He was stuck talking with an elderly woman who claimed her neighbor mowed his grass too early in the morning to suit her. Misty had known by the look on Morgan's face that his patience was about at an end. If she hadn't been required to be elsewhere, she very well might have hung around just to see what he'd do. "I left the station at three o'clock. But then I went to the diner."

"To meet someone?"

Her temper snapped. Did he always have to think the worst of her? "That's none of your concern."

She kept walking, but he had stopped. She didn't mean to, but when she turned to face him and saw his expression, her heart almost melted. He looked angry and frustrated and...hurt.

She'd never thought she'd see a look like that on the inimitable sheriff's face.

She didn't like it at all.

She stomped down the hall to glare at him, thrust her chin up and said, "No, I wasn't meeting anyone. I went there to work."

His confusion was almost laughable. "You're working at the diner? Since when?"

"Since yesterday. Ceily hired me." His mouth opened and she said, "Before you ask, yes, I told her about my record."

"Misty." He said her name so softly, like a reprimand, and she felt a lump gather in her throat. He took both her arms, his thumbs rubbing just above her elbows. "I hadn't even thought of that."

"Bull. You had that look on your face."

"What look?"

"The one that's full of doubt."

"That was just me trying to figure you out." His mouth tipped in a small smile. "What did Ceily have to say?"

"I told her the truth, that I was innocent but couldn't prove it, and that the whole thing had cost a lot so I needed to save up more money now. She believed me." Misty twisted her hands together, once again caught in a worry. Ceily was a very pretty, petite woman with long golden brown hair and big brown eyes. She looked to be around Gabe's age. She'd been very warm and welcoming to Misty from the onset. "She didn't strike me as the type to carry tales. She even warned me about telling any secrets to Howard or Jesse. She said they're both horrible gossips."

Morgan laughed. "She would know. Jesse is her grandpa."

"I hadn't realized. They don't look anything alike."

"Considering Jesse is old and cantankerous and Ceily is young and cute, I'm not surprised you didn't see the family resemblance. But you're right about Ceily, she doesn't gossip. You don't have to worry about that."

Without meaning to, Misty frowned at him. "You know her well?"

He shrugged. "As well as I know anyone here. Ceily and Gabe went through school together, and she used to hang out at the house when they were younger. They're both water fanatics. She's a good kid."

Misty relaxed the tiniest bit. It appeared her secrets were safe with Ceily, which had been her only concern.

Morgan asked, "Do you mind telling me how you figure on doing both jobs?"

"I knew you wouldn't understand," she muttered. He was strong and capable and respected...and it would have been so easy to lean on him and let him help her, to follow suit with the entire town and let Morgan handle her problems. But she wanted to regain what she'd lost on her own. It was the only way she could think of to restore her self-respect.

He let her go reluctantly and fell into step beside her as she headed for her room. "Tell me what I don't understand, babe."

She shook her head. "What I do for you can barely be considered part time, Morgan. It's only six hours a day."

"I didn't want you to overdo."

Why, oh why, did he have to say things like that? "I'm not breakable, you know."

"I would never suggest such a thing." He kept pace with her easily, then paused when she reached her door. "No one would ever doubt your strength or determination, Malone. If that's what this is about..."

Flustered, Misty shrugged. "There's no reason I can't work for the diner in the evenings, right? Ceily agreed to put me on at four. That gives me time to grab a bite to eat and then get in four or five more hours. Last night, I made fifty bucks in tips. It's a good job."

Morgan propped his hands on his hips, dropped his head forward and paced several feet. When he finally faced her again, he looked grim. "I'm going to let all that go for now."

"How magnanimous of you."

He didn't appreciate her dry wit. "I want to talk to you about something else. Will you ride into work with me?"

She regretted the need to refuse him. "I can't. I'll be going to the diner again after we finish at the station. I'll need my car to get home."

"I'll pick you up when you get off."

"That doesn't make sense, Morgan. You never know when you might get a call, and I don't want to interrupt things for you."

He did a little more jaw locking. Misty wondered why he didn't have a perpetual headache.

"All right. Then let me take you to my house tonight. I've been wanting to show it to you, anyway."

The idea was tempting. From afar, his house looked wonderful. It wasn't quite as large as the house he shared with his brothers, but it had just as much character. The exterior appeared to be cedar, and few of the mature trees had been displaced during the building. Every morning when she went to the lake, she looked at his house. Its position on the hill would prove a stunning view. "Why do you want to go there?"

He shrugged. "I just want your opinion, to see if you like it. No other woman has seen it yet, except for Honey. But the two of you are so different, I thought it'd be nice to get your reaction, too. The house will be done before much longer. Gabe works on it off and on, and I get up there whenever I can. All the major stuff is done, now it just needs the finishing touches."

Misty chewed her bottom lip. She wasn't stupid; she knew if she was alone with Morgan for any length of time, they'd probably end up making love. She'd honestly believed no man could ever tempt her again, but she hadn't counted on a man like him. She'd thought him incredibly sexy from the moment she saw him, and since then, she'd also discovered what a wonderful man he was, inside as well as out.

He was always honest with her, and she knew deep in her heart she'd never meet another man like him. She was through with lasting relationships, and as soon as she could save up a little money, she was going to move away. By the time she returned for a visit, Morgan might well be married and on his way to having his own children.

She shook her head, saying mostly to herself, "I don't know...."

His hands cradled her face. "I won't lie to you, Malone. I want some time alone with you. I want to be able to talk to you without one of my damn brothers nosing in, or someone at the station staring at us." He looked at her mouth. "And I want to kiss you again. We've barely seen each other all week. At this rate, no one is going to believe we're involved. Already I've had people questioning our relationship."

He said the last with a growl, and she almost laughed at him. "What people?"

His frown deepened. "No one you need to know about. I made it clear you weren't free—like we agreed, right?"

"Uh, right." Morgan was in a very strange mood, she decided. It was almost as if he was...jealous.

"It's Nate's fault. He's running around telling people we hardly talk, much less act involved."

"Nate, your deputy?"

"Yeah." Morgan looked suspicious. "And that reminds me, has Nate been flirting with you?"

Startled, Misty shook her head. She'd met Nate her first day on the job. He was a good-looking young man, not a whole lot taller than she was, with brown hair and green eyes and full of smiles. He'd asked her to lunch during her break, but she'd declined, choosing instead to eat at her desk—an apple and a peanut-butter sandwich she'd packed. After that, Nate usually brought a bagged lunch, too, and visited with her while they ate.

Morgan generally had appointments during that time and

ate on the road. The amount of community work he did astounded her.

Morgan gave her a long sigh. "Are you sure?"

She scoffed at him. "He's only a boy, Morgan."

"He's twenty-two years old, Malone, old enough to be my deputy, and only two years younger than you." Morgan's tone was exasperated. "Would you even realize it if Nate *was* flirting?"

"Well, I assume so."

Morgan put one arm on the wall beside her head. "For some reason, I think you're just oblivious to the way you affect men."

"Maybe that's because, so far, you're the only one claiming to be affected. That only makes you the oddity, Morgan, not the norm."

He didn't look at all insulted by her comment. His large hand spread out over her middle, making her suck in her breath as a shock of awareness rolled through her. His fingertips, angled downward, nearly touched her hipbones. His palm was hot and firm against her.

Very softly he asked, "Now, how can that be true, when I know for a fact at least one other man chased you down? You didn't get pregnant all by yourself."

She couldn't reply. So many feelings swamped her at once, it was difficult to sort them out. In the past, every relationship she'd shared had started because she wanted someone to call her own, because she'd believed women were supposed to share their lives with men. It wasn't because she found a man irresistible and craved his company.

She no longer felt she needed or wanted a man in her life, and she'd decided she was better off on her own. But how she felt around Morgan was so different from those other relationships. She *did* crave him, and ignoring Morgan was like trying not to breathe—impossible.

By reflex, she put her hand over his, intending to pull it away, but instead, she held it tighter to her. "Kent...Kent was like most men, saying the right things to get my attention. I wanted to believe that he cared, so I did. But he never really wanted me, not like—" She stammered into silence and blushed.

Morgan gave her a satisfied smile. "You mean, like I do?"

How could he expect her to answer that? "All he really wanted," she said, ignoring his question and her embarrassment, "was the convenience of being with one woman. He never really cared about me."

"He was obviously a goddamned fool."

She looked up at him, then felt snared in his gaze. "Men flirt by nature. It doesn't mean anything. And it doesn't matter who the woman is or what she looks like."

"There's flirting, and then there's flirting." Morgan gave her a small smile. "You can believe I've never disabled another woman's car, or dragged her into a gazebo."

Misty managed a laugh. "No, probably it was the women dragging you into private places."

Morgan's fingers on her abdomen began a gentle caress that made it difficult for her to remain still. "Let's try this from another angle, okay? Forget Kent—he's not worth mentioning. And he's hardly a good example of the male species. Agreed?"

"Agreed."

"So. Has Nate been hanging around your desk? Talking to you a lot? Has he asked you out?"

She could barely think with his palm pressed so intimately to her body. Her khaki slacks weren't much of a barrier. And she could feel his breath on her cheek, could smell the delicious scent of cologne and soap and man. His wrist was so thick where she held him, her fingers couldn't circle it completely. "Um, yes, yes and no."

He nuzzled his nose against hers. "Yes and no what?"

"Yes, he talks with me, and yes, he stops by my desk. Just about everyone who comes into the station does."

Morgan dropped his forehead to hers. "I need to put a paper sack over your head. I hadn't realized it, but I'd have been better off hiding you away here at the house."

Misty couldn't help but smile. "No, he hasn't asked me out. He invited me to lunch once, but that hardly counts as a date. That was just a friendly visit between employees. I think he gets lonely at lunchtime, because now he usually eats at the station with me."

Morgan looked at her like she was a simpleton. "He's *flirting*, Malone."

"No, he's not."

Morgan drew an exasperated breath and shook his head at her. "I'm going to put a stop to it."

"Jesse and Howard are always there. And don't you dare suggest they're flirting, too."

He tipped his head back and groaned. "I'm surprised every single male in the area isn't there hanging on your damn desk. From now on, I'm going to make sure I'm around to take you to lunch. And stop shaking your head at me!"

"Morgan, you're being unreasonable." But deep inside, she was pleased by his jealousy. She had to admit that maybe, just maybe, she was fighting a losing battle.

"I want to make sure you eat right."

"Uh-huh. I can tell that's your motivation." Misty quit denying him. "If you want to take me to lunch, that's fine with me."

"Then it's settled." Triumph shone in his gaze. "And about damn time, too."

"You know, Morgan, if everyone found out I was pregnant, that'd likely put an end to any interest—imagined or otherwise."

Morgan kissed her brow, then her nose. "Don't count on it. It didn't do a damn thing to make me want you less."

He was about to kiss her again, and she was about to let him, when Sawyer emerged from his bedroom and glanced at them.

"A little rendezvous in the hall?" he asked.

Misty felt like kicking Morgan. How did she always end up in these awkward situations when he was around? "Did we wake you?"

"Nope, I had early appointments this morning. The honeymoon is over now that a flu bug has started making the rounds."

That sounded innocuous enough, and Misty sighed. "Well, I need to get going, anyway. I was just on my way out."

Morgan tipped his head. "Didn't you need something from your room?"

She closed her eyes. She'd come to her room just to escape him, but she wouldn't admit that in front of Sawyer, who showed no signs of giving them any privacy. With a weak smile, she said, "Whatever it was, I've forgotten."

She darted around Morgan and made a beeline past Sawyer. She was almost out of hearing range when Sawyer said, "You've got her on the run, Morgan. I just wonder if that was your intent."

MORGAN GLARED at his brother. "I know what I'm doing."

"And what exactly is that?"

They both left the hall in the direction of the kitchen. The smell of coffee was tantalizing, and Morgan needed a shot of caffeine to boost him. Unfortunately, Jordan was still there, the cat on his lap.

"You," Morgan said, effectively distracted, "were ogling Misty when I walked in."

Jordan shrugged, then said to Sawyer, "She'd climbed under the desk to get the cat for me." His grin was unholy. "She has a damn fine bottom."

Morgan felt ready for murder. "Keep your eyes off her bottom."

"Why? You sure didn't." He rubbed the cat and said in an

offhand way, "Sawyer, I meant to mention it to you earlier. I think there's something wrong with Morgan."

Sawyer filled his coffee cup then sank into a chair. He blew on the coffee to cool it, showing no interest in Jordan's gibe.

Which of course didn't stop Jordan. "Yep, I think he must be sick. Half the time I see him, he's got this glazed look in his eyes. And once or twice, I've actually caught him smiling."

Sawyer laughed. "No! Morgan smiling? That's absurd."

Morgan came half out of his seat, and Jordan held up a hand, grinning. "No, don't throttle me. I'm on my way out the door right now. I just hung around to tell you...goodbye." He stood, the cat tucked under his arm, and grabbed his keys hanging by the door. "I'll see you all later."

As the door closed behind him, Morgan muttered, "Good riddance."

"Quit being such a grouch, Morgan. I survived, so I'm certain you will, too."

"Survived what? I don't know what you're talking about."

"Falling in love." Sawyer added quickly, "No, don't give me all your excuses. I've heard them all and even made up half of them. It'll do you no good."

Morgan felt like an elephant had just sat on his chest. He wheezed, then managed to say, "I am not in love."

"No? Then what would you call it? Lust?"

"What I'd call it is no one's business but my own."

"I think Honey might disagree with you there. She loves her sister more than you can imagine. I think they spent the longest time with no one but each other. Right now, Honey's convinced you're an honorable, likable gentleman. But if you hurt Misty, she'll take you apart. And I can tell you right now, there's not a damn thing I could do about it."

"I keep telling you that you should control your wife."

"Spoken like a true bachelor."

"Besides, I'd never hurt Malone."

"Oh? You think having an affair with you won't hurt her?

She's been through enough, Morgan. Did you know she went to her father and he offered not an ounce of comfort? Honey told me about it. It seems he was more disappointed with her than anything else."

Which, Morgan assumed, pretty much guaranteed she wouldn't bother him with her arrest and conviction. She'd known without asking that her father wouldn't assist her, or even take her side. Morgan shook his head, feeling that damn pain again. Misty had come to the only person she could really count on: her sister. And thank God she had.

Sawyer frowned at him. "She needs some stability, Morgan, not more halfhearted commitments."

Morgan downed half his coffee, burned his tongue and cursed in the foulest of terms. Sawyer never said a word. "Look, Sawyer, she doesn't want a commitment, all right? She told me that herself. She's sworn off men."

"Hate to break it to you like this, Morgan, but you're a man."

"That's not what I meant! What we feel—well, it's mutual. Only she doesn't want to get overly involved." Almost as an afterthought, he added, "Any more than I do."

"I thought you wanted to get married?"

He shook his head, wondering if Sawyer was rattling him on purpose. "I want a wife like Honey."

Sawyer spewed coffee across the table. Morgan gave him a look then handed him a napkin. "I said a wife *like* her, not Honey, herself. I want someone domestic and settled and sweet...."

"You don't think Misty fits the bill? What, she's not sweet? She's got a nasty temper?"

"I never said that," he ground out between clenched teeth. He thought Misty Malone was about the sweetest woman he'd ever met, even if her temper rivaled his own. Or maybe because of her temper. He almost grinned. "You keep forgetting, Misty doesn't want to get married. She's told me that plain as day."

Suddenly Sawyer's eyes widened. "Good God. You're afraid."

Morgan slowly stiffened, and he felt every muscle tense. In a low growl, he asked his brother, "Are you deliberately trying to piss me off?"

Sawyer waved a hand, dismissing any threat. "You're afraid you'll ask her and she'll turn you down."

Even his damn toes tensed. "You're a doctor of medicine, Sawyer, not psychology. There's a good reason for that, you know."

Sawyer started to laugh. "I don't believe this. Women have been chasing you for as long as I can remember, and now here's one you've got cornered, keeping her as close as you can get her, but you're afraid of her."

"Honey's not going to like you much with a bloody nose."

Morgan hadn't actually raised a hand in anger toward any of his brothers since his early teens. He assumed that was why Sawyer so easily ignored his warning.

Sawyer was still laughing, and Morgan decided it was time to change the subject. "She's taken another job."

That shut him up. "Misty quit working for you?"

"No, she took a second job. But should she be doing that in her condition?"

"Her condition isn't exactly debilitating," Sawyer pointed out, then with curiosity: "What job did she take?"

"She's working at the diner." Morgan knew he sounded disgruntled, but damn it, he didn't want her working two jobs. And he sure as certain didn't want her out there where anyone and everyone from town would be able to look her over. The woman didn't know her own appeal. Before she'd even be aware of it, she'd find herself engaged again. Morgan wasn't about to let that happen.

"From what she said, I gather she plans to work there an additional six or so hours, all in the evening. I think it's too much."

Sawyer frowned in thought. "She's a healthy young

woman, and her pregnancy is still in the early stages, so it probably won't bother her right now. But when she gets further along, there's a good chance her ankles will swell and her back will hurt if she stays on her feet for that long."

"Maybe you should try talking to her." Morgan thought it was a terrific idea, and his mood lightened. "You're a doctor. She'd listen to you."

"I'm not *her* doctor, so it's none of my business. Come to that, it's none of your business, either."

"Hmm. She hasn't mentioned seeing a doctor at all. And shouldn't she be taking vitamins or something?"

Sawyer gave it up. "Why don't you ask her about it. I can give her the vitamins, but she should have regular checkups with an obstetrician. Being she's new in the area, I could recommend someone." As an afterthought, Sawyer asked, "How far along is she?"

"I think she said around three months. Why?"

Sawyer finished his coffee and stood. "No matter." He looked his brother over carefully. "I've got to get to work. Are you going to be okay?"

Morgan immediately frowned again. "I'm fine, damn it."

"Just asking." He turned to go, but hesitated. "Morgan? At least think about what I said, all right? If you wait too long to figure things out, you could blow it. And I can only imagine what a miserable bastard you'd be in that case."

Morgan watched him go, thinking that marriage had made Sawyer more philosophical than usual. Then he thought of Misty at the office, with Nate and Jesse and Howard all sucking up to her. He saw red.

Howard and Jesse were old enough to be her grandfathers, and she was right when she said Nate wasn't much more than a kid.

It was a sad day when he got jealous over the likes of them, but Morgan admitted the truth—he *was* jealous. Viciously jealous. He didn't want anyone looking at her, because he knew good and well that any red-blooded male, regardless of his age, would be thinking the same erotic things he thought.

Jealousy was new to him. He'd been dating women since before he was Casey's age, and never once experienced so much as a twinge. If a woman wasn't interested, he moved on. If she was, they set up ground rules and had some fun. The twist with Misty was that she was interested, but she'd rather deny them both because she'd been burned and she didn't want to get *involved*. Morgan had thought that the promise of an uninvolved relationship might suit her, but so far she'd turned that down, too.

Was Sawyer right? Was Misty only trying to protect herself from being hurt again? He knew having a record wasn't something she'd ever be able to accept, so he'd set things in motion on that front. He didn't believe she was guilty, but he had a hunch who was. He'd hired a few men to check into it, and now it was only a matter of waiting to see if he was right.

Maybe once that was taken care of, she'd stop holding back on him. If he could only get her to see how good things would be between them.... What? He'd get her to marry him?

Morgan thought about that, then nodded. Life with Misty would be one hell of a wild ride. He grinned with the thought. She was spicy and enticing and sweet and stubborn, and he wanted her so bad he couldn't sleep at night.

Morgan stood and picked up his hat, then snatched his keys from the peg on the wall. It was well past time he got a few things clear with her. Tonight, when he took her to his house, he'd stake a claim. He'd show her that they were a perfect match and when she got used to that, he'd reel her in for the permanent stuff.

In the meantime, he'd shore up his cause by showing her how gentle and understanding he could be. He'd even make a point of not frowning and maybe, just maybe, she'd stop fighting him so hard and then he could quit feeling so desperate, because he sure as certain didn't like the feeling one damn bit.

9

MORGAN'S better intentions were put on hold when he found a woman with a car full of kids and a flat tire waiting on the side of the road. She'd been on her way home from grocery shopping when the tire blew. Unfortunately, her spare wasn't in much better shape. Morgan called in to Misty, told her why he'd be late and asked her to postpone his morning meeting with the town trustees.

She'd sounded a little frazzled when he called, but he didn't have time to linger and find out why. He bundled the woman, her children and her flat, as well as her worthless spare, into the Bronco and drove to her house. The kids, ranging in age from one year to twelve, had screamed and yelled and generally enjoyed the excitement of being in the sheriff's car. Morgan wondered if he ought to make that a regular part of the Blackberry Festival. He and his deputy could take turns giving the kids a ride around the town square.

His thoughts wandered from that as the woman tried to thank him in her driveway, obviously embarrassed that her children were loud and that he'd had his day interrupted. Personally, Morgan thought the kids were pretty cute, three of them girls, the youngest two boys, and he told her so even as he juggled a bag of groceries and a tiny three-year-old. The mother had positively beamed at him then.

All in all, they'd acted like children, which they were, so he saw no reason for her to be uncomfortable about a little noise.

After Morgan helped her get her groceries inside, he called

Gabe. His brother met him at the garage where they got both tires repaired. After they'd driven back out to her car and changed the tire, Gabe drove the woman's car to her house while Morgan took the Bronco. Finally, they both went back to the garage.

"I appreciate your help, Gabe. Could you believe those tires she's driving on? And with five kids in the car." Morgan shook his head, wondering if there was any way he could help her. She and her husband were both hard workers, but her husband had suffered an illness and missed a lot of work in the past year.

Gabe rubbed the back of his neck. "What's her husband do for a living?"

"He's a carpenter, I think."

"Maybe we could barter with him. You still need some trim put on the back deck, and if he could—"

Morgan grinned. "—do the work on a weekend, I could give them some tires." He clapped Gabe on the back, almost knocking him over. "Hell of an idea."

Gabe shifted his shoulder, working out the sting of his brother's enthusiasm. "If you want, I could get hold of the guy, tell him I'm not able to do the trim and see if he'd be interested. It'd probably sound more authentic coming from me."

Morgan started to clap him again and Gabe ducked away. "I'll take that as your agreement and get in touch with him tomorrow. I'll let you know what he says."

Morgan left Gabe with a smile on his face. But when he pulled into the station, Ms. Potter, the librarian, hailed him. She wanted to know if he'd agree to take part in their annual read-a-thon, where a group of leading citizens would each pick a day to read to the preschoolers and anyone else who wanted to listen in. Morgan agreed, though it wasn't one of his favorite tasks. The books for that age group tended to rhyme, and his tongue always got twisted.

Next it was two shop owners who wanted to know if he

was going to have the county take care of a massive tree limb that was likely to fall on their roofs if a storm hit. Morgan eyed the tree, agreed it needed a good trimming and made a note to get hold of the maintenance crew.

By the time he finally walked into the station he was hot and sweaty and frustrated. He looked forward to seeing Misty, to reassuring her, showing her what a great guy he could be and that she could trust in him. Little by little, he'd win her over. Then he'd talk to her again about her avoidance of commitments.

He walked into chaos.

The noise had reached him even before he opened the door. Laughter. Lots of male laugher and music and a banging noise. Morgan frowned and headed directly for the small desk that Misty occupied during her work hours. He found her sitting there—not in the chair, but on the edge of the desk, her long legs bare, crossed at the ankles. Casey was there, too, with a couple of his pals, and they had evidently supplied the music that was blasting from a portable CD player. Howard had pulled Misty's chair to the side of the desk and was seated in it. Jesse had his bony butt propped on the arm of the chair. Nate stood in front of Misty, dancing while she cheered him on.

Her tailored slacks had been replaced with shorts. Her white blouse was gone in favor of a loose T-shirt. She was barefoot, and of all damn things, she was licking an ice cream cone.

Morgan saw red.

No one had noticed him, and he watched silently while his temper seethed. When Nate made a turn, Misty shook her head, swallowed a large lick of ice cream and then handed her cone to Casey. Casey, the traitor, just laughed and held it for her.

Misty stood in front of Nate and executed the dance step herself.

Lord, she looked sexy.

Morgan glanced around at the other men in the room and saw his thoughts mirrored on all their faces. The last thin thread of his control snapped. "What the *hell* is going on here?"

His roar effectively stopped the dance. Nate nearly jumped out of his skin, Casey quickly handed Misty back the cone, and both Howard and Jesse jerked to their feet. The loud banging noise continued.

Morgan stalked into the room. His gaze slid over Misty, then shifted to Casey. "Turn that damn music off."

One of the kids with Casey hurried to obey. Nate stepped forward. "Uh, Morgan, we were just—"

Morgan cut him off with a glare. Nate stammered for a moment, then clicked his teeth together and went mute.

With a sound of disgust, Misty stepped forward. "For heaven's sake, Morgan. Stop trying to terrorize everyone."

Morgan stared at her and silently applauded her courage. No one else in the room would have dared call him to task. She obviously didn't realize quite how angry he was.

Her hair was mussed, her skin dewy, her eyes bright. She looked like someone had just made love to her. And she dared to stand there giving him defiant looks in front of everyone.

"Is this what I pay you for, Malone? To have a party?"

Her eyes narrowed. "We weren't having a party. If you'll just listen..."

The T-shirt clung to her damp skin, emphasizing her breasts and distracting him. Her cuffed walking shorts showed off her long, sleek legs. A pulse tapped in his temple, making his head swim. "Employees of this office," he said succinctly, "do not traipse around dressed like that."

She took a step closer to him and stared up, her brows beetled. "I had to change."

His gaze dropped to the large cone she held, now dripping on her hand. "Nor do they eat ice cream cones during business hours."

"Morgan." She said his name like a growl.

He ignored the warning, too angry to care that now she was angry, too. "I pay you to work, to answer the phone and take messages. It's little enough to expect that you might take those duties seriously."

Casey groaned, then mumbled, "Now you've done it."

Morgan paid no attention to his nephew. He was too fascinated by the way Misty's eyes darkened, turning midnight blue.

She went on tiptoe. "I'll have you know, I've worked my butt off today!"

He leaned to look behind her. "Looks to me like you've got plenty of ass left."

Her gasp was almost drowned out by the groans of the spectators. Misty turned around and snatched up a stack of notes scattered over the desk's surface. "These," she said, slapping them against his chest one by one, "are from your various girlfriends hoping for a date tonight." They fluttered to the floor to land around his feet. "They've been calling all day, tying up the damn phone."

"Malone—"

"And they were rather persistent that you reply right away." She gave him a sarcastic-sweet smile. "Before I leave, I'll be sure to let them all know you're most definitely free!"

"Malone..."

"And this," she said, throwing a yellow bill at his face, "is for the plumber, because everything backed up and soaked the floor. If it wasn't for Howard and Jesse helping me mop we'd still be six inches under."

He started to get a little worried. "Uh, Malone..."

"And that constant banging you hear," she practically yelled, "is the repair man working on the cooling system. In case you missed it, it's about ninety degrees in here."

So that was why she was all warm and damp. Not because she'd been playing so hard? His brow lifted, but she wasn't through yet. Morgan was aware of Howard and Jesse trying to slip out unnoticed. Casey's two friends had already slunk as far as the door. Nate was openmouthed beside him, not moving so much as a muscle. Casey, the rat, whistled.

"And finally," Misty snarled, in a voice straight out of a horror movie, "this is the first break I've had all day. The flooding water ruined my lunch, and with no air-conditioning I was too hot to eat, anyway, so Nate got me an ice cream cone to tide me over until dinner. But since you don't think I should be eating it, why don't *you* take it!"

And with that, she aimed the damn thing like a missile, ice cream first, into the middle of his chest. Morgan gasped as the chill hit him, then made a face when he felt the first sticky dribble soak under his collar and mingle with his chest hair.

Casey stopped whistling. "Uh-oh. The fat's in the fire now."

Howard and Jesse ran out the door, slamming it behind them.

Nate made a strategic turn and crept out.

Like a stiff, well-trained soldier, Misty tried to troop out after him. Morgan caught her by the arm, pulling her up short. "Oh, no, you don't." A clump of ice cream dropped to the floor with a plop. He dragged Misty closer.

He hated to admit it, but her temper turned him on.

He had an erection that actually hurt it was so intense, and every muscle in his body was pulled taut against the need to take her. He stared at her, aroused by the glitter in her eyes, by the way her chest heaved. "I think we should share the cone, Malone."

Misty reared back, but he caught her other arm, pulling her up close. She stared at his chest, covered in goo, and her lips twitched.

"You think it's funny?" But he fought his own smile. No, life with Misty would never be mundane.

"I think you got what you deserved." Her bare heels slipped on the floor as she tried to dig in. She giggled as another plop of ice cream fell loose. "Morgan, no! I mean it, Morgan. Don't you dare—"

Her words ended in a gasp of outrage as he squished her up against his chest. "Cold, isn't it?"

She tried to twist free, which only made her breasts slip and slide over his chest. Morgan groaned.

"You..." she started to say breathlessly.

Morgan kissed her. It was a funny kiss, since she was struggling so hard against him, but laughing, too, and they had the damn cone crunching between them, the ice cream fast melting with their combined body heat.

Casey cleared his throat. "I'll be on my way now. See you both later. No need to see me off."

Morgan lifted his head. "Get out of here, will you?"

Casey laughed. "I'm going, I'm going."

Morgan watched as Casey dragged his gawking friends out the door and quietly closed it behind them. Misty tried again to pull loose, and he tightened his hold. "Oh, no, you don't. I have a few things to say to you."

She twisted in his arms, realized she couldn't get free, and stopped squirming. "What?"

He kissed her again. Then against her lips, "I'm sorry."

"You should be."

"Mm." With her mouth open he deepened the kiss, tasting her, making love to her. He groaned when the banging noise suddenly stopped.

As he gasped for breath, she muttered, "You ruined my T-shirt. Now what am I going to wear to work?"

Morgan cradled her head in his palms and asked, "You were going to go to the diner dressed like this?"

"I'm perfectly decent, Morgan, so don't start again."

"Dear God, you'll start a riot."

"It was your plumbing that ruined my other clothes. Casey was nice enough to bring these to me when I called."

"I'll run home and get you something else, okay?"

When she hesitated, he waggled her head. "Have some

pity on me, Malone! I'm not used to being jealous, and it's taking some getting used to here."

"You really were jealous?"

"What did you think? That I just enjoy making an ass of myself?"

She mumbled, "Well, you do it often enough." Then she glared at him. "You have some explaining to do, insulting me like that in front of everyone."

He swallowed hard, still very aware of her soft body lined up along the length of his. "You're not going to quit on me, are you, just because I yelled a little?"

"I can't." She gave him a sad smile. "I need the job."

Morgan kissed her again, this time gently, because he hated to hear that, to be reminded of her position. "I'm sorry."

"For embarrassing me?"

"Yeah, though you didn't seem all that embarrassed to me. More like raging mad."

"True. On top of everything else, I was suffering my own share of jealousy. I mean, *eight* calls from women, Morgan."

"You were jealous?"

She frowned at him. "That, and annoyed. You have very pushy girlfriends."

He tried to look innocent. "Some of them are probably just friends."

"Probably? You don't know?"

He bit his lip, then chuckled. "It doesn't matter anymore, anyway. I swear. Now tell me you forgive me."

"Are you sorry for what you said?"

"About your sweet tush? Hell, no. You do have a great—"

"Don't say it, Morgan!" She laughed. "And about ruining my clothes?"

"Come into the bathroom and I'll help you clean up." Then he frowned. "I gather we do have running water now?"

"Yes, but I can clean up without your help. You," she said,

pointing to all the paper littering the floor, "have a lot of calls to return."

Morgan looked down and saw that he'd stepped all over the message slips.

"You know, Morgan, it suddenly occurs to me." Her frown was back, her mouth set in mulish lines. "You're running around insisting every male in the area believes we're involved, even to the point of putting on this caveman routine. But there seems to be an awful lot of females who don't know a thing about it."

"I've been too busy mooning over you to give other women a thought. And that includes thinking about them long enough to update my status from available to unavailable."

He loved how quickly her moods shifted, from mad to playful, from brazen to shy. Right now she looked uncertain. She stared at his chocolate covered chest. "Are you considered unavailable now?"

Morgan tipped her chin up. "For as long as you're willing to put up with me."

She stared at him a moment, then pulled him down for a hungry kiss. Her hands were tight on his shoulders, her mouth moving under his. Morgan felt singed. It was the very first time she'd ever initiated anything, and he wanted so badly to strip her naked and sate himself on her, he was shaking with need.

A sudden hum and the kick of cool air let him know the repairs on the system were complete. And just in the nick of time. A few more seconds and he'd have burned up.

"Tonight, will you let me make love to you, Malone?"

She touched his mouth, gave him a small smile, then nodded. "I do believe I'd like that."

His heart almost stopped. He reached for her, but the repairman gave a brief knock and stepped in.

"All done." He drew himself up short as Morgan stepped away from Misty and he got a good look at the ice cream mess on their clothes.

Morgan grinned. "Just leave me a bill."

10

IT SEEMED TO BE Morgan's day for chaos.

The rain was endless, coming down in sheets, and he was relieved and thankful when he saw that Misty's car was already parked around back by the kitchen door, as was her habit. He'd worried endlessly about her driving home in the pouring rain. She'd worked all day and had to be exhausted. He'd hoped to follow her home, then immediately sweep her off to his house. But then he'd gotten held up and the storm had started. He put the truck in park, close to where she'd left her car. Normally he would have driven the Bronco into the garage, but he wanted to be as close to the back door as he could, so Misty wouldn't have as far to run in the rain.

He sighed as he picked up his small bundle in the front seat beside him, wrapping his rain slicker around it to keep it dry, then dashed the few feet through the downpour.

The kitchen door opened before he reached it, so he figured someone had been watching for him. Unfortunately, it wasn't Misty. No, she was engaged in what appeared to be a heated argument with Sawyer. It was Honey who had opened the door.

He kissed her cheek to thank her, then turned to see what the hell was going on.

Misty went on tiptoe and said to Sawyer's chin, "If you don't take the money, I can't stay!"

Sawyer threw his arms into the air, spotted Morgan and let out a huge sigh of relief. "She's worse than Honey, I swear."

Rain dripped down the end of Morgan's nose. His shirt

stuck to his back. He glanced around the kitchen and asked, "Where's Jordan?"

Sawyer looked surprised by his question, then said, "In his rooms, why?"

Slowly, so as not to startle the creature, he unwrapped his burden. A fat, furry, whimpering pup stared at them all, then squirmed to get closer to Morgan. He said to Honey, "Can you get me a towel? I found the damn thing under the front steps of the gym. He's been abandoned awhile, judging by how tight his rope collar was."

Morgan was still so angry he could barely breathe. Cruelty to an animal sickened him, and it was all he could do to hold in his temper, but he didn't want to scare the poor pup more than it already was.

Sawyer picked up the phone and called Jordan while Misty inched closer. Her eyes were large, and she was looking at him in that soft, womanly way she had. He'd get her alone tonight if he had to carry her through the damn storm.

Honey skittered into the kitchen with a towel.

The back door opened, and both Gabe and Jordan came in. They wore rain slickers that did little enough to keep them dry. Jordan was all business, taking the pup without asking questions, ignoring his own damp hair and shirt collar. Gabe shook his head. "It looks pretty young. What kind of dog do you think it is?"

Jordan murmured to the frightened animal as he gently toweled it dry. "A mixed breed. Part shepherd by the looks of him, maybe with some Saint Bernard. He'll be big when he's full grown." Jordan investigated the pup's throat and scowled where the too small rope collar had rubbed off much of the fur. "I'll need my bag."

Gabe turned to the door. "I'll get it." He pulled the hood of his slicker over his head and stepped into the rain without hesitation.

Misty started unbuttoning Morgan's shirt as if she did so

every day. "You'll catch a cold if you don't get some dry things on."

Sawyer nodded. "Go change, Morgan. And take Misty with you. Maybe you can talk some sense into her."

Morgan stood still while Misty peeled off his wet shirt. "What have you been up to now, Malone?"

Sawyer didn't give her a chance to answer. He waved a few bills under Morgan's nose. "She wants to pay for staying here."

Morgan scowled. "I thought we had all that resolved."

Taking his hand, Misty tugged him from the room. "I won't be a freeloader. If I stay I have to contribute. I've been eating here almost every day...."

Morgan allowed her to lead him away from the others, but the second they were out of sight he pulled her around and pinned her to the wall, then gave her a deep, hungry kiss. Against her lips, he whispered, "Damn, I missed you."

She looped her arms around his neck and smiled. "I was starting to wonder. I thought you'd be home hours ago."

"I had to do a class, and one of the women got hurt, and then I found the pup." He groaned. "God, it's been a hectic day."

He knew his wet slacks were making her damp, too, but he couldn't seem to let her go. He'd thought about her all day long.

"What kind of class?"

Oh, hell. He hadn't meant to say that. He took her hand and now it was he leading—straight into his bedroom. He closed the door and turned the lock. "Let me change real quick and we'll run up to the house. I'll drive you straight into the garage so you won't get wet."

"Morgan." She crossed her arms and leaned against his door while he hunted for a towel to dry himself. "What class?"

Trying to make light of it, he said, "I teach some of the women self-defense two Fridays of the month. Especially the women who work as park guides for the mountain trails. Sometimes they end up alone with a guy, so they need to know how to defend themselves."

Eyes soft and wide again, Misty asked, "You said one of them got hurt?"

"Yeah, but not in the class. I'm careful with them, and the high school gym lets us use the mats. But she slipped on the front steps when she was leaving and twisted her ankle. She couldn't drive, so I took her to the hospital and then had to go fetch her husband because they only have the one car and it was still at the high school. The only good part is that I found the pup when she fell. If I hadn't bent down to lift her, I'd never have heard it whimpering."

"So you bundled them both up and did what you could?"

"Don't get dramatic, Malone. Anyone would have done the same."

"Obviously not, or that poor little puppy wouldn't have been there in the first place." She sauntered over to him and touched his bare chest, smoothing her hands over his wet skin. "I don't think you control things so much as you try to take care of everyone."

Morgan kicked off his wet shoes even as he bent to kiss her again. Her hands on his flesh were about to make him nuts. "Let me change," he growled, "so we can get out of here."

She nodded and stepped away, then sat on the edge of his bed. If she had any idea what that did to him, seeing her there, she wouldn't have dared test his control. Morgan opened a drawer and pulled out dry jeans and socks. He was just about to unzip his slacks when she asked, "Morgan, am I just another person you're trying to take care of?"

He halted, unsure of her exact meaning, but angry anyway. "You want to explain that?"

She shrugged, then quickly looked away when he jerked his pants open. Hands clasped in her lap, she said, "You wanted me gone until you thought I needed to stay. And you not only try to coddle me, you said you're trying to prove me innocent of stealing. I just wondered if I was...I don't know. Another project of sorts. Like the scholarship at the school, the puppy you just brought home, that other woman you helped today."

"What other woman?"

"Gabe told me about the woman with the flat. He said you do stuff like that all the time."

She looked at him with deep admiration again, when what he wanted was something altogether different. "Gabe has a big mouth."

His dry jeans in place, Morgan sat beside her on the bed. He bent to pull on socks and shoes, his thoughts dark. He could feel her looking at him as he hooked his cell phone to his belt and clipped his gun in place.

"You might as well save it, you know."

Startled, Morgan glanced at her. "Save what?"

"The look. I'm immune to it. You're not nearly as much of a badass as you let everyone believe. Ceily told me you haven't even been in a fight in ages, and the last one was over too quick to count."

Displeasure gnawed at his insides. "You were talking about me with Ceily?"

"Oh, quit trying to intimidate me." She waved a hand at him. "You got a reputation when you were a hotheaded kid, but even then, you were never a bully. I've heard plenty, and any fights you got into were because you were defending someone else. The last fight was in a bar in the neighboring town. Ceily said some guy tried to drag his girlfriend out of there and you stopped him. Rather easily, as a matter of fact, which I suppose only added to your reputation, right?"

Morgan decided that when he got hold of Ceily he'd strangle her. "Did she also tell you how that woman was most...grateful?"

Misty snorted. "Yeah, she did. But that's not why you did it, so don't even bother running that by me. You're the sheriff now because you hate injustice and abuse and you take a lot of satisfaction in setting things right and taking care of others. Admit it."

The hell he would. His reputation had worked to his advantage for most of his life, and he'd damn well earned it. He pulled a loose black T-shirt over his head then twisted to face her. "You still going to the house with me?"

Her dark, silky hair swung forward and hid her profile as she stared at her hands. She looked a tiny bit nervous. "If you want me to."

Morgan caught her chin and turned her face toward him. "What do *you* want?"

She bit her lip, took a deep breath, then smiled. "To be with you."

His heart punched up against his breastbone and his vision blurred. He stood up before he decided to forget about the tour and took her right now. They needed privacy, not for what he wanted to do, but for all the things he wanted to say. "C'mon."

Her hand caught securely in his, he led her out of the room. She looked cuddly in a soft, oversize sweatshirt and worn, faded jeans. Unfortunately, she wore sneakers, but he'd keep her feet dry. He looked forward to holding her close. When they got into the kitchen, everyone leaned over watching Jordan and the pup. Now that it was dry, the dog resembled a round matted fur ball with a snout and paws. A stubby tail managed to work back and forth, and it gave a squeaky bark at Morgan.

Morgan grinned. The dog was incredibly cute in an ugly, sort of bedraggled way. "Is it going to be okay?"

"*It* is a *he*, about three months old, I'd say, and yeah, he'll be fine. He just needs to be cleaned up and loved a little."

Morgan nodded. It was obvious the poor thing had been abandoned, and if he ever found out who'd done it, a very hefty fine would be presented. "I'll keep him. I was thinking of getting a dog anyway, for when I move into the house.

This one'll do as well as any." At his pronouncement, Misty squeezed his hand.

Honey predictably grumbled about him moving out. She protested any time he mentioned it, saying she wanted him to stay, then went on to tell him how wonderful his house was and offered to help him decorate. He adored her.

Jordan watched as Morgan pulled two raincoats off the hooks. "I can keep him with me tonight if you want, since you appear to have plans to brave the storm again."

"Misty hasn't seen my house yet."

The brothers all grinned and cast knowing looks back and forth.

Sawyer handed Morgan the money Misty had tried to give him. "Make her take this back."

Misty held up her hands, palms out. "I can't continue to eat here if you won't let me pay for my share of the food and stuff. That's just tip money—I can afford it. Honest."

Sawyer's eyebrows shot up. "Tips? You made this much in tips already?"

"According to Ceily," Morgan grumbled, "every male that came in wanted to show her his gratitude, even if she hadn't done a damn thing for him. She said Misty kept the restaurant packed most of the night."

Misty blinked at him. "You talked to Ceily? When?"

He flicked the end of her nose. "Before I came home. She felt the need to page me and let me know how...successful you were. She even suggested she might want to lure you away from the station so you could work more hours for the diner. She claims she wouldn't even need to show up with you there drawing in customers and raking in the dough."

Gabe laughed, Jordan bit his lip and Sawyer rolled his eyes. Morgan didn't think it was the least bit amusing. "I told her you were going to continue working for me. That's right, isn't it, Misty?"

Her eyes narrowed. "As long as you all let me pay my way."

She was the most cursed stubborn woman he'd ever met. He caught her chin on the edge of his fist. "Most of the time, the food is *given* to us."

With a wholly skeptical look, she murmured, "Uh-huh."

"It's true, damn it. Sawyer barters with his less fortunate patients. Hell, he gets paid more often with food than with money. That's why we're always overloaded with desserts and casseroles."

"You're serious?" When he nodded, she said, "I had no idea."

Sawyer looped one arm around Honey and added, "I have vitamins I can give her, too, so she won't have to go to the pharmacy, but of course she refused them."

And Honey piped in, saying, "I know for a fact she's embarrassed about getting them in town. Everyone will know she's pregnant if she does. Make her accept them, Morgan."

Morgan took one look at Misty's inflexible expression and laughed out loud. Were they all under the misguided notion that he had some control over the woman? Hell, she butted heads with him more than anyone else!

Knowing it would only prompt her stubbornness more, he said, "Yeah, sure, I'll take care of it."

Her brows snapped down, her mouth opened to blast him with invective, and Morgan kissed her—a quick, grinning smooch. She gave him a bemused look, and he dropped the coat over her head, then lifted her in his arms.

She fussed and wriggled, but he contained her with no effort at all and when she saw all the brothers watching intently, she made a face at them, but at least stopped struggling. "You have the worst habit of hauling me around."

"I don't want your feet to get wet going out."

"Oh."

Sawyer said, "Finally, he's listening to me."

Honey acted as if it was all par for the course. "Here, Misty, I packed a basket so you could both eat. I doubt if either of you have had dinner yet. Take your time. You'll love

Morgan's house and maybe the rain will have stopped by the time you head back."

Morgan watched Misty balance the large basket with one arm while looping the other around his neck. "Don't wait up for us," he said to the room at large.

He darted out the door and made his way cautiously to the Bronco. Misty opened the car door, and he slid her inside. The rain wasn't coming down quite so fiercely now, and Morgan hoped Honey was right, that it would stop soon. Too many wrecks happened in weather like this, and he didn't look forward to his evening getting interrupted. Already his anticipation was so keen he had to struggle for breath. He was semihard and so hot the windows started to steam the second he got behind the wheel.

"Will you accept the vitamins?" He drove from the driveway to the main road, hoping the conversation would work as a distraction. "Sawyer offered them because he wants to, you know."

With her arms around the basket, she grumbled, "He offered because I'm Honey's sister."

"Bull. If you'd just stumbled into our lives the way Honey did, he'd do the same. Sawyer cares about people and likes doing what he can. It has nothing to do with you being related. Except that he takes it more personal when you refuse."

She shook her head. "All right, fine. I'll take the vitamins, but I insist on paying my own way. I won't be swayed on that. Regardless of where the food comes from, I'm still staying there and taking up room."

Morgan smiled at her. "Stubborn as a mule." He pulled up in front of his garage and hopped out to open the door, then drove inside. "I'm going to have the driveway poured soon, and then we'll install a garage door opener, but that's stuff I can take care of after I move in."

Misty didn't wait for him to open her door after he'd turned off the engine. She hefted the heavy basket in her arms and climbed out. "I want to see the outside of the house, too. From down the hill, it looks gorgeous."

Morgan felt like a stuffed turkey, he puffed up so proud. "Let's go through the inside first and maybe the rain will let up." He opened the door leading into the house and reached in for a light switch. The first-floor laundry looked tidy and neat, a replica of the one in the house where he'd grown up, with pegs on the wall for wet coats and hats, a boot-storage bench and plenty of shelving. "All the fixtures aren't up yet, but there's plenty of light."

He turned to look at Misty and caught her wide-eyed expression of awe as she stared from the laundry room into the kitchen. "Oh, Morgan."

Like a sleepwalker, she went through the doorway and turned a circle. "This is incredible."

The kitchen had an abundance of light oak cabinets, high ceilings with track lighting and three skylights. Right now, the rain made it impossible to see anything but the blackness of the sky, but Morgan knew on a sunny day the entire kitchen would glow warmly, and in the evening, you'd feel like the stars were right on top of you.

"C'mon. I'll show you around." He took the basket from her and set it on the counter.

She kept staring at his cathedral ceilings. "I love the design. It's like you're in a house, but not, you know? Everything is so open."

"I don't like closed-in spaces." He laced her fingers with his own and said casually, "I figure it's easier to keep an eye on kids when they aren't behind doors getting into mischief. Other than the four bedrooms and the two baths, all the doorways are arches."

She stalled for a moment inside the dining room. He turned to look at her, and she shook her head. "How many kids do you plan on having?"

He held her gaze and said, "Three sounds about right. What do you think?"

Her fingers tightened on his and she said quietly, "I think I'll worry about raising this one before I even contemplate adding any more."

He wanted to tell her she didn't have to worry, that she wouldn't need to raise the baby on her own, but he had to bide his time. He didn't want to scare her off. "I don't have the dining-room furniture yet. I'm still working on that."

She went to a window and looked out. "The view of the lake is gorgeous."

"Yeah. Back here in the coves the lake is almost always calm, not like farther up where all the vacationers keep it churning with boats and swimming and skiing. It's peaceful, nothing more disturbing than an occasional fishing boat."

"I bet in the fall it's really something to see."

"Yeah. And in the winter, too, when everything is iced over. I figure I'll need to hire someone to keep all the windows clear, but what's the point of living on a hill with great scenery if you can't see it? The view from the master bedroom is nice, too." He slipped that in, then added, "The deck runs all the way around the house."

The next room was the living room and he watched her inspect his choice of furniture, wondering if she'd like it.

"Everything looks so cozy, but elegant, too."

Morgan rubbed the back of his neck. When he'd chosen the blue-gray sofa and two enormous cranberry-colored chairs, elegance hadn't entered his mind. It was the saleslady who'd suggested the patterned throw pillows to "pull it all together." He'd been going strictly for comfort. The softness and large dimensions of the furniture had appealed to him. "I'm glad you like it."

"You could fill this place up with plants. You know, like you did around the fireplace at the station."

Morgan watched her closely as he admitted, "One of the women I used to see on occasion brought in those plants. I'd never have thought of it. It's the cleaning lady that keeps them watered and healthy."

She sent him a narrow-eyed look over the mention of a girlfriend. "Well, I can just imagine a lot of plants really blending in here. With the stone fireplace and the light from the windows, it'd be great. What do you think?"

"I think maybe you should help me pick some out."

She blinked at him in surprise, then smiled. "I'd love to."

Satisfied on that score, he took her hand and continued on the tour. He opened the first door they came to. "This is the hall bath."

Misty stuck her head in the door, and her mouth fell open. "It's...decadent."

Grinning, Morgan gently shoved her the rest of the way in. "Yeah. I kinda like it. Other than my bedroom, it's my favorite room. It turned out just the way I wanted."

Morgan watched her run her hand over the cream-colored tiled walls, the dual marble vanity. A large, raised tub took up one entire corner, looking much like a small pool. You could see the water jets inside the tub, and all the fixtures were brass. There was a skylight right above it and a shelf surrounding it for lotions and towels and candles—things he'd noticed Honey was partial to, so he assumed other women would be, too. In the adjacent corner was a shower with two showerheads, one on either side of the stall.

Honey was a hedonist when it came to her baths—the woman could linger for hours. He'd assumed most women were the same, but Misty tended to take quick showers, just as he did. He frowned with that thought, until he considered showering with her, and then his breath caught. He eyed the shower. It was plenty big enough to make love in....

"It's beautiful, Morgan."

He shifted his shoulders, trying to ease the sexual tension that had invaded his muscles. "I still have to get towels and stuff, but I figured there was no rush on that."

Tentatively, without quite looking at him, she said, "I could help with that, too, if you want."

Morgan stared at her, then swung her around and gave

her a hard, quick kiss. "Thanks," he said in a gruff tone, his throat raw with some unnamed emotion that he didn't dare examine too closely. It was based on sexual need, but there was a lot of other more complicated stuff thrown in that he didn't understand at all.

Misty looked at his mouth, drew a slow broken breath and then licked her lips. Morgan was a goner. Backing her into the cool tile wall, he took her mouth again, this time more thoroughly, then didn't want to stop kissing her. She felt perfect, tasted perfect. She made him feel weak when that had never happened before, but she also made him feel almost brutal with driving need. He wanted to devour her, and he wanted to cherish her.

She arched against him and he cupped her rounded backside with a groan. "Damn, Malone."

In a husky, laughing tone, she asked, "Are you ever going to use my first name?"

She sounded a bit breathless, and he forced himself to loosen his hold. Sawyer was right; she'd been through a lot, and even the strongest woman in the world needed time to adjust. "Malone suits you. It sounds gutsy and sexy and a little dangerous."

She allowed him to lead her from the room, but she asked, "Dangerous? Me?"

With his arm around her shoulders, his heart still galloping wildly, he steered her to the first empty bedroom. "To my libido, yeah."

The first three bedrooms were empty, but still Misty oohed over the tall windows and the ultrasoft carpet and the oak moldings. Morgan felt as if he might explode by the time he got her to his room. There were no curtains yet on the French doors that flanked the tall windows, almost filling an entire wall. The doors led to a wide, covered deck. The overhang wasn't quite sufficient to shield them from the wind, and the rain blew gently against the glass. "Let me show you something."

Without hesitation she came into the room and went to the wall of windows with him. "Look at the lights on the lake. Isn't it beautiful?"

She stared into the darkness for long minutes, then finally nodded. "Yes."

"I've always enjoyed the lake, the way sunlight glints on every tiny ripple, and how the evening lights along the shore turn into colored ribbons across the water. Even on stormy days, it's great to watch. The waves lap up over the retaining wall and every so often the lake swells enough to cover my dock. The fish get frisky on those days and you can see them leaping up into the air and landing again with a splash. On my next day off I'll take you boating and we can swim in the cove. Would you like that?"

She continued to gaze into the rainy night. "I've always loved being outdoors, and around water. When I was younger, we had a sailboat. My dad would take us out about twice a year, but mostly he used the yacht for entertaining his guests or business associates."

Morgan hugged her from behind, knowing her relationship with her father had been far from ideal. "I don't have a yacht, but I think you'll like our boat. Or rather boats—we have three. An inboard for waterskiing, which Gabe uses more than anyone else. He's as much fish as man. And a fishing boat with a trolling motor, which is so slow you could probably paddle faster. And a pontoon. My mother bought the pontoon and left it here, but whenever she visits she takes it out."

Misty leaned her head back to look at him. "I didn't know you had a gazebo."

The gazebo was only barely visible in the darkening sky, a massive shadow on the level ground fifteen feet off the shore of the lake. He'd had electricity run down there so a bug light could hang inside the high ceiling, though it wasn't lit now.

Morgan kissed her temple and looped his arms around her middle so that his hands rested protectively over her belly. "I had Gabe build it for me." His fingers contracted the tiniest bit, fondling her gently.

She sucked in her breath, and her hands settled over his. "When?"

In a hoarse tone, he explained, "After that night I kissed you at the wedding. In the gazebo."

She twisted in his arms. "But...you'd asked me to leave then."

He searched her gaze. There was no accusation there, just confusion. "I wanted you to stay." Very gently, he pulled her closer. "Damn, I wanted you to stay."

Her smile was shaky, and then she touched the side of his face. "I have to tell you something about me."

Morgan leaned forward and nuzzled the soft skin beneath her chin. He felt wound too tight, edgy and aroused and full to bursting. He tasted the silky skin of her throat, her collarbone. He didn't say anything, waiting for her to continue.

He felt the deep breath she took. "You're a special treat for me, Morgan."

He grinned at that and continued to put soft, damp kisses on her throat, beneath her chin, near her shoulder. He felt her tremble and held her closer.

"I want you to understand what this means to me."

He leaned back to look at her. She appeared far too serious and solemn to suit him.

"I know that an unwed pregnant woman sort of gives the impression of being experienced—"

"Damn it, Misty, I didn't—"

She pressed her fingers to his mouth. "Just listen, okay?" He nodded reluctantly and she continued. "Truth is, I haven't had much experience at all. Back in high school I got very curious, and we experimented a little. Very little, actually. Things didn't last long with him, but it was no big heartbreak."

Very carefully, Morgan pulled her earlobe between his teeth. She shuddered.

"And then there was Kent. I'd only been with him a few times, but we were careful. It's just that the condom broke—"

He squeezed her tight, cutting off her spate of confessions. "Enough."

Jealousy washed through him. The idea of her with a kid in high school was bad enough; his brain nearly overflowed with visions of her being groped in the back seat of a car, making him hazy with anger. But to think of her as a grown woman with a man she'd thought she loved... A man who had gotten her pregnant, then turned away from her. He could barely tolerate the idea.

"I don't need to have an accounting for past lovers, Malone." He growled those words against her ear, then added, "I don't care about any of that."

She wriggled loose so she could see him. "But that's just it. I don't have much of an accounting to give. Not because I'm so particular, and not because I think it's wrong. It's because no one ever really made me want him. Not the way you do."

Emotion nearly clogged his throat. Morgan hugged her right off her feet. "You don't have to worry, baby. I'll take care of you. I won't hurt you."

She pushed against his shoulders. "Morgan, you don't understand."

Morgan lowered her to the floor with him so that they faced each other on their knees. Misty's eyes were dark and wide and even in the dim light he could see her excitement. He slipped his hand under the hem of her sweatshirt and stroked her bare waist. Very softly, he said, "Explain it to me then."

Morgan hoped she was about to give him a clue to her feelings. She hadn't balked at the idea of helping him decorate, but neither had she seemed to realize why he wanted her help. And his comment about kids had gone completely over her head: in order for him to have those three kids, he'd need her cooperation, because no other woman would do.

She hesitated, her chest rising and falling in fast breaths, then she blurted, "I want to get my fill of you."

A wave of lust washed over him, making him tremble. That was not what he'd been expecting, or even hoping for. *But it might do.*

"You're so open about sex and how you feel," Misty explained, "that I don't have to worry about my old inhibitions or any of that stuff. I don't have to worry about what you'll think of me, or if I'll offend you." She touched his face with a trembling hand. "I want to do everything to you that I've been imagining doing. I want to let go completely."

Morgan swallowed hard, struggling to come up with a coherent reply.

It wasn't necessary. Misty launched herself at him, her hands holding his ears while she kissed him hungrily. He felt her small tongue in his mouth, felt her sharp little teeth nip his bottom lip. With a harsh groan, he rolled to his back, keeping her pinned against his chest, and she touched him all over, her hands busy and curious and bold.

He thought of all the things he'd meant to say to her, but at the moment, none of them seemed important.

Morgan made a sound somewhere between a groan and a laugh. She didn't care if she amused him. "I've wanted you for so long," she told him between kisses. "It's awful to want someone that bad."

"Tell me about it." He worked her sweatshirt up until he could pull it over her head. She lifted her arms to help him, not feeling a single twinge of shyness. Not with Morgan.

As soon as the shirt was out of the way, Morgan reached for her. His hands were so large and rough and hot, and she moaned as he cuddled her breasts in his palms. His thumbs stroked over her nipples and she felt wild at the sweet ache his touch caused. "This is almost scary."

"No." Morgan brought her back down for another kiss, but she dodged him.

"I want your shirt off, too." He was such a big hulk that

there was no way she could get his clothes off him without his cooperation. She slid to the side and tugged his shirt free of his jeans. Morgan curled upward, making the muscles in his stomach do interesting things, and he threw the shirt off. She'd seen his chest many times, but now was different. Now she was allowed to touch and taste and have her way with him.

Misty attacked the snap on his jeans.

"Slow down, babe."

"No, I don't want to. I kept telling myself I couldn't do this, but then I realized there was no way I could *not* do it. I want you too much. I doubt I'll ever meet another man who makes me feel this way."

"Damn right you won't." Morgan caught her hands and pulled them away from his zipper. "Kiss me again."

She gladly complied. And while she was kissing him, licking his mouth, tasting his heat and feeling the dampness of his tongue, the smoothness of his teeth, Morgan rolled her to her back. The plush carpeting cushioned her.

"I don't want to hurt you, Malone."

She pulled him closer, breathing deeply of his scent. "You won't."

"The baby..."

Everything seemed to go still with his words. Morgan loomed over her, heat pulsing off him, his dark blue eyes burning hot, his hair mussed. There was so much concern and tenderness in his gaze that she felt tears well in her eyes. Misty touched his cheek, then his wide, hard chest. She let one finger drift over a small brown nipple and heard his sharp intake. "I want you naked, Morgan."

His head dropped forward and he labored for breath.

"You won't hurt me, I promise." She watched the way his wide shoulders flexed, how the muscles in his neck corded. "I've been thinking about this all day, and if I'm going to do this—"

His gaze snapped to hers. "*You are.*"

"—then I want to do everything. Why take a risk unless you make it worthwhile?"

The look on his face was almost pained before he deliberately wiped it away. "I'm not a risk, babe."

Misty didn't want to tell him that he was the biggest risk she'd ever taken. She loved him so much, even more than she desired him. Around him her heart felt vulnerable and soft and a little wounded because she wished so badly she could have met him months ago. He could break her so easily.

She shook her head, willing to tease him to chase her dark thoughts away. This wasn't a time for wariness, but a time to break free. "I've never had an excellent lover, Morgan." She slipped her fingers down his side, over his hip. "I want you to be excellent."

His teeth flashed in the darkness and his hand smoothed over her hair, then tucked it behind her ear. "You know how to put on the pressure, don't you?"

"Are you intimidated?"

He snorted. After staring at her for a long moment, he shifted to sit up. His gaze strayed to her body again and again while he pulled off his shoes and socks and laid his cell phone aside. "So you want to see all of me?"

"Yes."

"Should I turn on some lights?"

Misty laughed. How she could recognize humor while burning up with need was amazing. Morgan made her hungry, and he amused her, and he made her feel special and cherished in so many ways.

But then, he did that for a lot of people.

"With no curtains on the windows?" she asked. "Don't you think that might be unwise? What if someone is out there and they see you prancing around in the buff?"

He chuckled, but the sound was strained as he stared at her breasts. "I don't prance, Malone. And there's no one out there on a night like this."

She pretended to consider his offer, then said, "No, let's leave the lights off." She'd definitely be more daring without too much illumination. She needed the shadows to enjoy herself fully. At least this first time.

Morgan shrugged. "Whatever you want."

"That's the spirit." Her laugh ended on a gasp when he came to his knees and carefully pulled down his zipper, easing it around a rather large, hard erection. She didn't want to laugh now. No, she just wanted to watch. And touch.

And taste.

Without any signs of modesty, Morgan slowly shucked his jeans and underwear down his hips, then sat back and pulled them the rest of the way off. "Now you," he rumbled, and leaned forward to do the job himself.

Misty stared at his naked body and felt the warmth build beneath her skin, felt her womb tighten, her breasts ache. His hips were a shade lighter than the rest of his sun-darkened skin, the flesh looking smooth and hard, taut with muscle. Crisp curling hair covered his chest and tapered into a downy line on his abdomen. She felt a little lecherous eyeing his swollen erection and wondered how it would feel to touch him there.

Belatedly, Misty remembered that she wanted to be a full participant, not a passive one. She toed off her sneakers, then came up onto her elbows as Morgan worked the button of her pants loose and started on her zipper. "Would you rather I strip? It'll be easier."

Morgan froze for a heartbeat, then shook his head. "I'd never live through it. The fact you're not wearing a bra is already more than any man should have to deal with."

"You *wanted* me to wear a bra."

His hand opened over her belly and caressed her lightly, smoothing over her skin, dipping quickly into her belly button, then sliding beneath her open jeans to palm her buttocks. She reached for his erection and wrapped her hand around him.

He was hard and hot and silky. He flexed in her hand, and she tightened her hold.

With a groan, Morgan hooked his fingers into the waistband of her jeans. His voice was gravelly and low when he spoke. "Unveiling you slowly would have been better for my system. Saving me the shock, you know?"

Misty ignored his words, enthralled with the velvety feel of him. "Do you like this, Morgan?" She squeezed him carefully, heard his rough gasp. "You'll have to give me some direction, okay?"

He had her jeans as far as her knees and he paused to tilt his head back and suck in deep breaths. "Harder."

Misty's heartbeat drummed at his growled command. She tightened her hand and stroked him again. "Like this?" she whispered.

Morgan suddenly caught her wrist and pulled her hand away. "I'm sorry, but I can't take it." He kissed her knuckles and placed her hand next to her head on the floor. "You need to do some catching up, sweetheart, so keep those soft little hands to yourself for a few minutes, okay?"

Nodding, Misty lifted her hips so he could pull her jeans the rest of the way off. Morgan pushed them aside, and immediately bent down to kiss the top of her right thigh. "Damn, you smell good," he muttered as he nuzzled her hipbone, her belly, leaving warm damp kisses on her skin.

Misty shifted, not sure if she should protest or not. He'd taken the lead, but she loved how he looked at her, the husky timbre of his voice.

"Open your legs."

"Morgan..."

"Shh. Trust me, okay?"

It seemed as though her heartbeat shook her entire body. Around her nervousness, her excitement, she whispered, "I do trust you. I always have."

Morgan looked down at her, making her feel exposed and agitated and eager. He wedged her thighs apart and settled between them. He stared into her eyes and cupped her breasts. His solid abdomen pressed warmly against her mound, making her arch the tiniest bit. Her thighs were opened wide around his waist.

Misty nearly choked on a deep breath when he lowered his head and sucked one nipple deep into his mouth. Her back arched involuntarily, but Morgan took advantage of the movement to slip his arm beneath her, keeping her raised for his mouth. He shifted to her other breast, making her moan with the sharp tingle of a gentle bite.

"I could spend an hour," he whispered, "just on your breasts."

Misty tangled her fingers in his hair. "I told you I wanted to do some things."

"We'll take turns."

He went back to her nipple, and true to his word, he seemed insatiable, tasting her, licking her, sucking her deep. Each gentle tug of his mouth was felt in her entire body. His tongue was both rough and incredibly soft on her aroused flesh. When he finally lifted himself away from her, she could barely keep still. Her nipples were swollen and wet, and she covered them with her own hands, trying to appease the throbbing ache.

Morgan growled at the sight of her touching herself and began kissing his way down her abdomen. When he reached her belly, he paused, then rested his cheek there. "I can't believe there's a baby in here," he whispered. "You're so slim."

Misty choked on an explosion of emotion, so touched by the way he accepted her and her condition. "I...I'm bigger than I used to be. I've gained seven pounds." It amazed her that he didn't seem the least put off by her pregnancy. Kent had been disgusted and repulsed by the idea, but Morgan seemed more intrigued and concerned than anything else.

He placed a gentle kiss on her navel, then slipped his hands under her thighs and opened her legs wide. "Bend your knees for me, sweetheart. That's it. A little wider."

She felt horribly exposed with her legs sprawled so wide, his warm breath touching her most sensitive flesh. He was looking at her, studying her, and it embarrassed her even as it excited her almost unbearably.

Knowing what would happen, overcome with curiosity and carnal need, Misty dropped her head on the carpet and stared at the heavily shadowed ceiling.

The first damp stroke of his hot tongue felt like live lightning. She jerked, but he held her still and licked again. She groaned. Morgan used his thumbs to open her completely and tasted her deeply, without reserve.

"Oh God."

"So sweet," he murmured, and anything else he said was lost behind her moans.

She couldn't hold still, couldn't think straight. His fingers glided over her wet swollen tissues, dipping inside every now and again, but not enough to make the building ache go away. His tongue did the same, lapping softly, then stabbing into her.

"Morgan, please..."

"Tell me if I hurt you," he murmured hotly, and even his breath made her wild.

But then she gasped as he began working two fingers deep into her. Moving against him, she tried to make him hurry, tried to make him go deeper.

"You're so tight," he murmured and she heard the repressed tension in his voice.

"Morgan."

His mouth closed over her throbbing clitoris, sucking gently while his fingers stroked in and out, and she was lost. She cried out, thankful that they were alone, that he'd had the sense to insure their privacy, because she wanted to yell, needed to yell. Nothing had ever felt like this, so powerful and sweet and so much pleasure it was nearly too much to bear.

Morgan moved up over her, settling his hips gently

against hers. His hands cupped her face until her eyes opened. "I'm going to come into you now."

"Yes."

"Tell me if I—"

"You won't hurt me." If he didn't get on with it, she might be forced to rape him. A gentle pulsing from her recent climax still shook her, but she wanted more, she wanted it all, she wanted Morgan.

"Put your legs around me."

As soon as she'd gotten her shaky limbs to work, he smothered her mouth with his own and pushed cautiously into her. Her body bowed, trying to accommodate him, then wilted as he sank deep, entering her completely. His raw groan echoed her own.

A moment of suspended pleasure and building anticipation held them both, then he began moving in deep, gentle thrusts. He stayed slightly propped up on his elbows rather than giving her his weight. Misty tried to protest, wrapping her arms tight around him and doing her best to bring him to her.

"No, sweetheart. I'm too heavy," he panted, his jaw tight, his shoulders bunched. His eyes blazed at her and he kept kissing her, as if he couldn't get enough; deep, hungry kisses and gentle, tender kisses.

Even now, he was being so careful with her. Her heart swelled painfully. "Please, Morgan."

He squeezed his eyes shut, his jaw clenched, and the sight of him, so strong, so powerful, and so gentle, added to the physical pleasure and made her climax again with a suddenness that took her breath away. She strained against him, her thighs tightening, her fingers digging into his powerful shoulders. The second her muscles tightened around his erection, Morgan cursed, then gave up the struggle.

He allowed her to pull him down and pressed his face into her throat, hugging her closer still, his big body straining and shuddering as he came.

For long moments he rested against her, dragging in air, his body gradually relaxing. She felt him kiss her throat...and she felt his smile.

Misty squeezed him again. She didn't know what she had expected, but the contentment, the happiness, the peace nearly overwhelmed her. "That was wonderful," she whispered to him, needing to say the words. "You were wonderful."

As though it took a great effort, Morgan slowly struggled up onto his elbows and smiled down at her. "So you're satisfied?"

She bit her lip, then slowly shook her head. "No, never."

Morgan blinked at her, then threw his head back and laughed. "Damn, Malone, I never thought I'd like hearing those two words leave your lips."

She touched his mouth with a finger. She no longer vibrated with need, but the curiosity was still there, and the love. "What you did to me, Morgan? I want to do that to you, too."

Morgan jerked. He breathed deep and he cursed and he shuddered. Finally he just laughed again, the sound low and rough. "From the moment I met you I knew on a gut level exactly how things would be with you."

"Did you?" When Morgan smiled, he made her want to smile, too.

"Yeah. Why do you think I've been going so crazy? I'm glad to see I wasn't wrong."

He rolled onto his back so that she was perched above him. His grin was so wicked and so lecherous, she almost blushed. "Now," he said.

And before she could ask him, "Now what?" his cell phone rang.

11

IT WAS ALMOST two in the morning by the time he got home, and he felt exhausted down to his soul. A three-car mishap had dragged him out of Misty's arms. Luckily no one was seriously hurt, but he was still pissed off. A few idiots from the next county over drank too much and tried joyriding over their deeper roads. They'd taken out not only a length of fence along Carl Webb's property, but they'd also knocked over a telephone pole. Cows had wandered loose in the road and into the neighboring field. Carl had been infuriated—and rightfully so—and many people had been without phone service.

In the pouring rain, it was damn inconvenient trying to sort everything out. One of the fools had a concussion, the other a broken nose. Morgan thought they deserved at least that much, though they'd both whined and complained endlessly.

He hadn't had a chance to say anything to Misty. He'd made love to her, and he'd made her laugh, but he hadn't told her that he wanted her to stick around as a permanent member of the family. He hadn't told her that he wanted her to be with him forever.

And she hadn't said a thing about how she felt, other than that she'd enjoyed making love with him. That was just dandy, but it wasn't enough. Not even close.

He kicked off his muddy boots just inside the kitchen doorway and made his way through the silent house to his room. His wet clothes went into a hamper and a warm shower helped to relieve his aching muscles, but not his aching head. He needed some sleep, but as he threw back the top sheet, the thought of climbing into his big bed all alone didn't appeal to him one bit. He glanced at the door, thought of Misty all warm and snuggled up in her own bed, and it felt like that fat elephant was on his chest again.

He stood there undecided, at the side of the bed for a full three minutes before cursing and pulling on underwear. Grumbling all the way down the hall, he got to Misty's room and started to knock, then changed his mind. The doorknob turned easily and the door swung open on silent hinges. He could barely see Misty curled on top of the mattress, her room nothing but shifting moon shadows as the trees swayed outside with the wind. But he could hear her soft, even breathing. She was likely exhausted and he promised himself he wouldn't keep her awake, but he wanted to hold her and there was no longer any reason to deny himself.

When he stood next to her bed she shifted and yawned, then opened her eyes to look at him. Immediately she sat up, shoving her silky hair out of her face. "Morgan? What's wrong? Did you just get in?"

Her normally deep voice was even rougher with sleep, and sexy as hell. "Yeah." He bent and scooped her out of the bed, lifted her up against his bare chest, and started out of the room. She had on a thin knee-length cotton gown, and her warm, sweet scent clung to her skin, making him regret his resolve to let her rest.

She tucked her face under his chin. "Where are we going?"

"To my room. I want to hold you while I sleep."

She made a soft, humming sound of pleasure and curled closer. As he toed her door closed from the hallway, he heard another door open. He turned, Misty held tight in his arms, to see Casey leaving the bathroom.

Casey blinked, then quickly averted his gaze. "I didn't see a thing."

"Make sure you don't repeat a thing, either."

Casey waved him off, too sleepy to care. Misty groaned. "How do you always embarrass me like this?"

"Why would you be embarrassed?" He went down the hall to his room and once inside he nudged the door closed. He didn't immediately put her in the bed; he liked the feel of her in his arms, the trusting way she accepted him.

"What will Casey think?"

"That I've got too much sense to sleep alone with you nearby." When she didn't comment on that he turned her slightly to see her face. Her eyes were closed, her expression relaxed. Not really wanting to, he gently lowered her to the mattress and climbed in beside her. "Sleep, sweetheart. We'll talk in the morning."

Before he could pull her against him, she had her arm around his waist, her head on his shoulder and one thigh covering his. And damn, it felt right. He wanted to sleep this way every night for the rest of his life.

Misty kissed his chest. "I'm awake now, you know."

Her voice was even huskier, and he eyed her in the darkness. "Shh. Don't tempt me. It's late and we both need some sleep." And he fully intended to explain a few things to her before he made love to her again.

Her soft little hand slipped down his stomach, making him suck in a deep breath. "Malone," he growled in warning. "Behave yourself."

She sat up, and he expected her to start arguing. He grinned, wondering what she would say, if she'd come right out and admit that she wanted him enough to force the issue.

Instead, she shifted around, and when she curled up against him again, she was naked. She shimmied onto his chest, cupped his face in both hands and said teasingly, "Don't make me get rough with you, Morgan."

He stroked the long, silky line of her back to her lush bottom and gave up. "All right, but be gentle with me. I've had a trying night." She laughed at that, her first kiss kind of ticklish and silly. But he had both hands on her bottom now and the second his fingers started to explore she groaned, and for the next hour neither one of them thought of sleep.

MORNING SUNLIGHT nearly blinded him when he heard Misty's soft, pain-filled moan. He immediately sat up to look at her. She had both hands holding her middle, her mouth pinched shut and her eyes closed. She looked pale. He said very quietly, "Morning sickness?"

She gave a brief nod. "It hasn't been this bad lately. But I don't usually wake up with a hairy thigh over my belly, either."

"Oh. Sorry." Morgan shifted away from her, trying not to shake the bed overly, then said, "Don't move. I'll be right back." When she didn't answer, he said, "Malone?"

"All right."

He pulled on jeans and darted into the kitchen. Honey was there, and Casey and Gabe. They all smiled at him and treated him to a round of inanities. He grumbled his own greetings, then stuck bread in the toaster and water on to boil. He glanced at Casey, who pursed his mouth, silently assuring Morgan he hadn't said a word about Misty.

Not that it mattered now, anyway. The world would soon know how he felt about that woman.

"What exactly are you doing?" Gabe asked as Morgan dug out a tea bag. Everyone in the family knew for a fact he wasn't a tea drinker.

"Misty has morning sickness. Mom said nibbling on dry toast and sipping sweet hot tea before she got out of bed would help."

"Ah."

Honey started to rise from her chair. "If Misty's sick—"

Gabe caught her arm, earning Morgan's gratitude. "It's nothing Morgan can't handle. Isn't that right, Morgan?"

"It's under control." He set the toast and tea on a tray and left the room. He heard Gabe chuckling, then some whispering, but he didn't care. He was going to ask Misty to marry him, so they could gossip all they wanted.

Misty was still flat on her back in the bed when he reached her side. "I have a remedy here. First, nibble a few bites of toast...that's it. No, don't argue. I promise, it'll help."

Crumbs landed on her chest, and he brushed them away. He imagined he'd have to change his sheets more often if this ritual continued, though his mother had claimed the morning sickness usually didn't last that long. Generally not past the first trimester, and Misty should be about through that.

"Now some hot tea."

"I hate tea."

"Tough. It'll help. And I made this real sweet."

She sipped carefully while he held her head, then sighed. "Not bad."

After several minutes of repeating the procedure, she cautiously sat up and smiled. "You're a miracle worker. I won't even need to sneak off to the lake."

Morgan smoothed her hair, thinking she was about the most precious-looking woman first thing in the morning, with her eyes puffy, a crease on her cheek from the pillow. He frowned at himself. "If you ever do want to go to the lake, let me know and I'll keep you company, okay?"

Instead of answering him, she asked, "You've taken care of a lot of pregnant ladies, huh?"

"No, you're my first. Why?"

"How'd you know the toast and tea would help?"

She was naked under the sheet, which barely kept her nipples concealed. Now that she no longer felt sick, talking required major concentration on his part. "I asked my mother."

She jumped so hard she spilled her tea. Yep, his sheets were in for a lot of washing.

He eyed the spill on the top sheet and started to pull it away from her before she got soaked, but she gripped it tightly to her chin and glared at him. "You did what?"

She sounded like a frog. "I asked my mother. I figured she had four kids so she had to have had morning sickness, right? She told me what worked for her. And by the way, she sends her love."

Misty pulled her knees up and dropped her head. "I don't believe this," was her muffled complaint.

Morgan smoothed her hair again. He loved her hair, shiny black and silky. Between the two of them, they'd likely have dark-haired children. He wondered if their eyes would be dark blue like his, or vivid blue like Misty's. It didn't matter to him one whit. "Will you marry me, Misty?"

She jerked upright and thwacked her skull on the headboard. With a wince, she rubbed her head, then eyed Morgan. "What did you say?"

Damn. Morgan took in her expression of stark disbelief and faltered. Her eyes were narrowed, her pupils dilated. Her soft mouth was pinched tight.

And he was hard again.

"I said," he muttered through his teeth, "will you marry me?"

"Why?"

Morgan stiffened, and he knew his damn face was heating. He hadn't blushed since sixth grade! "What the hell do you mean, *why?*"

She didn't blink, didn't look away from him. As if talking to a nitwit, she asked slowly, "Why do *you* want to marry *me?*"

A knock on the door saved him from trying to give a stammering reply. He sure as hell hadn't expected her to answer his proposal with an interrogation. He gave her a glare, waited until she'd pulled the sheet higher, then called out, "Come in."

Gabe stuck his head in the door. He kept his gaze resolutely on Morgan, and not on Misty. "You have a phone call."

"Take a message."

"Uh, Morgan, it's from out of town. I think you'll want to take it."

He could tell by Gabe's tone who the caller was. Hating the interruption, even while he was relieved by it, he stood. "I'll be right back."

Misty nodded, her face almost blank.

He put his hands on his hips. "We'll finish this conversation when I get off the phone."

"All right."

She sounded far from enthusiastic, and he wanted to demand to know how she felt, but knew he'd do better to bide his time. Patience, more often than not, wasn't his virtue.

He didn't look at her again as he left the room.

Twenty minutes later he was lounging against the wall outside the hall bathroom when Misty finally emerged, fresh from her shower. She put on her brakes when she saw him and stared at him warily without saying a word.

Morgan noticed her wet hair, her pink cheeks, her bare feet. She had on a T-shirt and loose cotton drawstring pants. "You going somewhere?"

"I have to be at the diner in about an hour."

He wanted to curse, to insist she skip work today, but he knew without even asking that he'd be wasting his breath. The woman was bound and determined to make all the money she could. Well, that'd be over with soon enough.

"All right. Then I guess we ought to get right to it."

"You're going to tell me why you want to marry me?"

There was no one else in the hallway, but he'd definitely prefer more guaranteed privacy. He took her arm and led her to his room. When he closed the door, he leaned against it and watched her. "Do you remember a woman named Victoria Markum?"

Misty backed up until her knees hit his mattress, then dropped onto it. "Yes. She was Mr. Collins's girlfriend."

He nodded. "Well, I hired some people to talk to her."

She frowned in confusion. "You hired people?" At his nod, she asked, "But why?"

"To prove your innocence. And don't give me that look, Malone. I didn't tell you because I didn't want you to start squawking about me spending my money. This is something I wanted to do, all right?"

"I'll pay you back—"

"The hell you will." Morgan went to her and sat beside her, then took her hands. "Can't you just accept that I care and I want to help?"

She searched his face for a long time before she grudgingly said, "Thank you. I don't know what to say."

"You could ask me what I found out."

"All right." She bit her lip, her face filled with anxiety. "I hope, judging by the way you're acting, it's good news?"

"As a matter of fact, it is. You see, Malone, I believed you when you said you hadn't taken the money. That meant someone else did, of course. I wondered if perhaps Ms. Markum might have done it."

Misty squeezed his fingers; her hands were ice cold. "I never even considered that. I kept wondering if someone had managed to slip into the store and open the register while I was in the rest room, or if maybe the money had just been miscounted, but... Victoria didn't seem like a thief to me. She was...I don't know. Too ditzy. And I think they were planning on getting married, so she'd have been sort of stealing from herself, right?"

Morgan held both her hands between his own to warm them. "Actually, they were planning on marrying, or at least, Ms. Markum was. But we found out that Ms. Markum and your boss had a falling out. He, it seems, took the money she'd been holding for him in her own savings account, and ran with it, so she was more than willing to talk to us. It didn't even take much prodding, from what the investigator told me. You see, she didn't steal the money...but he did."

"*What?*"

"Collins had been skimming from himself. Ms. Markum may be a ditz, but she has facts and dates and exact amounts that should corroborate her testimony. All we need to do now is contact your lawyer, who can file for a motion for the first trial to be declared a mistrial, based on the new evidence. The second trial should be scheduled quickly, probably within a month, because they won't want you serving more of a sentence than you've already had to."

She shook her head. "It can't be that easy."

"Actually it is." He smiled, trying to reassure her. "Well, you'll have to see the judge again, of course, but this time I'll be with you."

She stared at him in amazement, her bottom lip starting to quiver.

"Now, Malone," he said uneasily, "don't cry. I can't stand it."

Big tears welled in her eyes anyway. "I can't believe you did this for me."

He pulled her close and kissed the tip of her nose, which was starting to turn red. "I want you to be happy."

She launched herself against him, knocking him back on the bed. She kissed his face, his throat, his ear. Morgan laughed even as he felt himself harden. There was no way Misty Malone could crawl all over him without turning him on. He caught her mouth and held her still for the deep thrust of his tongue, but pulled back slowly before he completely lost control.

He held her head to his shoulder and smiled. "That's one problem taken care of."

She squeezed him tight. "You are the most amazing man."

Laughing, Morgan growled, "So you keep telling me. Now answer my other question. Will you marry me?"

She went still. Very slowly she raised her face. "You still haven't told me why you want to marry me."

Because he'd had a few minutes to come up with a reply, he said easily, "You're sexy and beautiful."

Her smile was radiant. "You're sexy and beautiful, too, but that's not a good reason to tie yourself to someone for life."

He snorted at her compliment. "We have great sex together. Hell, I still feel singed."

Her smile melted away and her eyes darkened. "Me, too. It was the most incredible thing. I'd never imagined sex could be like that." She brushed a kiss over his jaw, then added, "But we don't have to get married to have great sex. For as long as I'm here, I'm willing, Morgan."

His stomach started to cramp. She wasn't saying yes, and in fact, she was making a lot of excuses to cancel out every reason he gave her. But there was one reason she couldn't refute. "You're pregnant."

"The baby isn't your responsibility."

"It is if I want to make it my responsibility."

"Oh, Morgan. You're not thinking straight. You can't really want to be a fill-in for another man's child."

"The baby will be mine if you marry me."

She touched gentle fingers to his mouth and her expression was one of wonderment. "You say that now because you're feeling protective of me, just like you feel about everyone. But I don't need you to take care of me, Morgan. I can take care of myself, and the baby."

Morgan moved swiftly, rolling her beneath him before she could draw a deep breath. "Let me tell you something, Misty Malone. What you know about men doesn't add up to jack. And for your information, I don't care that the baby isn't mine. It's yours, and that's all that matters to me."

She shook her head, making him curse. He caught her hands and raised them over her head. "I'm going to tell you a little story."

"I have to be at work soon."

"Tough. Don't rush me." She wisely didn't push him on that score. Morgan drew a deep breath, then admitted, "Sawyer isn't Casey's natural father."

Misty's eyes widened and her mouth opened twice before she sputtered, "That's ridiculous!"

"No, it's true. If you want all the details, you can ask Honey. I'm sure Sawyer told her the whole story."

"But..." She searched his face, then looked away. "She's never said a word."

"Likely because it doesn't matter. Not to Sawyer, and sure as hell not to the rest of us. No one could love that boy more than we do. Sawyer knew all along that Casey wasn't his. But he'd been married to Casey's mother, and she didn't want him. So he brought Case home, a squalling little red-faced rodent, and we all went head over heels. Hell, a baby is a baby. It doesn't matter who planted the seed. All that matters is who loves him and cares for him and shelters him. I want to do that with you, Misty." He swallowed hard, his hands gripping her shoulders. "Marry me."

He could feel her shaking beneath him, saw the tears gathering in her eyes. She bit her lip and sniffed.

"Malone?"

"I...I can't."

Never in his life, Morgan thought, had anything hurt so much. He'd been in brawls, he'd been injured by cars and animals. He'd had broken limbs and a broken nose and more bruises than he could count. But nothing had ever hurt like this.

He stared at Misty, not wanting to believe that she'd refused him. She'd told him all along that she didn't want commitment, that she was through with involvement. But he hadn't believed her, not really. He hadn't *wanted* to believe her.

His head throbbed and his blood boiled. He wanted to rage, he wanted to shout. But he'd made a big enough fool of himself already.

He rolled to the side of the bed and stared at the ceiling. He started to ask her why, but wasn't at all sure he wanted to know the answer. Misty scampered off the bed, and her bare feet made no sound on the carpet. His door closed very quietly.

By the time he followed her, she'd already left for work.

Gabe gave him a questioning look, but Morgan didn't even bother to acknowledge him. He left for work and didn't come home until late that night. He didn't see Misty at all.

MISTY WAS SITTING by the lake when Honey found her. She glanced at her sister, shielding her eyes from the sun. "Hey. What's up?"

"That was my question." Honey lowered herself onto the edge of the dock beside Misty. She pulled off her sandals and dangled her feet in the water. "Morgan has looked like a thundercloud all day, growling at everyone, ready to spit nails. We're all avoiding him. The only one not afraid is the puppy."

Misty looked at the dark lake water and promised herself she wouldn't cry. "The dog has really taken to him, then?"

"Amazing, isn't it? Do you know what he named that little wad of fur? Godzilla. And the dog seems to like it."

Misty summoned up a smile, when in truth, it was all she could do not to bawl like a baby.

Honey made an exasperated sound. "So Morgan is more feral than ever and you're so morose the sun won't even shine on you. What's going on?"

Misty turned her face away, resting it on her bent knees. Hoping Honey couldn't hear the strain in her voice, she said, "Nothing. I just wanted some peace and quiet."

"Funny. That's just what Morgan said."

"Oh?"

"Yeah. He sent Gabe and Jordan running, and Sawyer was ready to hit him in the head, but I insisted he talk to me. He won't growl at me, you know. I think he's afraid it'll break me or something."

Funny. Morgan had never hesitated to shower her with his

bad moods, not that she'd minded. He hadn't scared her at all, because she'd seen through him.

Honey cleared her throat. "He told me he just wants to finish up the house so he can get moved out. He's been spending every spare minute up there." Honey hesitated, then said with a dramatic flair, "Tomorrow he's moving in."

Her stomach cramped, because she knew she'd chased him away, but what else could she do? Marry a man who didn't love her?

"I hate to see him go," Honey admitted softly. "The house won't seem the same without him."

Misty didn't reply to that. What could she say? She'd barely seen Morgan in two days. Even today, at the station, he'd not taken much notice of her. When he had looked at her, his expression had been flat. There'd been no teasing, no lust, no tenderness, none of the things she was used to and that she had begun to expect. Oh, he'd still been courteous, telling her to go to lunch, to take her time, to make sure she ate right. It was as if what had been between them was no longer there.

Misty couldn't bear to think about that, so she decided to do something she should have done already. "I have a confession."

Honey's arm slipped around her shoulders. "I'm still a good listener, you know."

"You're going to be angry," Misty warned her.

"I doubt it."

But when Misty explained all about the theft, how she'd been found guilty, Honey was absolutely livid. Not at Misty, so much, but that her boss had dared to accuse her and that the judge hadn't believed her.

It took some fast talking on Misty's part to make Honey understand that all was well now, or at least on the way to being well, thanks to Morgan, and to explain why she hadn't told her sooner.

"So Morgan is the one that got it all straightened out?"

Misty nodded, once again confounded by his generosity. "He's pretty wonderful, isn't he?"

"*I've* certainly always thought so."

She'd always thought so, too, but what she felt wasn't enough to make a marriage work. Misty heaved a sigh. "I have to leave tomorrow morning. I might be gone overnight. I'm not sure."

Honey stiffened. "Leave where?"

"My lawyer needs to see me. There're some things that have to be done to set up the new trial. Everything should go well, so I'm not worried about that. I already told Ceily, and I told Nate. I know I should have told Morgan that I wouldn't be in, but I just couldn't. Things aren't great between us right now."

Very gently, Honey asked, "Why not?"

Misty squeezed her hands into fists. "He asked me to marry him."

There was a moment of stunned silence, then Honey gasped theatrically. "Well, that bastard! How dare he?"

Shaking her head at her sister's mocking outrage, Misty said, "You don't understand."

"I understand that you love him, sis. Isn't that what's most important?"

"No." Misty dropped her feet into the water with a splash, then watched the ripples fan out until they disappeared. "What's important is that two people love each other. But Morgan doesn't love me. He likes to take care of people, and he thinks I need a husband because I'm pregnant. You've said yourself how old-fashioned he is. But that's not good enough anymore. I've learned a lot through all this, most importantly that you can't cut corners. If there isn't love, then there's nothing."

"And you think Morgan doesn't love you?"

Misty lifted one shoulder, not sure what to say. "I asked him why he wanted to marry me. He gave me a lot of good reasons, but not once did he say he loved me."

"So ask him outright."

Misty stared at her, appalled. "I can't do that!"

"Why not?" Honey kicked her feet, too, splashing them both. "Morgan is a hard-headed man. Actually, he's just hard, period. All over."

"I know, I know." Misty hadn't been able to sleep at night, remembering how wonderfully hard Morgan was. She loved everything about him, but she was crazy nuts about his big, solid body. And after only making love with him twice, she was addicted. She didn't think she could have ever gotten enough of him.

"Hard men are usually sensitive men."

Misty snorted over that bit of nonsense. "Morgan is about as blunt as they come. He always tells me what he's thinking or feeling, even if it embarrasses me to death."

Honey looked at the sky and pondered that. "Well, then, don't you think you owe him the same courtesy?"

She shuddered at just the thought. "I'm a horrible coward. Morgan's made it clear from the first that he's attracted to me. But that's all."

"How can you say that?" Honey frowned at her. "Morgan's done everything he could to keep you close by. He even made up that ridiculous story about the two of you having an agreement."

"You knew that wasn't real?"

Honey smiled. "It was plain on your face."

Bemused for a moment, Misty wondered if all his brothers had known he was just making up their involvement. Then she shook her head. "It doesn't matter. He kept me here because he was trying to take care of me—whether I wanted him to or not. He does that for everyone, Honey." She turned to face her sister, wanting her to understand. "Morgan is about the most giving, caring man I've ever met. That's why being a sheriff is so perfect for him. He loves taking care of other people's problems. He's a natural caregiver—though he'd choke if he heard me say that, and probably frown something fierce. He tries to hide his gentleness behind a big tough exterior."

Honey waved that away. "I know. But still—"

"No. If he loved me, surely he would have said so."

"Will you at least think about it? Maybe he's not quite as tough or as confident as you think he is."

The idea of Morgan being insecure would take some getting used to, but to appease her sister, she agreed to think it over. What would Morgan say if she blurted out that she loved him? Would he be embarrassed? Would he lie and say he loved her, too, just to keep her from embarrassment? She closed her eyes, not sure at all what his reaction would be.

"I was looking for you for another reason, too."

Honey's serious tone pulled Misty out of her contemplation. "What's wrong?"

After a deep breath, Honey said, "Father wants to visit us. He called a few minutes ago."

That was the very last thing Misty had expected to hear. Incredulous, she stared at her sister. "You must be kidding."

"Unfortunately...no."

Misty narrowed her eyes. "He wants to come here? To Kentucky?"

"Yes. That's what he said. I'm supposed to call him back and tell him when it'd be convenient."

A summons from her father wouldn't have thrown her so badly. But a visit? It didn't make any sense. Unless... "What are we being accused of now? Is he mad about something?" Then a horrid thought intruded. "Oh, God. He found out I'd been arrested, didn't he?"

"I don't think so. Actually, he told me he wants to meet my husband. Sawyer is afraid he's going to bring up his will again, and you can just imagine how that'd go over."

Misty nodded. All her life, her father had claimed to want a son to carry on the family name. Since their mother had died without giving him one, he'd decided that Honey, as the oldest child, would have to supply a husband to fill the role of masculine heir.

Sawyer had flatly refused to accept anything from him. And their father had been peeved ever since. He hadn't even attended the wedding.

"Father said he was intrigued by the notion of men who would blindly turn down money and power. When I mentioned to him that he should have come to the wedding, he actually said he regretted missing it. Can you believe that?"

"Uh...no."

Honey softened her tone. "He also said he was worried about you."

"Since when?" Misty couldn't help but feel bitter over her last conversation with her father. He'd been very disappointed that she'd gotten pregnant, and he hadn't bothered to try to hide that disappointment.

"Here's what I think." Honey pulled her feet from the water and stood, then looked at Misty. "I think I'm so happy that I don't mind hearing him out, seeing what he has to say Sawyer told me that not everyone is as capable of expressing love as we are. He asked me about Father's upbringing, our grandparents, and you know, I think he might be onto something there. Father was always a cold, detached man, just as his parents were and as they expected him to be. After Mom died, he was all alone. That couldn't have been easy for him, Misty. I'm not saying we have to be all loving and hugging." She shuddered, then laughed. "That would be too weird after all this time. But I'd at least like to make my peace with him. And you're going to be giving him a grandchild. Maybe he'll look at things differently, but either way, I want to know that I gave our relationship every chance."

Honey walked away, leaving Misty to think things over. True, her father had never been the type to hug or even give a quick compliment. But he'd made certain they were always well dressed and well fed, and they'd never wanted for anything material. Just the fact that he wanted to meet Sawyer and the brothers showed a bending on his part, a sort of olive branch. She supposed it wouldn't hurt to listen to him.

As she walked up to the house, dodging stones on the ground and the occasional bee feasting on clover, she smiled. She couldn't begin to imagine her father's reaction to the brothers. They were overwhelming and dominating and they spoke their minds without hesitation.

Her father would be in for a surprise.

EARLY the next morning, Morgan stared at his bedroom ceiling, a habit that had replaced sleeping in the past few days. No matter how hard he worked, no matter how he exhausted himself, he couldn't sleep. He was so damn tired he could barely see straight, but when he closed his eyes, all he could think of was Misty.

Hell, even with his eyes open, she was all he could think of. He alternated between fantasies of making love to her until she begged him to marry her and throttling her for turning down his proposal in the first place. Not that he would ever really hurt her, he thought with disgust. Hell, no.

There was one bright side to all his recent labors; his house was done. He could now move in and live in comfort—and solitude. But he didn't want to. He'd come to think of the house with Misty in it. Without her, it didn't seem complete no matter what he did to it.

Sawyer was right, he was a miserable bastard. He never should have given in to his needs. He should have avoided her instead of finding out for a fact how sweet she was, how right it felt to be inside her, holding her, talking with her, loving her. Now she was still here, a damn relative, and he had to look at her and know she was close, but she didn't want him.

He closed his eyes and groaned.

Two seconds later his bedroom door flew open and bounced off the wall. Morgan leaped out of bed, automatically reaching for his gun. The overhead light came on, nearly blinding him in the gray morning shadows, but showing his brother's angry face clear as day. Sawyer stalked in, grabbed Morgan's discarded jeans and flung them at him.

"Get dressed."

Morgan began pulling on his pants without hesitation. It wasn't often Sawyer issued commands that way. "What's wrong?"

"You blew it, that's what."

He stumbled, his jeans only to his knees. "What the hell does that mean?"

"It means Misty is gone."

Forget the elephant, it felt like his heart was smashed flat. Wheezing, a little light-headed, he asked, "Gone where?"

Sawyer jutted his chin toward Morgan and growled, "She *left*, Morgan. What did you expect her to do with you moping around, ignoring her, acting like she didn't exist? I thought you loved her!"

Morgan dropped onto the edge of the bed. "I asked her to marry me," he said, feeling numb. "She turned me down."

"You must have misunderstood."

Sawyer and Morgan both turned to see Jordan standing in the doorway. Morgan shook his head. "No, I asked and she flatly refused."

Jordan crossed his arms over his chest and frowned. "I can tell she cares about you."

Gabe walked in. "She's crazy about him, if you ask me."

"Oh, for the love of—" Morgan stood and finished pulling on his pants. "If that's true, why wouldn't she marry me?"

Honey pushed Gabe out of her way and glared at all of them. "Because she said you didn't love her."

"*What?*"

"She said you were just trying to take care of her, but without love, it wasn't worth it."

Morgan cursed so viciously that Gabe backed up and Jordan rolled his eyes. Sawyer pulled Honey protectively to his side. "Get a grip, Morgan. Are you going to go after her or not?"

His head shot up. "Go after her? When did she leave?"

Honey tapped her foot. "About two minutes ago."

Before she had finished, Morgan had snapped his jeans, shoved his gun in his pocket and started out of the room. But his brothers had all congregated inside, blocking his path at the end of the bed, so he bounded over it instead, bouncing on the mattress as he dodged past them. He ran out the doorway, not bothering with a shirt or shoes. Gabe trotted after him, waving a shirt. "Wait! Don't you want to finish dressing?"

Morgan ignored him, but he couldn't ignore the loud guffaws from his other brothers. He snatched his keys from the peg by the back door and ran into the yard.

"Damn irritants," he muttered, then winced as his bare feet came into contact with every sharp stone on the dew-wet grass. He slipped twice, but within thirty seconds he had the Bronco out, lights flashing and sirens blasting. When he caught up to her...

Morgan filled the time it took to get to town by plotting all the ways he'd set her straight.

She was in front of the sheriff's office when he spotted her. She slowed when she noticed his flashing lights, and after a few seconds she pulled over.

Unfortunately, Ceily was just coming to the diner to start preparing the food, and she paused on the front stoop to watch as Morgan climbed out of the Bronco and slammed the door. Nate was at the station already, and he and Howard and Jesse also walked out to see what was happening. It wasn't often that Morgan pulled anyone over with so much fanfare.

By the time he'd circled the front of the Bronco, Misty had already left her car. She gaped at him, then demanded, "What in the world is wrong with you? Has something happened?" She gazed at him from his shaggy hair, his bare chest, to his naked feet.

Morgan stomped up to her, ignoring the sting to his feet and the way the sidewalk was quickly beginning to crowd with curious onlookers. He hooked his hand around the back of her neck and drew her up to her tiptoes. "Where in hell do you think you're going?"

She blinked at him. "I have to meet with my lawyer today."

Morgan prepared to blast her with his wrath—and then her words sank in. "You're not leaving?"

"Leaving, as in for good?"

He nodded.

"Why would you think that?"

He seriously considered going home and choking Sawyer. But first, he had a few things to straighten out. "You should have told me you were leaving."

"You," she said, beginning to show her own pique, "haven't shown the slightest interest in talking to me lately!"

"Because I asked you to marry me and you had the nerve to say no."

A loud gasp rose from their audience.

Morgan pretended he hadn't heard them. "Do you know how many other women I've asked to be wife? Do you? *None!*"

"Well, I'm honored," Misty sneered, then poked him in the chest and her own voice rose to a shout. "But I'm not marrying a man who doesn't love me."

He sputtered in renewed outrage. *"Who the hell says I don't love you?"*

Misty caught her breath, panting, then said with deep feeling, her gaze intent, *"Who says you do?"*

Morgan growled, ran a hand roughly through his hair, then he picked her up. He held her at eye level and said, "Damn woman, I asked you to marry me! Why would I do that if I didn't love you?"

Someone on the sidewalk—it sounded like Ceily—called out in a laughing voice, "Yeah, why would Morgan do that?"

Morgan jerked his head around to face them all. "Can't you people find something to do?"

"No!" was the unanimous retort.

Morgan growled again. "Nate, arrest anyone who doesn't scatter."

Nate promptly looked dumbfounded. "Uh..."

Misty regained his attention by saying softly, "You just want to help me, like you helped that woman with the flat tire, and the dog, and the school kids and the elderly."

Morgan walked to her car and plunked her down gently on the hood. He braced his hands on either side of her hips, then leaned in so close his nose touched hers. "Listen up, Malone. I didn't ask the damn dog to marry me. I didn't ask Howard or Jesse to marry me."

Jesse shouted, "He's speakin' the truth there."

Misty opened her mouth twice before she got words to come out. She spoke so softly, Morgan could barely hear her. "You said...you said you were looking for a wife."

He gave a sharp nod. "You."

"But..." Her voice faded to a shy whisper. "You said you wanted three children."

"Three total." His hand covered her belly, and he smiled. Breathing the words so no one else would hear, he explained, "This one and two more. I was trying to hint to you that I'd be a good father."

"Oh, Morgan." She cupped his face, and tears filled her eyes. "I already know you'd be an excellent father."

He straightened and put his hands on his hips. "I swear, if you start crying again, Malone, I won't like it." He drew a breath and added, "Hell, it just about kills me to see you unhappy."

She sniffed loudly. "I'm very happy."

"So you won't cry?"

"I won't cry."

A fat tear rolled down her cheek, making him sigh in exasperation. The woman was forever turning him in circles. But since she seemed in an agreeable mood for a change... "Tell me you'll marry me."

She nodded. "I'll marry you."

She started to put her arms around his neck, but he held her off. "Not so quick, Malone. I told you I love you. Don't you have something to say to me?"

With everyone on the sidewalk cheering her on, she grinned around her tears and said, "Morgan Hudson, I love you so much it hurts."

He scooped her into his arms for a fierce hug, then turned to the crowd, laughing out loud. "You heard her. Consider me an engaged man." Then to Misty, "Damn. Do you think we have time for me to go home and get dressed before we go see your lawyer? I'd probably make a better impression that way."

_____ Epilogue _____

MORGAN HAULED MISTY into his lap after her father had left. She protested, saying, "No, Morgan, I'm too fat now!"

Three months had passed. She was rounded with the child growing inside her, but still so sexy he could barely keep his hands off her. Every day he loved her more.

He kissed her cheek and smiled. "I promise to bear up under the weight."

Honey, a little subdued and cuddled up against Sawyer's side, said, "Misty, you look wonderful. Not at all fat."

Gabe laughed. "When I start looking like you two did, you'll have to give me some pointers so I can find my own beauty."

Sawyer blinked. "I wasn't looking. That's why Honey sort of...blindsided me." Honey playfully punched him for that remark, making Sawyer laugh.

Shrugging, Morgan added, "I wasn't looking, either."

The feminine weight in his lap gasped over his statement. "What an outrageous clanker! You even told me you wanted a wife."

Morgan shook his head. "That was just lip service. Sawyer seemed so tamed, I thought I should give it a try, too. But I wasn't putting much effort into it, not until I saw you."

Gabe nodded. "As I said, they're both gorgeous."

"Looks don't matter, Gabe." He tilted Misty's chin up and kissed her lips. "It was Misty's mouthy bluster that reeled me in."

Gabe made a face. "You can say that _now_."

Jordan shook his head. "Your day will come, Gabe."

"Ha! But not before yours, old man. If we're going in order, you're doomed."

Jordan made a face at him. "If you keep using words like 'doomed,' Misty or Honey are going to flatten you."

Casey flopped down on the sofa. "So, Dad, what do you think about me visiting Mr. Malone?"

Morgan hid a smile. Mr. Malone had surprised them all. True, the man was so rigid he bordered on brittle. But he had made the effort to unbend a little more on each visit. His first had been horribly strained, but with all the ribald teasing going on, he could hardly stay puckered up indefinitely. This time, he'd actually kissed each daughter's cheek.

And rather than trying to offer his money to Sawyer again, he'd asked—actually *asked*—if he could put a good portion of it in a trust for the baby. Morgan and Misty had discussed it, then agreed, as long as equal money was put in for each child either of the sisters had.

That had settled one problem, but then the man had fixated on Casey. All along, he'd seemed very impressed by Casey's manners, his maturity, and within a few hours of this visit, he'd damn near adopted him as a pseudo heir. None of them were overly pleased by it, especially not Honey, but when the man had invited Casey to visit, to look over his enterprises, Casey had shown some interest.

Sawyer pursed his mouth, then hugged Honey closer so she wouldn't protest. Morgan knew Honey hated to let Casey out of her sight. She had a hard time thinking of him as a young man, despite the fact he was exactly that. "I suppose we could all make a trip up there. If after that you want to hang around for a short visit, it'd probably be all right."

"Great." Casey didn't seem overly enthusiastic either way, and when he said he had a date, Morgan understood why. The male brain had a hard time focusing when females were being considered.

They all watched Casey leave with indulgent smiles. Seconds later, Honey and Sawyer left to begin dinner. Jordan had a few calls to make, and when Morgan started kissing his wife, Gabe left the room whistling.

"You about ready to head home?" Morgan asked.

"I thought we were staying for dinner."

"We'll come back," Morgan promised, then gave her a lecherous grin. He picked her up in his arms and suffered through her complaints.

"I'm too heavy now for you to keep doing this!"

Morgan just grinned at her. "Do you know, you're the only one who's ever doubted my strength."

"That's not true." She kissed his chin. "I just like to match it."

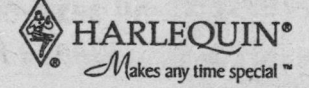

Romance is just one click away!

online book serials

- *Exclusive* to our web site, get caught up in both the daily and weekly online installments of new romance stories.
- Try the Writing Round Robin. Contribute a chapter to a story created by our members. Plus, winners will get prizes.

romantic travel

- Want to know where the best place to kiss in New York City is, or which restaurant in Los Angeles is the most romantic? Check out our Romantic Hot Spots for the scoop.
- Share your travel tips and stories with us on the romantic travel message boards.

romantic reading library

- Relax as you read our collection of Romantic Poetry.
- Take a peek at the Top 10 Most Romantic Lines!

Visit us online at

www.eHarlequin.com
on Women.com Networks

If you enjoyed what you just read,
then we've got an offer you can't resist!

Take 2 bestselling
love stories FREE!
Plus get a FREE surprise gift!

HARLEQUIN®
Temptation

COMING NEXT MONTH

#793 RULES OF ENGAGEMENT Jamie Denton

Jill Cassidy needs a fiancé—fast! Morgan Price needs a savvy lawyer—immediately! The gorgeous contractor agrees to pretend he's madly in love with her and attend her sister's wedding. In turn, Jill will settle his case. But drawing up the "rules of their engagement" brings trouble. For starters, they have to practice kissing. Then there's the single hotel room they *have* to share....

#794 GABE Lori Foster
The Buckhorn Brothers, Bk. 3

Gabe Kasper, the heartthrob of Buckhorn County, can have any woman he wants. But it's prickly, uptight college woman, Elizabeth Parks, who gets under his skin. She thinks Gabe's some kind of hero and wants an interview for her thesis. He doesn't consider pulling a couple of kids out of the lake heroic, but will answer her questions in exchange for kisses...and more.

#795 ALL THROUGH THE NIGHT Kate Hoffmann
Blaze

Is it love...or just a one-night stand? Advice columnist Nora Pierce can't answer that for sure. An unexpected night with warm sexy sportswriter Pete Beckett thrills her to the core. But the ex-jock is too laid back and a real ladies' man to boot. Nora can only read between the lines...and decide where to draw the line with Pete!

#796 SECRETLY YOURS Gina Wilkins
The Wild McBrides

Trent McBride is known for being brash, cocky and very, very reckless. But when a horrific plane crash leaves him grounded, he doesn't know what to do with his life. Then he meets spirited, *secretive* Annie Stewart and suddenly, he feels alive again. Especially when he learns that Annie desperately needs a hero....

CNM0700